Ghost Light

Also by E.J. Stevens

Ivy Granger World

Ivy Granger
Urban Fantasy Series
Shadow Sight
Blood and Mistletoe
Ghost Light
Club Nexus
Burning Bright
Birthright
Hound's Bite
Blood Rite (coming soon)

Hunters' Guild
Urban Fantasy Series
Hunting in Bruges

Beyond the World of Ivy Granger

Spirit Guide
Young Adult Series
She Smells the Dead
Spirit Storm
Legend of Witchtrot Road
Brush with Death
The Pirate Curse

Poetry Collections
From the Shadows
Shadows of Myth and Legend

Super Simple Guides
Super Simple Quick Start Guide to Self-Publishing
Super Simple Quick Start Guide to Book Marketing

IVY GRANGER PSYCHIC DETECTIVE

Ghost Light

E.J. STEVENS

Published by Sacred Oaks Press
Sacred Oaks, 221 Sacred Oaks Lane, Wells, Maine 04090

First Printing (trade paperback edition), July 2013

Copyright © E.J. Stevens 2013
All rights reserved

Stevens, E.J.
Ghost Light / E.J. Stevens

ISBN 978-0-9842475-9-2 (trade pbk.)

Printed in the United States of America

PUBLISHER'S NOTE
This is a work of fiction. Names, characters, places, and incidents either are the product of the author's imagination or are used fictitiously, and any resemblance to actual persons, living or dead, business establishments, events, or locales is entirely coincidental.

The scanning, uploading and distribution of this book via the Internet or via any other means without the permission of the publisher is illegal and punishable by law. Please purchase only authorized electronic editions, and do not participate in or encourage electronic piracy of copyrighted materials. Your support of the author's rights is appreciated.

PRONUNCIATION GUIDE

Pronunciations are given phonetically for names and places found in *Shadow Sight, Blood and Mistletoe*, and *Ghost Light*. Alternate names and nicknames have been provided in parentheses. In some cases, the original folklore has been changed to suit the city of Harborsmouth and its environs.

Athame: *ah-thaw-may*
Barguest: *bar-guyst* (Bargheist, Black Dog)
Bean Tighe: *ban tig*
Béchuille: *Beh-huh-il* (Bé Chuille)
Blaosc: *blee-usk*
Boggart: *bog-ert*
Brollachan: *broll-ach-hawn*
Brownie: *brow-nee* (Bwca, Urisk, Hearth Faerie, Domestic Hobgoblin)
Bugbear: *bug-bayr* (Bug-a-boo, Boggle-bo)
Bwca: *bu-ka* (see Brownie)
The Cailleach: *kall-ahk* (The Blue Hag, Cailleach Bheur, Queen of Winter, Crone, Veiled One, Winter Hag)
Cat Sidhe: *kat shee* or *kayth shee* (Faerie Cat, Cait Shith, Cait Sith)
Ceffyl Dŵr: *Keff-eel Door* (Kelpie King)
Clurichaun: *kloor-ih-kon* (clobhair)
Daeva: *day-va*
Demon: *dee-mon*
Each Uisge: *erkh ooshka* (Water Horse)
Faerie: *fayr-ee* (Fairy, Sidhe, Fane, Wee Folk, The Gentry, People of Peace, Themselves, Sidhe, Fae, Fay, Good Folk)
Fear Dearg: *far dar-rig* (The Red Man)
Forneus: *Fore-nee-uss* (Demon, Great Marquis of Hell)
Fuath: *Foo-ah*
Galliel: *Gal-ee-el* (Unicorn)
Ghoul: *gool* (Revenant)
Glaistig: *glass-tig* (The Green Lady)
Gnome: *noh-m*
Goblin: *gob-lin*
Griffin: *griff-in* (Gryphon, Griffon)
Grindylow: *grin-dee-loh*
Hamadryad: *ha-ma-dry-ad* (Tree Nymph)

Henkie: *hen-kee*
Hippocampus: *hip-po-cam-pus*
Hob-o-Waggle *Hob-oh-wag-l* (Brownie, son of Wag-at-the-Wa)
Jenny Greenteeth: *Jen-nee Green-teeth* (Water Hag)
Kelpie: *kel-pee* (Water Horse, Nyaggle)
Lamia: *lay-me-a*
Leanansídhe: *lan-awn-shee* (Lhiannan Sidhe, Leanhaun Shee, Leannan Sìth, Fairy Mistress)
Leprechaun: *le-pre-khan* (leipreachán)
Mab: *Mab* (Unseelie Queen)
Melusine: *Mel-oo-seen*
Mermaid: *mer-mayd* (male Merman)
Merry Dancer: *mer-ree dan-ser* (Fir Chlis)
Murúch: *mer-ook* (Merrow, Moruadh, Murúghach)
Nixie: *nix-ee*
Oberon: *O-ber-on* (Seelie King)
Peg Powler: *Peg Pow-ler* (Peg Powler of the Trees, Water Hag)
Peri: *per-ee*
Pixie: *pix-ee* (Pisgie)
Pooka: *poo-ka* (Phooka, Pouka, Púca, Pwca)
Redcap: *red-kap* (red cap)
Saytr: *say-tur*
Selkie: *sel-kee*
Shellycoat: *shell-ee-cote*
Sidhe: *shee* (see Faerie)
Succubus: *suk-you-bus* (male Incubus)
Tech Duinn: *tek doon*
Titania: *Ti-tayn-ee-ah* (Seelie Queen)
Troll: *trol*
Tuatha Dé Danann: tootha day da-nan
Tylwyth Teg: *till-with teeg* (Seelie Court)
Unicorn: *you-ne-korn*
Vampire: *vam-pi-r* (Undead)
Will-o'-the-Wisp: *Wil-oh-tha-Wisp* (Gyl Burnt Tayle, Jack o' Lantern, Wisp, Ghost Light, Friar's Lantern, Corpse Candle, Hobbledy, Aleya, Hobby Lantern, Chir Batti, Faerie Fire, Spunkies, Min Min Light, Luz Mala, Pinket, Ellylldan, Spook Light, Ignus Gatuus, Orbs, Boitatá, and Hinkypunk)

Now it is the time of night,
That the graves all gaping wide,
Every one lets forth his sprite,
In the church-way paths to glide.
—William Shakespeare, *A Midsummer Night's Dream*

What wild heart-histories seemed to lie enwritten,
Upon those crystalline, celestial spheres!
...Lighting my lonely pathway home that night,
They have not left me (as my hopes have) since.
They follow me - they lead me through the years.
They are my ministers - yet I their slave.
Their office is to illumine and enkindle -
My duty, to be saved by their bright fire
—Edgar Allan Poe, *To Helen*

INTRODUCTION

Welcome to Harborsmouth, where monsters walk the streets unseen by humans...except those with second sight.

Whether visiting our modern business district or exploring the cobblestone lanes of the Old Port quarter, please enjoy your stay. When you return home, do tell your friends about our wonderful city—just leave out any supernatural details.

Don't worry—most of our guests never experience anything unusual. Otherworlders, such as faeries, vampires, and ghouls, are quite adept at hiding within the shadows. Many are also skilled at erasing memories. You may wake in the night screaming, but you won't recall why. Be glad that you don't remember—you are one of the fortunate ones.

If you do encounter something unnatural, we recommend the services of Ivy Granger, Psychic Detective. Co-founder of Private Eye detective agency, Ivy Granger is a relatively new member of our small business community. Her offices can be found on Water Street, in the heart of the Old Port.

Miss Granger has a remarkable ability to receive visions by the act of touching an object. This skill is useful in her detective work, especially when locating lost items. Whether you are looking for a lost brooch or missing persons, no job is too big or too small for Ivy Granger—but you may be on her waiting list for awhile. Hopefully, you are not in dire need of her immediate services. After her role in recent events, where she was instrumental in saving our city, Miss Granger's business is booming.

If matters are particularly grim, we can also provide, upon request, a list of highly skilled undertakers. If you are in need of their services, then we also kindly direct you to Harborsmouth Cemetery Realty. It's never too early to contact them, since we have a booming "housing" market. Demand is quite high for a local plot—there are always people dying for a place to stay.

CHAPTER 1

What do the names g*host light, friar's lantern, corpse candle, aleya, hobby lantern, chir batti, faerie fire, min min light, luz mala, spook light, ignus fatuus, orbs, boitatá,* and *hinkypunk* have in common? They are all names for wisps. Corpse candle? Now that was bound to give a girl a complex.

I had recently discovered that I was half fae. My faerie half is wisp, as in Will-o'-the-Wisp—my father, king of the wisps. It was a lot to digest.

Dealing with my newfound princess-of-the-wisps status was stressful, but business was booming and I didn't have time for random panic attacks. I used to see a therapist to help deal with my anxiety. Lately, I visited Galliel at Sacred Heart church.

Galliel wasn't the priest at Sacred Heart, though I usually stopped and said hello to Father Michael while there. Father Michael had helped me with my recent demon trouble, but spending time with him didn't relieve my anxiety like Galliel did. It wasn't Father Michael's fault. He was a good priest, as far as I could tell, but he was only human. Galliel was a unicorn.

I was indulging in my guilty pleasure, Galliel's adoring head resting in my lap, while Ceff spoke with the priest. This was bliss. I had always wondered what true happiness was like, but never thought I'd have the opportunity to experience it for myself. Somehow, during a catastrophic week that nearly brought my city to its knees, I had found my own. Galliel was a big part of that. So was Ceff.

If I were looking for love on Craig's List, my singles ad would begin something like, "Must Love Unicorns." Of course, I didn't have to look for love online. My heart now belonged to Ceff.

Ceffyl Dŵr, or Ceff, was a kelpie. In fact, he was king of the local kelpies. Since discovering my wisp princess birthright, that seemed somewhat fortuitous. It was also extremely dangerous. The kelpie king had plenty of enemies. He also had a murderous, sociopathic wife.

I didn't care. For the first time in my life, I felt like I truly belonged. I had so much to be thankful for; a gorgeous date; an amazing best friend, business partner, and roommate; a wonderful mentor; fabulous new friends; numerous clients; and a pet freaking unicorn.

I should have known that something bad was coming. I have said it before and I'll say it again; Fate is a fickle bitch.

*****

Most people have skeletons in their closets. I wasn't born yesterday, and I am fully aware that my boyfriend was born more yesterdays ago than I can count. Since Ceff is a few millennia old, I expect some dusty bones lurking behind the perfectly pressed shirts, faded jeans, and tailored suits—no shoes of course. What I didn't expect was for Ceff's skeletons to come storming from the dark corners of his closet with finger bones raised in anticipation of clawing my eyes out.

Ceff was married once. To put it nicely, the woman was a freaking bitch. I'd say the chick was a harpy, but that would insult harpies everywhere and I didn't want to piss off potential clients. Melusine, Ceff's ex-squeeze and former queen, was pure malicious evil.

Judging from the memories I witnessed in a psychometric vision I had while hunting for Ceff's bridle, the woman was also bat-shit-crazy. Coming from me, that's really saying something. But seriously, what other reason explains a mother murdering her infant child in front of her husband?

Their union, an arranged marriage based on fae politics, may not have been based on love, but Ceff hadn't been a bad husband. He was attentive to his wife and lavished her with gifts befitting a queen. But his true love was reserved for his sons. Unfortunately, that love would spell their doom.

Melusine became so filled with jealousy that she began scheming how to remove her eldest son from his prized role as heir to the kelpie throne. She framed him as a traitor—a crime punishable by death under kelpie law—and watched with glee as her husband meted out the punishment. But her eldest son's public execution was not enough.

Melusine wanted Ceff's love and undivided attention, but even in his grief, Ceff didn't turn to his wife. Instead he shone his affections on his youngest son who was then still just a babe.

Melusine seethed with envy for the love she felt was rightfully hers. What kind of child steals a parent's love from the other? Enraged, she dangled the child over a pit of flames and watched as Ceff struggled to save him. His attempts to plead with her, for the sake of their child, only maddened her further. She threw their baby into the fire and, with a flick of her serpent tail, disappeared into the sea.

I had hoped that the bitch had been eaten by a shark, or run over by a motor boat. Maybe she'd remarried some other poor guy and was making big with the crazy in his ocean. I didn't care, though I was fond of the shark scenario, so long as Melusine was out of the picture.

Too bad she didn't stay that way.

Have you ever taken pictures with friends and everyone is smiling, but when you see the photos later they are dotted with white orbs? Okay, sometimes those are my people, wisps, but more often they appear like ghosts haunting the picture's inhabitants and making the smiles seem grotesque rather than cheerful.

Melusine was like one of those photographic ghosts. She was back in the picture, haunting me and tainting the near-perfect relationship that Ceff and I had with painful memories and the threat of violence. The honeymoon was over before it began—and that really pissed me off.

I'll be turning twenty-five soon and I have never dated anyone until now. I've also never been intimate with anyone. The closest I've come to intimacy was one magical night with Ceff during the winter solstice. Jinx thinks I'm nuts for cuddling on the couch all night when I had the chance for something more, but for me being held was a huge first step. Nearly twenty-five and never been kissed. But I was getting closer to achieving that with Ceff, until his ex-wife showed up.

She better hope she had a leprechaun somewhere in her family tree, because that bitch was going to pay.

CHAPTER 2

Fog rolled in off the harbor to smother the Old Port and strangle The Hill with its embrace. I trudged through the chill mist beside Jinx, lamenting the shopping bags filled with shoes hanging from every gloved finger. I hate shopping. The threat of getting an unwanted vision without the reward of a payday was too high, but my roommate and business partner wanted to celebrate our newfound success and I was a sucker for tears.

Now I was acting as a shopaholic's Sherpa while Jinx scaled Joysen Hill in six-inch platform pumps. I figured carrying the bags was slightly better than having to carry an injured BFF. Jinx was the most accident prone person I'd ever met. Just watching her teeter on those shoes, while tripping over cobblestones, made my ankles hurt and teeth ache.

I tried to rub my jaw with my shoulder, but gave up with a grunt. My neck and shoulders were tight and I'd likely pull a muscle. Walking around Joysen Hill always made me tense, even during daylight. The oppressive gloom of the incoming fog made my ears itch, as if I were being watched.

I spun on the balls of my feet, suddenly sure that someone was approaching from the gloom, but when I scanned the street behind us I saw only harmless shoppers out on a chilly spring afternoon. I peered through the pea soup fog further down the hill, my gaze darting into shadowed doorways and alleys, but couldn't spot the source of my unease.

The alarm bells going off in my head could be good old-fashioned paranoia, but worrying about being hunted in this part of the city wasn't necessarily my imagination. The big baddies of Harborsmouth, both supernatural and human, have holed up in the warrens of Joysen Hill for decades. It's a fact of life in Harborsmouth that bad things happen daily on The Hill. Vampire slumlords suck their tenants dry, djinn provide favors for those who...rub their lamps, and carnivorous fae find creative ways to bait humans into their lair.

That was the other reason why I had agreed to go shopping. Jinx had access to faerie ointment which allowed her to see through a basic faerie glamour, but the stuff was expensive. She'd rather spend her money on shoes than on the potions my witch friend brewed. So I tagged along to make sure Jinx stayed out of trouble. Jinx may only be able to see shopkeepers hocking their wares, but I could see the fangs and mandibles behind the glossy smiles.

I steered Jinx away from a display of pottery bowls, that beneath a shimmering glamour were actually hollowed out skulls, and into the shop next door. The smell of leather filled the air and a hiccup erupted from behind the till. I smiled and let the tension ooze out of my neck and shoulders. We had entered a clurichaun's leather goods shop.

My hands were currently sheathed in a pair of clurichaun crafted gloves, a Christmas gift from Marvin. I smiled and flexed my fingers, trying not to drop the bags I was holding. Marvin had gone to a lot of trouble to bargain with one of the perpetually inebriated faeries, but I was glad that he did. The gloves were beautiful, fit me perfectly, and hadn't given me terrifying visions.

Clurichauns, cousins to the infamous cobbler faeries, maintain a constant state of intoxication. In other words, the little drunkards are too merry and their minds too unfocused to pass along unpleasant visions. Marvin had found the perfect gift for me. I smiled thinking how lucky I was to have had the young troll stumble into my life. I'd have to buy the kid some honey before heading home.

I shifted my bags and the clurichaun behind the counter snorted and fell off his stool with a crash. Jinx gasped and I hurried forward to take a look. The red-nosed faerie stumbled to his feet, shook his head, rubbed his face, and grinned from ear to oversized ear. I wondered, not for the first time, how the bleary-eyed creature could craft such beautiful leather goods. I shrugged a shoulder. It was just another faerie mystery.

Jinx, no longer concerned about the shopkeeper, rifled through a bin of leather belts.

"This one is gorgeous," she said, holding a red belt aloft. "Do you have shoes to match?"

Jinx turned to the man behind the counter and I winced. Leprechauns make shoes, clurichauns make everything else. It was a sore point between the two faerie races.

The red of the clurichaun's nose spread across his face and down his neck. I half expected steam to come out of his ears. Of course, that was silly. He wasn't a phoenix.

The clurichaun stumbled out from around the counter shaking his fist.

"Now, I'll tell you..." he said.

The little man stopped in front of Jinx, mouth falling open. His silly grin returned and the heat rising in his face shifted to his rosy cheeks. Clurichauns don't stay mad for long and this one was obviously smitten at the sight of my roommate. Of course, at his height, he was looking up her skirt.

"Clurichauns are master tailors and leather craftsmen, not cobblers," I said, filling the uncomfortable silence. I reached for the belt in Jinx's hand and pulled her away from the enthralled faerie.

"No shoes?" she asked.

"Nope, no shoes," I said.

Jinx sighed and released the belt, letting it drop into the display bin. With dangerously weaving steps, the clurichaun carried over a burgundy leather halter top. I tuned out the conversation as the faerie tried to pour on the charm. The clurichaun was using the merchandise as an excuse to look at my roommate's chest. Jinx leaned in and started haggling over the price.

I rolled my shoulders, shifting bags and boxes, and turned to look out onto the street. There, beside a lamppost on the opposite sidewalk, Melusine stood upright on her coiled serpent's tail. Here on dry land, I could see that her lower half was covered in snake skin, not the fish scales I had assumed when I observed the lamia in my vision.

She was staring right at me.

Hatred burned in Melusine's eyes and a forked tongue shot in and out of her mouth. Fangs lengthened as she thrashed from side to side in a weaving motion and stared daggers at me between passing cars.

I gasped, dropped Jinx's bags, and ran for the door. An enraged sea serpent was not something I wanted to tangle with, but my chances of survival would increase if I had room to move. If Melusine crashed through the shop window, we'd be like fish in a barrel.

"Keep her safe," I shouted over my shoulder. I dug into my pockets and tossed a wad of cash and our business card at the tipsy shopkeeper. "Glamour my friend and take her to your bolt-hole until I return. Do this and I will owe you a debt. Private Eye detective agency will work one case of your choosing, free of charge."

As far as faerie bargains went, it wasn't that solid, but it was the best I could do on the run. I just hoped I'd live to regret any loopholes I had left in the agreement.

The clurichaun snatched up the items and eyed our card curiously. The money disappeared into one of his many pockets.

"Agreed," he said with a nod.

I staggered, dizziness blurring my vision as the debt between us settled onto my soul. Faerie oaths were binding, especially between fae. My wisp blood was responding to the agreement, and the weight of the multiple debts I'd accrued. I probably shouldn't be so quick to ask another faerie for help. Too bad I didn't have any other options.

I shook my head, clearing my vision. Seeing double was something I was used to, but this was more than catching a glimpse of glamour draped over a monster's true form. I blinked rapidly, trying to regain my sight, and lunged for the door.

I fought down nausea and ran outside, keeping my eyes on the lamia. Melusine's fanged face swam before me once more. The dizziness passed and my vision cleared as the faerie bargain nestled in for the ride. What I saw wasn't much of an improvement. Melusine looked pissed.

At least as the image solidified, the lamia now only had the one head. Thank Mab for small favors. Too bad I didn't have time to relax and enjoy the improved view.

Melusine leapt off the sidewalk and slithered at blinding speed into the street, rush hour traffic the only thing between me and her dripping fangs. I ran to the edge of the sidewalk and dug a glass vial filled with iron shavings from one of my many pockets.

It was time to see how the bitch liked our local weather. My lip lifted in a sneer. I was going to bring a rain of iron down on Melusine's head. I raised my arm, ready to throw the vial as soon as I caught a break between vehicles.

I edged down to the pavement, but a city bus honked twice, horn blaring dangerously close to my ear. I jumped back a step, narrowly avoiding a future as a road pancake. My boot heels hit the concrete sidewalk, but I never took my eyes off Melusine as she waited for her chance to strike. With a rush of heated air and diesel exhaust, the bus drove past just inches from my face. Gripping the vial tightly in my gloved fist, I blinked against the swirl of debris.

I stepped forward as soon as the bus passed, but Melusine was gone.

A car swerved around me, but the driver's curses were lost beneath the roaring in my ears. My heart tried to pound its way out of my chest and into my throat.

Where the hell was Melusine?

I spun in a circle, but there was no sign of the lamia. My arm shook with the strain of holding the vial aloft while I scrambled for my target. It shouldn't be hard to spot a sea serpent on a busy city street, but Melusine had completely disappeared into the growing fog.

Tendrils of mist snaked around my feet and choked the mouths of nearby alleyways. Could the lamia have called up the fog to cover her escape? It seemed like more than an unhappy coincidence.

But why would she have run? If Melusine had returned with some grudge against me for dating her husband, why not have her revenge? I'd been alone and lightly armed mere yards away from her crushing grasp. I took a deep breath and sighed. All I had were more questions.

I lowered my arm and shoved the vial of iron shavings back into my pocket. None of this made any sense. I stepped up onto the sidewalk and turned to face the clurichaun's shop. It was then that I noticed the wall of people whispering and pointing. I looked over my shoulder, half expecting Melusine to materialize out of the mist, but traffic continued to flow past. A cold ball of ice settled in my stomach as I turned to face the crowd. They weren't gawking at something in the street.

They were all staring at me.

I winced and hunched my shoulders, ready to walk away into the fog and wait until the crowd dispersed. I could double back for Jinx after I made my escape. I took a step to my right, avoiding a lamp post, but the sidewalk was blocked by a wall of curious shoppers.

Unfortunately, the afternoon shoppers weren't alone. A man in uniform scowled at me from beneath his navy blue hat. Great, I had attracted the attention of the Harborsmouth police. Could this day get any worse?

Stupid question, of course it could. My chest tightened and I took a shaky breath. More than a dozen sets of eyes stared at me, making my skin burn hot. I wanted nothing more than to run and hide from their disapproving looks. Would I make it across the road in one piece if I dove into the traffic rushing at my back?

A slight shake of the cop's head answered that question. My desire for escape must have been written all over my face. His hand shifted to his hip where a baton and handgun hung from his belt. Running away was definitely not an option.

"Stay where you are, ma'am," the cop said, squaring his shoulders. "I have more than one witness who claims you just stepped out into moving traffic, potentially endangering motorists and yourself. Some of them say you raised your hand as if to throw something into the road. One witness says you did throw something. Can you explain your behavior, miss?"

The cop, Officer Hamlin according to his uniform, was all sweet as pie, but his hand lingered over the butt of his gun. From his opposite hip hung a shiny pair of handcuffs, taunting me with the threat of their cold embrace. I had to come up with a reasonable explanation for stepping in front of a bus that didn't include attempted suicide, public vandalism, or chasing down a vengeful sea serpent, and find a way to convince the cop that I wasn't dangerous, destructive, or crazy. If I didn't think of something quick, I'd be riding in the back of a squad car with those shiny bracelets around my wrists.

I was sure the handcuffs would slam me with a vision whammy. It would be hard to convince a judge that I was both sane and not a threat to society while in the clutches of a vision.

I tried to swallow, but my tongue stuck to the roof of my mouth. I willed saliva and words back to my mouth, but all that came out was a squeak as something brushed against my leg.

I looked down into the all too intelligent eyes of a cat sidhe. The faerie looked like a scrappy street cat, but the eyes, and the way parts of his body seemed made of smoke and shadow, gave its fae nature away. Not that anyone else could see the difference.

"Glamour yourself!" the cat hissed.

The words seemed to come from the cat sidhe, but its mouth didn't move. Since the surrounding crowd didn't gasp at the spectacle of a talking cat, I figured the creature must be a telepath. Just what I needed—a bossy faerie cat in my head.

Go away. Can't you see I'm in the middle of something here? I thought the words at the cat. Hopefully, the telepathy worked both ways.

My pulse sped up as the animal pressed his furred body against my boot. With only a thin layer of leather between the cat sidhe and my flesh, the faerie was starting to look like another potential problem. The cop cleared his throat, obviously waiting for the crazy lady to answer his question. I'd have to worry about the cat later.

"You're glowing," the cat sidhe said. "Which, Princess, I shouldn't have to remind you is against fae law. Exposing our existence to humans is punishable by death. Turn off the light show before these folks realize it's not a trick of the light and fog."

I can't. And don't call me Princess.

I was glowing in front of a human audience? Great. Just perfect. My wisp father, king of the wisps, hadn't bothered to teach me anything useful, like how to cast a life-saving glamour, before ditching me and my mom and hitting my mind with a memory spell to forget he ever existed. My chest tightened and sparks of light filled my vision.

Something scratched my boot and I looked down to see the faerie cat roll his eyes.

"Calm down, Princess, and follow my lead," he said. "First, act pleased to see me and give me a cuddle."

Give you a cuddle? I bet you say that to all the girls.

"That's better," he said. "Your glow is dampening. Take deep breaths, smile, and act happy to see me. I'm your lost cat—THE ONE YOU'VE BEEN DIVING INTO TRAFFIC FOR."

Oh, that makes sense. And it did, kind of. I pasted on a smile that made my cheeks hurt and clapped my gloved hands together in faux glee.

"Kitty!" I said.

"If you really want to sell it, and get the police off your back, you're going to have to pick me up," he said.

I snuck a glance at the crowd and the faerie was right. Frowns were replaced by raised eyebrows and tentative smiles, but no one was going to believe this was my lost cat if I just stood here grinning like a pooka. If your pet just had a brush with death in a major roadway, would you leave it sitting within inches of moving traffic? No, most people would clutch their precious pet to their chest and make sure that it was safe.

Of course, this wasn't my pet, he wasn't even a real cat, and most pet owners don't risk being assaulted with a vision when holding their furry babies. The urge to run was overwhelming, but I forced my grin wide and lifted the cat sidhe into my arms.

If you scratch the leather, I'll turn you into a pair of slippers. The coat was new, one of the perks of a booming business, but it was an empty threat. I'd never skin a cat, not even a cat sidhe, but I hoped to keep the faerie's claws from puncturing my sleeve. The creature's claws could slice through leather as easily as warm butter, leaving nothing between my skin and an immortal faerie—and a nasty vision.

"You can try," he said, flashing a lazy crocodile smile. He flexed one paw and the tips of its claws pressed against my arm. Each needle-sharp claw slid into leather, but, so far, didn't touch flesh. The claws had struck the blade strapped to my forearm.

I stifled a shudder and lifted my head to face the cop.

"Sorry officer," I said. I kept the cat perched in my arms, but lifted my gloved hands in supplication. "This is all a misunderstanding. I was just trying to find my lost cat and bring him home."

The cop looked from me to the cat in my arms and back again. I couldn't have conjured the cat from thin air, but the guy looked reluctant to let me go.

"And you were standing out in traffic because?" he asked.

"When I finally found my cat, he was playing in the road," I said. The faerie's claws squeezed my arm, making tears well up, though not drawing blood. He let out a chuckling purr. The cat bastard was enjoying this. I blinked away the tears and ground my teeth. If I lived through this day, I swore to never again pick up one of the foul creatures except to wring its neck. "A bus was coming and I didn't think...I just stepped out into traffic. I couldn't let my sweet Butterball die. I had to try to save him."

A chorus of *awwwwww*s escaped the crowd. Someone in the rear of the crowd clapped their hands and someone else cheered.

"Butterball?" the cat sidhe asked.

That's what you get for putting holes in my jacket. I warned you not to scratch the leather. Plus, you could stand to lose a few pounds. What do cat sidhe eat, lead weights? I tried not to picture the cat playing with a mouse twice his size. Were there huge rat fae in our city too? *On second thought, I don't want to know.*

While the cat sidhe and I bantered telepathically, the crowd began to disperse. A lady in a baggy sweater and matching knit scarf called me an angel and I hoped she hadn't noticed my glowing skin. My skin looked normal now, and I wasn't seeing any more flashing sparks of light behind my eyelids, so hopefully my wisp glow had fully dissipated. I'd have to learn how to control my fae powers, but that meant a foray into my wisp heritage. That would have to wait.

There was still one person from the crowd who hadn't budged. I stared at the uniformed figure and sighed. He was below average height and weight, but looks can be deceiving. I should know. I assessed the threat he posed—gun, baton, cuffs, wide stance—just as Jenna had taught me. I ran multiple possible fight scenarios through my mind, drawing some satisfaction from each. But I wasn't here to pick a fight with the city's finest. We were technically both on the same side and I wanted to keep things that way.

Trouble with the local authorities wasn't just foolish—it was bad for business. If I landed myself in jail, my PI license could be revoked. If I couldn't legally work cases, Jinx would have my head.

"I'm really sorry if I worried anyone," I said. "I'll keep Butterball inside from now on."

The cat sidhe stopped licking his paw long enough to skewer me with a nasty look.

"There's just one more thing, ma'am," the cop said. "How about you empty your pockets and show me what you were about to throw into the road."

Crap! I had some very unorthodox items in my pockets. How would I explain the bottles of potions and bags of herbs? Heck, the cop would probably think the herbs were drugs. Even though they'd discover their benign nature once tested, I'd still be looking at cuffs and a ride in this guy's squad car.

I may not have inherited the family allergy to iron, but being cuffed and trapped in a metal box was not how I wanted to spend my evening. And if I was hauled downtown, they'd frisk me for weapons. I may eventually talk my way out of the herbs and charms, and the stakes at my back were only pencils to anyone but the undead, but the concealed silver throwing knives strapped to each arm, not to mention the iron dagger in my boot, could cause some serious trouble.

I looked into the cop's face and struggled to remain calm. His eyebrow twitched and his hand slid onto his gun. I tried not to stare at the handcuffs hanging from the officer's belt as I adjusted my grip on the cat. If I started glowing again, I'd probably wind up getting shot.

Mab's bloody freaking bones.

"You surprise me, Princess," the cat sidhe said. "You swear like a lubber fiend."

Shut up. I juggled the cat onto my left arm and slowly reached into my right pocket. I slid the vial of iron shavings from my coat with shaking fingers. I held it out to the officer as something fell from my pocket onto the damp pavement.

"What's this?" the cop asked, reaching for the vial.

"Glitter, um, for the holidays," I said.

He raised an eyebrow as he lifted the "glitter" for a closer look, but the glass vial only contained metal shavings.

"And this?" he asked.

The cop bent down, eyes narrowing as he glanced at the baggy at my feet. *Oh crap, oh crap, oh crap.*

"Catnip," I said, hoping the herb wasn't something obviously poisonous. "I was using it to get Butterball to come to me."

With a thrust of his hind legs "Butterball" launched himself from my arms, startling the cop. The cat sidhe snatched the bag of herbs with his teeth and dropped it at our feet where he began rolling and rubbing himself on the baggy.

"See," I said, shakily. "He really likes it."

St. Mary's church bells tolled the hour, a reminder that night would soon replace the foggy day. I didn't want Jinx out here much longer. The Hill was no place for humans come nightfall. The cop tipped his head back to look skyward and grunted.

"Go on then and get your cat home," he said. "These streets are no place to wander alone at night."

Not one for counting gift horses, I pasted a smile on my face and turned to walk away. My best option was to get out of sight before the cop changed his mind. I scooped up the cat sidhe, tossed the packet of herbs in my pocket, and strode south toward Congress Street. Claws dug into my leather jacket and I swore under my breath. I kept the smile on my face and moved stiffly down Joysen Hill while a wheezing snicker echoed inside my skull.

CHAPTER 3

I found an empty lot behind a pool hall and set the cat on the lid of a trash bin. Grass grew incongruously through broken pavement, seeming to glow green in the fog and thickening shadows. The apparent glow was a reminder that I had unfinished business regarding my fae heritage. The cat sidhe may enjoy goading me by calling me Princess, but the title was apt. My father was the king of the wisps and I was a half-breed with no knowledge of how to glamour myself. I needed to remedy that problem before I ended up enslaved or dead.

If I continued to lose control as I did earlier, risking humans witnessing my glowing skin, someone or something would come for me. I could be forced to live in the Green Lady's realm, if they let me live at all. Faerie assassins could be watching me now, waiting for their chance to take me out. I hunched my shoulders and dragged my eyes away from the shadows.

The cat sidhe's claws scraped the metal can lid as he shook vigorously. His fur stood on end making him look all the more scrappy. An overhead street lamp flickered on, illuminating white ribbons of wax-like flesh which laced the fur along his sinewy body. But the scars were nothing compared to the condition of his face and head.

A ragged scar above the faerie cat's left eye bisected the brow ridge, leaving him with a perpetual look of disdain. He was, in fact, lucky to still have the remaining eye. His ears were not so fortunate. The cat's left ear was filled with holes and tears, like the storm ravaged sail of a ship lost at sea. But the damage to the cat's tattered left ear was outdone by a lump of scar tissue where his right ear should have been. The ear looked to have been torn savagely from his head.

I looked away. This cat sidhe had obviously seen battle and had the scars to prove it. That was something I'd be smart to remember.

"I can't believe you made me roll around like some drug-crazed house cat," he said.

"What?" I asked. "I didn't make you do any of it. Though I appreciate you turning up when you did, I never asked for your help."

Which now that I think of it was strange indeed. Most fae don't lend their assistance without making sure they get something out of the deal, but the cat and I had entered no pact for his help. I'd know if I sealed another faerie bargain. It wasn't the kind of event that went unnoticed. The debt I already carried was wrapped around my soul like choking vines.

My gaze returned to the scars that striped his body and I swallowed hard. I definitely didn't want to owe this faerie a boon. I was pretty sure that fulfilling that kind of favor would get me killed.

"No, but you didn't leave me much choice, Princess," he said. The cat sidhe stretched forward, resting his chin on his front paws, tail waving hypnotically above his head. "Your clumsiness sealed my fate. As soon as you dropped that bag, I had one chance to snatch it back or you'd have been hauled downtown—with no glamour. I'm thinking that the stress of such a trip would have set your wisp skin to glowing."

"But what do you care?" I asked.

"Who says that I care?" he asked. He lifted a paw to his mouth and yawned. "I do, however, believe in self-preservation. Letting humans know we exist would be foolhardy, especially in light of recent events."

"Such as?" I asked.

I wasn't sure what recent events might have stirred up human suspicion. Vamps had erased the memories of all the humans who stumbled onto the waterfront during the *each uisge* invasion. Hadn't they?

"Don't you listen to the mortals?" he asked. The cat sidhe's tail danced an archaic pattern above his tattered ears and I forced myself to look away. Becoming ensnared by a cat sidhe was not on my to-do list. Fae blood may run through my veins, but my human genes left me vulnerable to faerie enchantments. I gripped the vial of cold iron in my pocket. Thankfully, my human half did have its perks—an immunity to iron being one of them. "Sightings of spectral beings have been reported all over the city. Graves are rumored to have been disturbed in local cemeteries. If street corner gossip is to be believed, the dead walk the streets of Harbormouth."

"But ghosts don't exist," I said, body going rigid.

"Does it matter?" he asked. "If mortals go poking their noses into shadows looking for ghosts, they may just discover who they really share this city with. That is one secret I'd rather we kept."

"So you helped me back there to protect the secret of our kind," I said. "To save your own hide."

That scarred hide was beginning to wink in and out of existence as if made of shadow. Watching parts of the cat sidhe's body appear and disappear made me dizzy, as if the ground at my feet were becoming less solid with each flickering wave of shadow. I wrenched my gaze from the faerie cat's body and focused on his face.

"Yes, Princess," he said. The faerie leapt gracefully from the metal bin to the pavement and began crossing the empty lot toward the main road. "And let me give a free word of advice, since I'm in a generous mood. Don't go throwing cold iron around these streets. You're likely to attract the wrong kind of attention."

The cat sidhe flashed a razor sharp smile in my direction then melted into the fog. The last I saw of him, he was a shred of shadow twining around the ankles of shoppers on Market Street.

"And what kind are you?" I muttered.

The bored kind. His voice whispered in my ear. I spun around, but the faerie was nowhere in sight.

"Wait," I said. "The iron shavings were for self-defense. Didn't you see the seven-foot tall, angry lamia?"

The sound of rush hour traffic was my only reply. I'd waited too long to ask my question and now the cat was gone. But the realization nagged at me as I trudged through back lots and alleys, avoiding throngs of shoppers as I made my way back to the clurichaun's shop.

Unlike the crowd of humans who only witnessed my side of the near-battle, the faerie cat should have seen through Melusine's glamour. So why hadn't he mentioned her? Ceffyl's ex had been there, hadn't she?

I shoved gloved hands into my pockets and ducked my head, avoiding the curious stares of dish washers and line cooks as they each sucked down one last cigarette before the busy dinner rush. The alleys of Joysen Hill were never completely empty, but at least there were no obvious threats in sight. Of course, that didn't mean I was safe.

Melusine was out there somewhere. She was in Harborsmouth, wasn't she? I'd seen the bitch with my own two eyes, so why was doubt creeping in like an unwelcome guest?

I bit the inside of my cheek and shook my head. No, I trusted my second sight. No one else had witnessed a seven foot tall woman with a serpent's tail on a busy city sidewalk? So what, that was business as usual. I was used to being the only person who could see the monsters who roam our streets.

I rounded the corner onto Catch Lane behind Dead Man's Catch and dropped into a crouch. Knives slid into my gloved hands from custom sheaths hidden beneath my coat. Clurichaun's were good at crafting more than gloves. The sheaths had been skillfully designed with two functions in mind; protecting my skin from contact with my new weapons and easy release. The grip end of twin throwing knives, balanced silver blades with sharp iron tips, hit my palms before I could blink.

Was that…? A large form loomed, emerging from a gap in the thick fog. I adjusted my grip on the knives, spinning each knife a half turn, and pinching the tips of the blades with shaking fingers.

I breathed in slowly, filling my nostrils with the fetid smell of frying fish and stale beer, relaxed my stance, and assessed the distance to where Melusine loomed in fog thickened shadow. The decision to switch my hold on the knives from the grip to the blade depended on range. If I misjudged the distance, the knives would bounce off my target. I'd lose the element of surprise and end up with one pissed off lamia.

I squinted at Melusine who hadn't moved since my intrusion into Catch Lane. That was weird. When the bitch stared daggers at me through the Clurichaun's shop window, her serpent tale had lashed back and forth like a cat watching a tasty bird just out of reach. But the only thing moving now was a mouse as it scurried beneath a rusting dumpster.

Still holding my knives, wrists cramping, I peered through the shifting mist at the unmoving form. I shook my head and slid my blades back into their custom sheaths. It wasn't Melusine leaning against the brick building, just a large coil of rope beside a stack of wooden barrels. I rubbed my eyes and straightened, cheeks blossoming heat. I'd nearly murdered a pile of rope. What the hell was wrong with me?

Time to retrieve Jinx and get off this damned hill before I got myself arrested. I didn't think Officer Hamlin would take too kindly to a second run in with me, not in one day.

CHAPTER 4

I rubbed my arms as I walked up Joysen Hill, comforted by the blades that hid beneath my leather jacket. Jenna had been trying to convince me to start weapons training since we met last summer, but I didn't take her up on the offer until the holidays. I had worked a job that could have gone south, fast. Even with Jenna's expert assistance, the faeries we were hunting had managed to ambush us. I was lucky to be alive and had the nightmares to prove it.

I still woke to the smell of burning flesh, the awful memory of that night seared into my subconscious. The memories left me feeling weak and vulnerable. Facing a horde of bloodthirsty redcaps will do that to a girl.

So I had treated Jinx and myself to a month of battle training with Jenna. Four months later, we were still attending classes. Jinx was a perfectionist and an adrenaline junkie and I was determined to gain the skills necessary to protect this city, and my friends. I don't make friends easily and wasn't about to let those precious few I had get hurt because I wasn't prepared.

I knew basic self-defense, ran through a routine of moves to disarm and immobilize an opponent every evening while Jinx cooked dinner, but this was no ordinary self-defense class. Having a skilled Hunter as a teacher was both enlightening and embarrassing. Jenna had discovered our weaknesses before our butts hit the practice mat.

I learned that my aversion to touch was a dangerous weakness when it came to hand-to-hand combat. I may know the moves, but when it came to executing those thrusts, flips, and punches, I held back. In close quarters fighting, a second's hesitation can get you dead. Kicks and foot sweeps were less difficult, but I was a total mess when it came to using my hands. Forget grappling or throws. If a move involved getting up close and personal, and risking a vision, I froze. No matter how hard I drilled technique, I didn't have the chops.

Jinx, on the other hand, was willing to follow through with her moves, but she lacked strength and experience. She was also the clumsiest person on the planet. Not that that stopped her. Jinx doesn't give up easily. She still puts up with me, after all.

Thankfully, Jenna could spy our strengths as easily as weaknesses. That's when she finally wore me down on my argument against the use of weapons. She put my physical strength and agility and Jinx's enthusiasm to good use.

Jinx, surprisingly, had a skill for projectile weapons. With her steady hand and tenacity, I wouldn't put it past my partner to master them all by next Christmas, but her current favorite was the crossbow.

Too bad she wasn't carrying one right now. I'd be less worried knowing my roommate was armed. Instead, I pushed my legs to climb the hill faster. Night was closing in.

I reached the clurichaun's shop and balked at the closed sign hanging in the window. Behind the sign, the shop lay dark and unwelcoming. Had the faerie locked up shop before taking Jinx into his bolt-hole? If so, I'd have a hard time getting my partner back. When someone has a secret hiding place they tend to keep it, well, secret. My only chance of finding Jinx was to enter the shop where I'd last seen the clurichaun.

In my haste to keep my friend safe, I'd put her life in the hands of a notorious drunkard. That was beginning to seem like a bad decision. I paced in front of the shop, trying to think. I needed to get inside.

I stepped forward and focused on the door, the letters on the sign swimming in my vision to reveal it hadn't been flipped after all. The sign read "open" and the shop lights became visible, banishing the darkness. I let out a whoop of breath I hadn't realized I'd been holding. The closed sign and lack of interior lights were an elaborate glamour. The spell was probably cast by preset wards that were tripped when the clurichaun opened his bolt-hole. If the shop wasn't actually closed, then perhaps the door wasn't locked either. A girl could hope.

I reached out trembling fingers. Was the glamour the only defense activated when the clurichaun left the shop? I was about to find out. I took a deep breath, the knob turning easily beneath my gloved hand. So far so good. I pushed the door inward and flinched as a small bell rang overhead.

Every time a bell rings, an angel gets its wings. The movie quote rose unbidden and I stifled a giggle. Thankfully, the shop wards hadn't triggered the lock mechanism on the door—or any potentially deadly spell traps, yet. I cleared my throat and stepped inside.

"Hello?" I asked.

The shop was empty. I breathed in the pungent smell of leather and tried to remain calm. Jinx was fine. I just had to contact the clurichaun, right? I spun in a slow circle looking around the store's well-lit interior. More than once I hesitated, mistaking a display of leather jackets for someone standing in my peripheral vision. And don't get me started on the mannequins. I could swear that their dead eyes followed me as I walked around the room. The damn things were creepy.

I stifled a shudder and searched for anything out of place. For a barfly, the clurichaun kept a tidy shop. Leather goods were displayed artfully around the room. As far as I could tell, everything was in its place. Even the boxes and shopping bags I'd dropped to the floor were stacked in an orderly row.

I rifled through the bags, lifting shoe boxes and folded clothing looking for a note or some indication as to where Jinx had gone, but they contained only the remnants of today's shopping trip. I thrust the items back into the bags and growled like a barguest. There were no clues to indicate where the clurichaun had taken Jinx.

I left the main showroom and examined the counter at the rear of the shop. Something seemed to be missing. The memory of my previous visit niggled at me. I tried to conjure up an image of the counter from earlier today, but the memory slipped away like smoke. I'd been too focused on Melusine and the threat she posed.

I scanned the countertop and stopped to examine the register. Kaye had a secret button on her till that opened the back door of her shop. Maybe the clurichaun had a similar setup. I pressed each button with a gloved finger, but nothing happened.

I risked a glance outside. The sun was setting and it was getting dark. The shadows and fog seemed to swallow the city lights, leaving only darkness and the denizens who lurk within.

I spun back to the register and pounded my fist on the counter. I had to be missing something. There had to be a way to contact the clurichaun. I slouched and let my head roll forward, hiding behind the curtain of hair. If I couldn't find a way into the faerie's bolt-hole, I'd have to start seeking visions. I stared at my gloved fist and did a double take.

I slid my hand back across the counter to reveal a circle scratched into the wood. The marks were faint, as if from something sitting there for years. Suddenly, I remembered what was missing from the counter. When I was here earlier, there had been a shiny silver bell—the type you ring for service.

A slow smile spread across my face. I knew what to look for. Where had the clurichaun hidden his bell? I dug around behind the counter, turning waste baskets and drawers upside down.

"Come on bell, where are you hiding?" I muttered.

I walked back out to the showroom and something shimmered in my second sight. I focused and the bell appeared, sitting on top of a creepy mannequin head. I lunged forward and grabbed the bell. It was solid beneath my gloved fingers.

I hurried to the counter and placed the bell on the circle of scratches. Raising my hand and holding it out flat, palm side down, I hit the bell. A loud clang rang throughout the shop. Should I ring it again, perhaps three times? Kaye was always explaining how three was a powerful number when it came to magic...

"Hell-o," a voice hiccup burped behind me.

I spun to see the clurichaun wave his hand and totter toward me. Jinx was sprawled on the floor behind him. *Jinx.*

I rushed to my friend's side and knelt on the polished wood floor. I steeled myself to remove my glove and check for a pulse—I'd never touched Jinx before, her secrets were her own business and not something I wanted to plunge into—when a lazy grin spread across her face. Jinx cracked opened her eyes and smiled even wider.

"Hey, girl," she said. "Let's go, *hiccup*, dancing!"

"Dancing," I said. "Seriously? I doubt you can even walk."

I imagined myself stumbling down Joysen Hill carrying my tall friend all the way home. The Old Port was a long walk from here and if I had to carry Jinx, my arms and legs would be useless in a fight. Running would also be impossible. I'd have to stumble down The Hill slow and defenseless. I grunted and sat back on my heels.

I raked a hand through my hair and pushed it out of my face while examining my friend. This wasn't the first time I'd seen Jinx drink too much, but she didn't usually get this trashed. Oh shit.

"I asked you to protect her," I said. I looked over my shoulder and narrowed my eyes at the clurichaun, and pointed at Jinx. "What did you give her?"

Turning back to Jinx, I nudged her with my knee.

"Hey, wake up," I said. "Did you drink faerie wine?"

I'd drilled three things into Jinx's head since I learned about faeries, demons, and the undead. Never give your blood to a vampire. Never sell your soul to a demon. If you find yourself in the Otherworld, do not eat or drink anything. And don't ever, EVER drink faerie wine.

Okay, that was four things. So sue me.

The point was that breaking these basic rules was worse than death. Letting a vamp drink from you, no matter how beautiful you think they are—and trust me beneath their glamour vamps are not sexy—results in addiction. The experience is so pleasurable, due to a combination of vamp pheromones and chemicals in their saliva, that many humans become addicts after only a few bites. The result is to become a hapless blood slave, passed around the vampire community like a bottle of cheap beer.

Selling your soul to a demon is even worse. No matter how good the bargain, you'll be headed to Hell sooner or later. Capital H, e, double hockey sticks. It's not a nice place to visit and you'll be a full-time resident for eternity—a slave to demons. And demons? They're not called horny because of those protrusions on their heads.

Eating or drinking while in the Otherworld holds a similar fate. Humans who eat or drink enough faerie food become addicts trapped in the faerie realm. Even if they escape, food from our world turns to ash on their tongues. Faerie wine is stronger than any human draught and is rumored to have the most addicting effects even if the smallest glass of the stuff is imbibed. To drink faerie wine is to become a slave to one of the faerie courts—a plaything for bored immortals.

I'd been told that the boundaries of Faerie had been sealed, but there were always loopholes and Jinx was unlucky enough to fall into one. If the clurichaun's bolt-hole was a gateway to Faerie, Jinx could have drunk faerie wine without realizing what she'd done. If she had, would she become an addict forced to live in Faerie?

I stood up, hands shaking, and nudged Jinx again with my boot.

"Did. You. Drink. Faerie. Wine?" I asked.

"Beer," she mumbled. "Lots and lots of beer."

"Is that true?" I asked, glaring at the clurichaun.

"'Tis true," he said, nodding.

I leaned in, sniffing at Jinx's clothes. She didn't smell like wine. Before I could straighten, Jinx burped in my face.

"Oberon's eyes," I said, wrinkling my nose. "You smell like a brewery."

Jinx giggled. I wanted to kick her, but instead crossed my arms and glared down my nose.

"That's 'cause we were in a brewery," she said. "This guy's hiding spot is in the basement of Old Shoal's brewery."

It sounded like she said "bashement o' Old Shhhhoalsh bwewewy," but I got the idea. My friend had been in her version of Heaven, surrounded by kegs of microbrew beer. She'd been partying in the basement of a local brewery, not Faerie. I shook my head and nudged her again with my boot.

"Come on," I said. "Get up. We need to get you home before full dark."

I hesitated, then reached down and pulled Jinx upright. I grit my teeth and slid an arm under her shoulders for support. Most of my skin was covered in leather and denim, but all it took was a small patch of bare skin to trigger a vision. This made carrying my roommate far from ideal. If I got slammed with a vision from Jinx's past, it would be her fault, but I hoped that could be avoided. We didn't need any more delays.

"What about my bags?" she asked.

Jinx looked so sad and lost, I melted just a little.

"Can you walk?" I asked.

Jinx shrugged me off and stepped forward. She was wobbly, but remained upright.

"See, I'm fine," she said.

She staggered and started to fall backward. Crap.

"Here, take these," I said. I passed Jinx a fistful of shopping bags for each hand, careful to keep her balanced. I had a feeling I'd need my hands free. "Ready?"

Jinx managed to nod without falling over. We were making progress.

"Thanks, I guess, for keeping her safe," I said to the clurichaun.

I tried not to grump, much. I hadn't included a clause regarding Jinx drinking alcohol, so he hadn't done anything to breach our agreement. The faerie had held up his end of the bargain. I could feel the debt between us heavy on my shoulders. I almost hoped he called in his favor soon. I'd have to work a case for free, but that was better than this feeling.

"Safe travels," the clurichaun said.

He waved a stubby hand, smiling eyes gazing over the spectacles he wore on his red, bulbous nose.

"Safe travels," I said.

I sighed and pushed Jinx out the door and into the night.

"Oh, crap," Jinx said, pulling to a halt.

"What?" I asked. "Did you leave something back at the shop?"

"I forgot about my date with Hans," she said. Jinx frowned at her feet and started to pitch forward. "Guess I won't be going out dancing."

Her words were so slurred it sounded like she said, "guesh I won't be going out danshing" so I was pretty sure she wasn't making it out on the dance floor tonight. Jinx was clumsy when she was stone cold sober. Drunk she'd be a menace.

"What's Hans' number?" I asked. "I'll call and tell him you can't make it."

She blinked at me and stuck her tongue into her cheek.

"It's in my phone," she said.

Jinx dropped the shopping bags to the sidewalk and fumbled for her phone. I didn't want to touch it, but I wanted to get this over with. I reached for the phone with thumb and index finger and scrolled through her contacts list. I found Hans' number and hit call.

"You're early, woman," Hans said.

Woman? Mab's bones, I wanted to shove the phone down the Hunter's oversized, Nordic throat.

"Um, this is Ivy Granger, Jinx's friend," I said. "Jinx has to cancel her date tonight."

"Why would she cancel and why are you the one to call?" he asked. "I know she doesn't have to work late. Jinx had this afternoon off. I checked."

They'd only gone out on a couple of dates and already this guy was keeping tabs on my best friend? I held the phone so tight I'm surprised it didn't explode into dust.

"Look, Hans, she had a few too many drinks with a clurichaun," I said. "Give the girl a break."

"She was drinking with a clurichaun?" he asked. Hans started breathing heavy and his tone was menacing. "With a FAERIE? That worthless bi..."

"Get over yourself," I said.

Hans made a strangled sound and spit. The guy had the temperament of a berserker and was known for his rages in the heat of battle. But he wasn't in battle now and he was talking about my friend.

Apparently, Hans thought the only good faerie was a dead faerie. Some Hunters are like that, a fact I'd be smart to remember. I'd become used to Kaye and Jenna's acceptance of my half-breed status, but thinking that all Hunters would be as accepting of my kind was foolish.

If I'd known the guy had such a hard-on for faeries, I never would have mentioned the clurichaun. Though I can't say I'm completely sorry. The Hunter was bad news. If he got this enraged at the thought of Jinx sharing a drink with a clurichaun, what would he do when he found out her best friend, roommate, and business partner was a wisp princess?

"Tell that faerie lover she can lose my number," he said.

Hans hung up and I handed Jinx back her phone.

"He cool?" she asked.

Jinx was smiling and I didn't have the heart to tell her that her boyfriend was a racist dick. She'd be better off hearing about the phone call when she was sober. It could wait.

"Sure, he's cool," I said, as Jinx picked up the shopping bags she'd dropped and we started our descent down the hill.

Hans was cool alright. His heart was cool as the blade of cold iron I wanted to skewer him with.

CHAPTER 5

Getting home had been a trial, but we were still in one piece. I couldn't say the same for Jinx's footwear. She'd puked into one of her shopping bags before making it home, fouling a brand new pair of shoes. And the platform sandals she'd been wearing? Those she threw into the harbor saying they were hard to walk in. Yeah, it couldn't have had anything to do with the keg of beer she drank.

When my roommate woke up, she wasn't going to be happy with herself. A grin slid across my face. Maybe destroying two of her treasured pairs of shoes would teach her a lesson.

Jinx slept, snores echoing from her room. I was tempted to bang around the kitchen, but settled for leaving the bag of shoes, the ones with sick all over them, in her bedroom. Oh, sweet revenge.

I pulled my hair back into a ponytail, dropped a note on the kitchen counter, and slid out of the loft apartment we shared. As much as I'd love to see Jinx's face when she woke up, I had questions that needed answering.

I considered going to see Jenna, but shook my head. No, hunters keep odd hours. My teacher, and sometimes backup, would probably be out prowling the streets for rogue supernaturals. Woe the creature she caught feasting on a human. Jenna might only be one-hundred pounds soaking wet, but the petite redhead was whip fast, armed, and deadly.

Instead, I turned right onto Water Street avoiding the drunks lingering in doorways or staggering to the next seedy bar or raucous pub. It would be just my luck to avoid being hit by Jinx's sick, only to have a stranger puke on me. Ah, the joys of living in the Old Port. I hunched forward, hands in jacket pockets, and walked faster.

I took Wharf Street and started to relax slightly. The bar crowd tended to stick to the sidewalks here, avoiding the cobbled street. "Ankle twisters" Jinx called cobbles and for good reason. I'd stuck to the comparatively smooth, brick sidewalks myself while guiding Jinx home, but now I strode down the center of the road, only stepping to the side when a car entered the narrow, one-way street.

At the top of the hill, I rang the buzzer beside the door of The Emporium. The store was closed, but Kaye never left the place unprotected. Someone or something manned the door, ready to carry a message back to their boss. I preferred coming to the store during business hours when Arachne, Kaye's human employee, ran the shop. Visiting after hours was...unpredictable.

I think Kaye liked playing with her visitors just as much as she enjoyed toying with her employees. Bothering the witch at night only added to her fun. I suppose I should be glad she didn't blast me into dust for the intrusion.

I waited, itching to press the buzzer again, but not wanting to push my luck. I raked a gloved hand through my hair and sighed. Patience was not my strong suit and, in my defense, it had been a very long day. As my sigh puffed out to mix with cool night air, I heard a scratching sound overhead.

I held my breath and listened, slowly tilting my head back to look up. I untangled my hands from my hair and lowered them to hip height, keeping my arms loose and hands ready to receive my knives.

Click, click, scratch.

There it was again, like claws tapping and scratching at stone. And it was definitely coming from above, not from the street below. That ruled out a human taking their dog for a walk. No, this was not a normal city sound at all.

The door to The Emporium stood at the corner of the building, walls towering overhead and roads running back at angles to the left and right. I scanned the stone and brick walls, searching for what was making the sound. My mouth fell open at the sight of a gargoyle crawling down the building toward me, stone nails clicking on brick, stone, and mortar. Though the creature must weigh a ton, it moved with surprising agility and speed—like a bat out of Hell.

A giggle rose in my throat and I snorted. The idiom was apt. Bat-like wings sprouted from the back of the demonic form. If the faerie hadn't been made of stone, I might have wondered if it was indeed Hellspawn—a bat demon rushing out of Hell and straight at me.

The gargoyle's face was grotesque, an amalgam of canine, bat, and goat. Ram's horns rose from its head and large teeth protruded from a rounded snout. The teeth were impressive, but I focused on the muscled arms and legs racing toward me, each ending in sharp claws—claws that rent through brick and stone.

I longed to palm my knives, but traffic continued to swish past on my right and left, humans oblivious to the creature rushing toward me. Not to mention the futility of stabbing a gargoyle with a common blade. If I resorted to violence, I'd have to wait for the gargoyle to suffer the effects of iron poisoning from the iron tips of my knives. I didn't think I'd survive that long.

I blinked away stone dust, and risked a glance at Kaye's door. I shouldn't have to face the gargoyle alone. Where was the doorman? Unless... Could the gargoyle be working for Kaye?

When dealing with the supernatural it can be difficult to tell friend from foe. The best indication of enemy is when the creature with big teeth tries to eat you. And I wasn't about to wait that long. I had no desire to be a gargoyle's chew toy.

I also didn't want to disembowel one of Kaye's employees, if the creature was in fact working for the witch. I had a nagging suspicion that doing so would piss her off. With only seconds left before the beast was on top of me, I did the one thing I could do. I screamed at the wall.

At least, that's what passerby would witness. A crazy lady yelling at a brick wall.

"Halt!" I yelled. "Identify yourself."

Jenna's military-style phrasing was starting to rub off on me. I suppose that's what happens when you spend too much time with Hunters. Next, I'd be referring to the gargoyle as my target. Though honestly, if the gargoyle wasn't friendly, I was screwed. I brushed the fingertips of my glove along the grip of my throwing knife, wishing I had a jackhammer up my sleeve instead.

"Thaaat isss myyy liiine," the gargoyle said. He grinned. At least, I hoped it was a grin. His lips pulled back to reveal more teeth. "Madammme Kaaaye willll seeee youuu nowww."

His words were like rocks grating on one another. The sound made my head ache, but at least the creature wasn't going to kill me. There was that. The gargoyle made a bowing motion, even though he was still hanging upside down on the vertical wall, and waved toward the door with one paw. At his gesture, the door clicked open.

Kaye's love of theatrics was really starting to piss me off. She could have spelled the door to unlock when I first knocked. I grunted at the gargoyle sentry and trudged inside. The faerie raised a stone eyebrow at my rudeness, but I didn't have the energy or patience for pleasantries.

My shoulders slumped as the last rush of adrenaline bled away. I'd put my body through too many fight or flight situations for one day. I wanted to be sleeping in my bed, not rousing a powerful witch from hers.

CHAPTER 6

The door snicked shut behind me, closing out the night and sealing me in. I paused and waited for my eyes to adjust to the dark. The Emporium was black as the inside of a closed coffin, but I was able to make out the clutter of obstacles in my path. My fae heritage had recently endowed me with exceptional night vision.

It was a good thing, since Kaye's shop was nearly impossible to navigate even in daylight. Without night vision I'd likely end up tripped by a witch's broom, tangled in imitation spider's web, and my head wedged inside a cauldron filled with plastic vampire teeth. Not my idea of a fun way to spend the night. And make no mistake; Kaye would leave me there until Arachne rescued me in the morning. She'd think it was a hoot.

I scowled at the tangle of foam reaper scythes, plastic skeletons, monster masks, and herb displays crowding my path. The Burning Times had left its mark on those with magical talent. Some witches hid their home high upon a cliff or within a tunnel of thick briars. Kaye chose to live in the back of her shop, a location just as insurmountable especially to anyone, or anything, she wanted to keep away.

And to those of us she deemed welcome visitors? We had to be careful where we stepped or risk breaking our necks. Even the welcome mat was unwelcoming with its message, "Abandon all hope, ye who enter here."

I wiped my boots on the mat and stomped deeper into the shop.

*****

I found Kaye in her spell kitchen, alone. She stood, fully dressed, eyes bright, holding a book under her arm and a mug of something steaming in her hands. She looked completely awake, which didn't seem quite fair. I felt like something the cat sidhe dragged in, half dead and nibbled around the edges.

"Where's Hob?" I asked.

I glanced around the kitchen, eyes searching for the small brownie, but he was nowhere to be seen. Of course, the little imp was adept at hiding. Hob loved ambushing unwary visitors. I hoped he wasn't offended by the late hour of my visit. Hob's pranks were legendary.

"Asleep, below the hearth," she said softly. "Let's leave him be, for now."

I nodded, pulling a small gift for Hob from my pocket. I tiptoed to the hearth and set the shiny package on the mantel where he would see it later. Brownies expected an offering for entry into their territory. I wouldn't risk Hob's ire by visiting without leaving a gift.

The hearth area was quiet. Hob may be sleeping quietly below the hearthstone, but where were Marvin's snores? I searched the floor, but we seemed to be missing one large bridge troll.

"And Marvin?" I asked.

Hob, and Kaye, had been letting the orphaned troll crash here until he'd recovered from his injuries. Though Marvin's face seemed to have healed, I suspected the kid had emotional scars that ran deeper. Those wounds would take longer to heal.

"Trying out a newly vacated bridge," she said.

She said the news as if it was nothing, but an unoccupied bridge meant Marvin could be getting new digs. I pressed a hand to my stomach where a pang of pain gnawed deep in my gut. I knew the kid needed his own place eventually, but hoped he wasn't rushing into things too soon. The streets were a hard place to live on your own, and…I wasn't ready to see him go.

I felt my mouth go dry and cleared my throat.

"In Harborsmouth?" I asked.

"Yes, dear," she said. "Don't worry about the lad. He's just around the corner along Myrtle Street where a footpath crosses the old stream bed. He'll be fine."

I shrugged, looking away.

"Who said I was worried?" I said.

"Nobody, dear," she said.

I glanced up to see her eyes twinkling. Caught in her gaze, I shifted from foot to foot wondering where to begin.

"Jinx went shopping today," I said. I let out a heavy sigh. "Which means I had to go shopping too."

"Why would you...?" she asked.

"She went shopping on Joysen Hill," I said.

"Oh, well then," she said. Kaye harrumphed and shook her head. "I don't see why you like the foolish, clumsy girl so much anyway. She's likely to get you into trouble."

"Is that prescience or just your dislike for her?" I asked.

"It doesn't take a toss of the bones to know the girl's trouble," she said. "But I'm guessing you didn't come knocking at my door, rousing me from my bed, to talk about roommate troubles."

Kaye didn't look like she'd tumbled from her bed, but I grit my teeth and kept the thought to myself. Starting things off with an argument wouldn't get me answers. In fact, it wouldn't be good for my health. Whether or not Kaye had been asleep, I was calling on her at an inconsiderate hour. Her wry amusement could easily turn to annoyance if I didn't pick my words carefully.

"I have questions," I said.

Kaye sighed and tossed a hand in the air. She waddled over to a wood table and dropped onto a long bench to hunch over her mug.

"Questions, questions, questions," she muttered. "Go on then, ask away before I change my mind."

I remained standing and focused on the mug in Kaye's wrinkled, tattooed hands. It was easier than meeting her eyes.

"I need to find a cat sidhe," I said. "I'm hoping you can help me find him."

"The streets are crawling with faerie cats," she said. "I'll need more to go on, but why would you want to find a cat sidhe? Start at the beginning, girl."

I told Kaye about sighting Melusine, the lamia's apparent anger, my descent into traffic, Melusine's sudden disappearance, my glowing skin, the crowd of bystanders, the human cop, and the appearance of the cat sidhe.

"I started to glow out on a public street today with a crowd of people, and a cop, watching," I said. I wet my lips and met Kaye's eyes. "I didn't even realize that I was doing it. I need to learn how to control my wisp abilities."

"And you think this cat sidhe can help you with that?" she asked.

"So far, we've had no leads in locating my real father, but the cat was aware of who and what I am," I said. "He knew I was both fae and a princess. That's more than I knew up until this year. So I want to know who he is and what else he knows about my past." I clenched my fists, the leather creaking loudly as I squeezed. "If he has information about my deadbeat father, I need to talk to him. I have to learn how to create a glamour, and control my wisp powers, before one of the faerie courts decides I'm a threat to their secret. They won't hesitate to kill me or, worse, send me to live in the Green Lady's realm."

I shuddered while imagining what it would be like having humans gawk at me all day, a carnival freak for their petty amusement. The Green Lady provided asylum to those fae who could not conjure a glamour to hide their true forms, but the price was eternal servitude. Working forever as an indentured freak in her carnival was not the future I wanted. It didn't feel like a future at all.

But if the fae courts discovered I was an unglamoured faerie living amongst humans, the alternative was death.

"Yes, this does seem serious," she said. Kaye stared at me over her mug, the steam giving her face an eerie cast. "Looks like I won't have to turn you into a frog for interrupting my sleep after all."

I was pretty sure that Kaye was yanking my chain. There was that twinkle in her eyes again. But the sorry fact was that she could have me eating flies faster than I could run out the door. I swallowed hard.

"So you'll help me find this cat sidhe?" I asked.

"Yes, but I'll need a more detailed description," she said. "As I've said, there are many of the cat faeries in Harborsmouth."

I described the cat sidhe, from his torn ear and scarred face to his shadow-winking tail. Kaye closed her eyes and nodded as I spoke. Would she be able to identify the faerie cat? I felt foolish in hindsight for not asking his name. I stared down at my boots and clenched my fists. Not asking the cat sidhe's name was a rookie mistake. A good detective relies on information, no matter how small. I should have asked, but I was too distracted by the disappearance of Ceffyl's ex.

Kaye opened her eyes and smiled.

"Few cat sidhe can speak telepathically to a human," she said.

Kaye placed a finger alongside her nose and winked, but I had no idea what she was getting at. I crossed my arms and tapped my foot against the kitchen floor. Why did faeries and witches take so long to get to the point?

"But I'm half wisp," I said.

"Yes, but most cat sidhe cannot speak to any fae outside their own race," she said. "Only those in the top echelons of the cat sidhe hierarchy have the ability. Even fewer have the ability to shapeshift into human form."

"But he was in cat form the entire time," I said. I shook my head. "How would I know if he can shift or not?"

"Yes, I get ahead of myself," she said, waving a hand. "You said the cat sidhe spoke telepathically, had a scar above his left eye, and his right ear was a lump of scar tissue where it had been torn from his head."

I nodded.

"That would be Torn," she said.

"Torn?" I asked.

"Sir Torn, Lord of the Harborsmouth cat sidhe," she said.

Oh. I'd held a faerie lord in my arms—and insulted him. I swallowed hard, not so sure I wanted to find him now after all. But, of course, I didn't have much choice. I had to learn if he knew where my father was.

"Where can I find this Sir Torn?" I asked.

"The Lord of Cats can be found holding court at Club Nexus," she said.

"Club Nexus?" I asked. "In Harborsmouth? Never heard of it." Which was weird since I knew the city well and I'd never heard Jinx, who had a fondness for nightclubs, mention a club by that name either.

"Yes, Club Nexus is in Harborsmouth, but it's not surprising that you haven't heard of it," she said. "It is a very secretive club. It is glamoured against prying eyes and only allows entry to a small number of humans. And until recently, you were more human than fae."

"So, this Club Nexus is a fae meeting place?" I asked.

"Yes and no," she said. "Nexus is not exclusive to the fae folk. It is a meeting place for all magical creatures. All of those who wish to see and be seen. Nexus is a place of power and so it draws those with power."

"Are you saying this place is some kind of black hole for supernaturals?" I asked.

Kaye nodded.

"There are forces in this world which act upon us, pulling and pushing," she said.

"Like gravity?" I asked.

"Yes, like gravity or your black hole," she said. "These forces hold sway over all things, but there are some which have more influence over magic than the mundane. Ley lines are such a force. These lines of power run over this world, like a grid, and where these lines intersect great or terrible things may happen. And so there have always been those of us who try to protect these places of power, to maintain a balance."

"And Club Nexus is a place of power?" I asked.

"All of Harborsmouth is such a place, a rare convergence of great power, where three ley lines intersect," she said. "Club Nexus is a crossroads, sitting on the very point at which the lines meet."

"Drawing every magical race to it, like pixies to salt," I said.

Details clicked into place. Things I'd never been able to understand, until now. Like why Harborsmouth attracted so many fae, both Seelie and Unseelie, and why the vamps had made this a settlement so many years ago.

"Yes," she said, lips lifting in a grin. "Like pixies to salt."

I had a lot to think about, and questions raced through my head, but now was not the time. I had to focus on the problems at hand.

"How do I get inside?" I asked. "Will I even be able to find this place?"

"Your second sight should cut through the glamour the fae folk use to keep curious humans away, and I can give you a map of its location," she said. "For most humans and lesser fae entry to Nexus is by invitation only, but if you are truly the daughter of Will-o'-the-Wisp, king of the wisps, then you may enter at will. But make certain that entering Club Nexus is worth risking your anonymity. Until now, your true identity has been known to very few. Entering Nexus will change everything. By using your birthright to gain entrance, you formally announce your existence to the fae community."

Crap. I rubbed the back of my neck, leather gloves cool against hot skin.

"Like a coming out party?" I asked. I tried to make the comment sound light and humorous, but it came out in a choked squeak.

"Precisely," she said. "You will lose what remaining anonymity you have. Your royal status will be known to all local fae. With that status comes grave danger and responsibility."

"Peachy," I said.

I let out a long sigh. The storybooks had it wrong. Being a faerie princess was not what it was cracked up to be.

"Think it over before making a decision," she said. "You have gone this long without the knowledge of your father's whereabouts. A few more days will not hurt."

Yeah, a few more days wouldn't hurt, so long as I didn't start glowing around humans. Then I wouldn't have to worry about finding my father, or the perils of becoming a princess. I'd be dead.

"Right, thanks," I said. "I'll sleep on it."

I took a step toward the door and swayed. I put a hand to my forehead and took a shaky breath. I was burning up, the heat evident even through my glove. The joys of keeping covered up, even while inside a warm kitchen. I pulled back my sleeve to examine my skin, but, thank Oberon, it wasn't glowing. Nothing a cold shower and good night's sleep wouldn't fix.

"Oh, and Ivy," she said. I sighed. I'd nearly made it out of the kitchen. "Be wary of Melusine. The former kelpie queen is dangerous. But if you must face her, keep in mind that her serpent half is capable of regeneration."

Regeneration? Good to know.

"Cut off her tail and it grows back again?" I asked.

"Yes," she said.

If anyone knew how to take down a lamia, it was Kaye. Not only did she have the largest library on magical creatures, she'd also been an accomplished Hunter. I filed the information away for later.

"Thanks for the tip," I said.

"Safe travels, dear," she said.

"Safe travels," I said.

CHAPTER 7

I decided to take the long way home, organizing my thoughts as I walked. I was a girl in need of a shower and a bed, but I'd never get any sleep with my mind racing. It was best to sort through the storm of facts and questions.

I'd learned a lot from Kaye, but I still had unanswered questions. Other than my guess that she sought revenge, I had no idea what Melusine was doing in Harborsmouth. That was something I needed to find out, preferably before she made her next move. I also needed to warn her ex-husband that she was in town.

Ceff wasn't going to be happy. Melusine had murdered his infant child and tricked him into the execution of his eldest son, leaving Ceff, and his kingdom, with no heir to the throne. Those were his most painful memories and by warning Ceff of Melusine's return, I'd be casting him into the darkness of those times. Melusine was hurting Ceff with her very presence here.

My hands rubbed at the knives hidden beneath my jacket. I wanted to make her pay for what she'd done to Ceff. I'd lived through those memories myself when I'd touched his bridle. I knew how the death of his sons had nearly destroyed him.

I shook my head and pulled my hands from my knives. I wouldn't lose myself to revenge, not like Melusine. Melusine was selfish and evil. I was nothing like her. But if she tried to harm the ones I cared about, I'd be happy to try out some of the moves Jenna had been drilling into me.

I continued to walk, boots nearly silent on bricks and cobbles. My fae heritage may be a liability, especially if I didn't learn to create a glamour, but I was beginning to discover a few beneficial talents. My second sight and psychometry had emerged during childhood, but my improved night vision, increased agility, and ability to move silently were new. What other changes did my fae blood have in store?

My thoughts turned to my father. I had few memories of him, due to a spell he'd cast over my mind before he left us. According to Kaye, it was a powerful spell. It had caused me to forget my own father, but now memories were breaking through—and so were my powers. Had he meant to keep my wisp abilities safely hidden away until I was an adult? What had he thought would happen when the spell broke? Who would teach me to use and control my new abilities?

Would he come for me? That thought scared me most of all. Since my memories emerged, I'd held onto the hate I felt for my father. He'd abandoned me and my mother and left me ignorant and defenseless. Now I had to find him because he had the information I needed to survive, but I didn't expect a happy family reunion. A piece of me wished for my father to rush in to save the day with a story of how his leaving was to protect my mother and me from some form of evil, but that was a child's wish, foolish and naïve. It was more likely that the wisp king had grown tired of his mortal wife and child. He'd probably ditched us for someone shiny and new. It was best not to get my hopes up.

But no matter my abandonment issues, I did need to find the wisp king. And my best chance for that was talking to the cat sidhe, Sir Torn. Too bad that meant entering Club Nexus—and being outed as a faerie princess.

Becoming a fae leader? Not on my bucket list.

If I accepted my role as wisp princess, I would also have to acknowledge my alignment in the world of faerie politics. Wisps, like kelpies, were members of the Unseelie court. Ceff had insisted that one's court did not dictate all of one's actions. He believed in free will, but I was less optimistic. Unlike Ceff, I did not have loyal guards and a royal entourage to back me up should I ruffle some feathers.

Walking through the doors of Club Nexus could change everything. It would mean acknowledging my royal responsibilities and my allegiance to the dark.

It was too much to think about, but, thank Mab, at least I didn't have to act tonight. Tomorrow or the next day, but not tonight. Maybe I could find another way to locate my father before then. I drew in a steadying breath and let the tension melt from my neck and shoulders.

While inside The Emporium I'd begun to worry that I was coming down with something. My body had flashed hot and feverish, as if my skin were too tight and about to burst into flame. But now, with the cool air from the harbor on my face, the heat bled from my skin. I took a deep breath and looked up at the night sky. Ceff was right. It was soothing for Unseelie fae to walk beneath the stars.

Ceff. My feet had carried me to the harbor. The fog which had shrouded the city had dissipated, crawling back into the dark places from which it had sprung. Stars danced on the water and the moon left a sparkling trail leading out into the ocean. Too bad I couldn't place my feet upon the moonlit path and simply walk to Ceff's domain.

I let out a sigh. I wasn't used to having someone to care about other than Jinx, but Ceffyl Dŵr, king of the local kelpies, had strode into my life and stolen my heart. I sometimes wonder how Ceff snuck past the walls I'd spent a lifetime constructing. It may have been how unguarded he was at the time. I never saw him as a viable threat.

It was strange, but I'd known Ceff's most personal secrets before I'd even met the man himself. And when we did meet, it was during a battle when he was at his most vulnerable. I'd held Ceff's fate when a pooka dropped the kelpie's bridle into my hand. Ceff pled for his release and I had returned his bridle, and tended his wounds while he sat dressed only in a tablecloth. After the battle, Ceff had asked me out on a date. Against my better judgment, the handsome thief had slipped past my defenses and stolen my heart.

I raised a gloved hand to my lips, powerless against the goofy grin spreading across my face. Even tonight when it seemed like my entire world was crashing down, the thought of Ceff could make me smile. Silly heart.

I bit my lip, pulled the tie from my ponytail, letting my hair fall across my shoulders, and smoothed my clothes with my hands. I could still feel the goofy grin on my face, but it would have to do.

Ceff and I didn't have a date scheduled for tonight, but he had posted sentinels along the waterfront. The system was in place to keep Harborsmouth safe and to rebuild peace between the land and water fae, but Ceff's kelpie soldiers and selkie allies would relay any message directly to his ears. If I called out for him, he would come.

I strode to the railing, cupped my hands around my mouth, and called out Ceff's full name. There's power in a name, especially for those with fae blood. I heard an answering splash near a pylon to my right and knew my message had been received. Now there was nothing to do but wait.

A flutter in my belly made my stomach churn. Should I have come to the harbor? It was selfish to take Ceff away from his duties just because I'd had a bad day. And telling him about Melusine would only cause him pain. I pressed my lips together, wishing I hadn't called out for Ceff. Wishing I could take it back.

My eyes scanned the calm waters of the harbor and the ocean waves beyond. After what seemed an eternity, a dark form emerged. I gasped. I was always startled to see Ceff in his horse form. Kelpies are Unseelie fae who can shift into human form, but their natural shape is that of a water horse.

The horse swimming toward me had a glossy coat, dappled grey like a harbor seal. Ceff's lustrous coat was marred by terrible scars, a parting gift from his *each uisge* captors. But instead of detracting from his beauty, the scars seemed to draw the eye and show off his smooth coat and rippling muscles by contrast. As he drew near, I could see the gill slits along Ceff's neck move with the exertion of swimming a long distance in such a short time. I looked into his large, dark green eyes and smiled.

He was beautiful, and he was mine. My hands fisted and skin flushed hot at the memory of Melusine on the street today. How dare she come into my city and threaten our happiness?

Ceff tilted his head to the side, studying my reaction. I shook off my anger as he approached the dock. Ceff shimmered and hands replaced hooves. He gripped the side of the dock and pulled his, now human, body from the water.

Ceff's water horse form was beautiful, but his human body was drop-dead gorgeous. Even in human form, he bore the scars from his abduction by *each uisge*, and the subsequent battle, but those scars didn't detract from his beauty. Water ran down his chest, though his dress slacks appeared dry; just another peculiarity of fae magic.

I looked up from his chest—I was looking at the scars, really—and into his eyes. Ceff's eyes were the one thing that remained unchanged when he shifted, large, midnight green pools in a handsome, otherwise human, face.

Ceff winked and I blushed, heat rising to my cheeks.

"Did you miss me already?" he asked.

His voice was like a burbling stream sliding across stones worn smooth with time. It made things churn and heat low in my belly. He started to reach toward me, responding to the heat rising between us. I flinched and took an involuntary step back.

"Sorry," I said, sounding breathless.

I bit my lip. The apology was automatic, though heartfelt. I did feel guilty about my touch phobia—god knows I wanted to run my hands over his chest and fingers through his wet hair—but I'd nearly lost my sanity while touching his bridle. I didn't know what would happen if I touched the man himself.

Immortals tend to accumulate painful memories in their long lives, and Ceff had experienced more loss and terror than most. Part of me wanted to reach out and share all of that with him, but most of me was a sniveling mess, rocking and shaking in the back of my mind. I wasn't prepared, not yet.

Thankfully, Ceff was patient.

"Do not apologize," he said, lips quirking upward. "We have all eternity."

That sounded like a promise.

I stepped forward slowly, Ceff meeting me partway. We stopped within inches of each other, his hands in his pockets. Perhaps to keep them from straying? The weight of them pushed his pants lower on his hips and it was all I could do not to reach out myself. I drew in a calming breath and smiled at the peculiar mix of salt brine and cool skin that was Ceff's personal scent.

Tension eased from my shoulders and I sighed. Ceff's presence was calming, though I slid my gloved hands into my pockets as well.

"Thanks for coming," I said. "I know you just left."

Ceff traveled like the tides. He spent time here on land with me, but inevitably returned to the water and his people. Currently, we were trying a schedule of one day on land followed by six days at sea. It worked well for both of us. I was used to being on my own, and work kept me busy. Plus, Ceff had his royal duties as king.

Speaking of royal duties...

"I will always come when you call," he said.

Yep, I was melting—big puddle of sappy goo over here. Ceff had that effect on me. But I did have questions which only he may be uniquely qualified to answer. I tried to decide where to begin. Focusing on my current problems helped to pull me back on track, and feel less like a love-struck puppy.

I nodded and took a deep breath.

"I met a cat sidhe today who may know something about my father," I said. Ceff raised an eyebrow, but I pushed onward. "Kaye believes the cat to be Sir Torn, Lord of the local cat sidhe. If it's the same cat, he holds court at a place called Club Nexus. But getting inside the club will be tricky."

"Cat sidhe," he said, wrinkling his nose. "I do not trust the shadow-walkers."

Right, cats and fish probably weren't the best of friends.

"I don't trust him either," I said. "But I need to learn how to control my wisp abilities, and that means finding my father."

"Why did you not ask this cat sidhe earlier?" he asked.

I sighed. This was the part of the conversation I'd been dreading. I turned toward the harbor, but continued to watch Ceff from the corner of my eye.

"I ran into him while I was chasing after a perceived threat, someone from your past," I said. I cleared my throat, swallowing hard. "Melusine is in Harborsmouth. I'm so sorry."

Ceff's face paled and he slumped forward as if the words struck a blow. But when he looked up again his face was flushed, eyes dark with fury. He thrust his shoulders back and held a clenched fist to his lips.

"Did she threaten you?" he said. "If so, she will pay."

"Not...exactly," I said. I thought back to the encounter. Ceff's ex had looked like she wanted to rip my body to shreds and eat me. But since none of that actually happened, I didn't bother to mention it. "She started to rush toward me through heavy traffic, but once I got Jinx to safety and stepped out to meet her, Melusine had disappeared."

He didn't ask how I had known it was Melusine. He knew I'd shared in his memories of his ex-wife when riding the visions from his bridle. I'd recognize the crazy bitch anywhere.

It wasn't like lamias typically slithered the city streets of the north eastern US. There were two types of serpent fae, desert dwellers and ocean dwellers. Melusine was the latter, a half-woman half-sea serpent who normally spent her time in water. A lamia should not have been seen coiled and ready to strike on the busy, non-desert, non-ocean streets of Harborsmouth. The woman really was crazy, or I was chasing ghosts.

Crap. Where the hell was my brain? The cat sidhe had mentioned ghosts, and I'd been too keyed up to ask the right kinds of questions. I needed to get Melusine out of town. Being able to think quick on my feet and problem solve under pressure was what made me a good detective. But now I was making foolish mistakes because my head wasn't in the game. Having that bitch in my city was too much of a distraction.

Not only had I missed an opportunity to ask Torn about my father and the ghost sightings, but I'd also forgotten to mention the ghosts to Kaye during my late night visit. I'd have to remedy that soon, but it could wait until morning—which was fast approaching. I wasn't risking the witch's wrath again in one night.

"Melusine ran, but you remain unharmed?" he asked.

"Yes," I said. "I'm fine, really. But seeing Melusine stressed me out enough to kick-start my wisp powers. I...I started glowing on a busy city street, in front of a crowd of humans, and a cop. If it wasn't for the fog, and the cat sidhe, I'd be in deep trouble right now."

Ceff knew all about fae law and the implications of my skin glowing unglamoured. He grew restless, running a hand through damp hair, bare feet shifting on the wet sidewalk. I froze, waiting for his reply.

As kelpie king, he had a duty to uphold fae law. I held my breath while myriad emotions shifted across his handsome face. This time Ceff held my fate in his hands.

"Melusine will pay one of these days, but you are right," he said. "First we must find this Sir Torn and learn what he knows of your father. The wisp king was reputed to be a solitary man, a lone traveler often seen wandering the moors and fen land before his disappearance. With no known friends or allies to contact, my own inquiries have turned up dry. The cat sidhe must be found. We must find a way into this Club Nexus."

I let out the breath I'd been holding.

"We?" I asked.

"Of course," he said. "I will help, if you will have me."

Need stirred low in my belly, but I tamped it down. Thoughts of taking Ceff home to my bed rose unbidden. I bit the inside of my cheek to clear my head. I was just feeling grateful that Ceff wasn't going to report my crime to either fae court. By turning a blind eye, he had saved me from possible execution. And now he was offering to help me on my quest to find my father, starting with questioning Sir Torn. I felt grateful, that was all.

I looked down to see my traitorous hands start to reach for Ceff, and shoved them back into my pockets. I was tired and emotional, a natural reaction to the day's adrenaline rollercoaster. I needed a shower and my bed, alone.

My stomach growled and I mentally added food to my list. Ceff laughed, dispelling the serious mood that had settled on our conversation. I grunted and turned away from the harbor.

"Are you coming with me then?" I asked. "Or should we meet here in the morning? I need a few hours sleep. If you're coming along, you'll have to sleep on the couch."

"I like the couch," he said, eyes glowing green.

Mab's bones. Ceff's eyes had glowed like that, with passion, once before. It was during the Winter Solstice and we had been sitting on that very couch. In fact, that one piece of furniture had become a repository for the memories of that night. Sometimes, when no one was around, I'd sit there, remove my glove, and place it against the upholstery. My own private movie of that night imprinted there.

I swallowed hard and waved for Ceff to follow.

CHAPTER 8

The smell of the harbor was left behind, replaced by the unpleasant combination of stale beer, grilled meat, and urine. We were firmly in the Old Port quarter when my phone rang. According to the ringtone, it was Jinx. But she was calling from our office phone, not her cell.

What was Jinx doing at the office this early in the morning? Even if she hadn't been nursing a hangover, Jinx being at the office at this hour was odd. We occasionally stay late for clients with a sun allergy, but Jinx never opened early. She wasn't a morning person. For that matter, neither was I.

I stifled a yawn, frowned, and took the call.

"Hey," I said. "I'm almost home. Ceff's with me, and we're on our way to the loft. What are you doing at the office?"

"We've got a problem," Jinx said. "Hold on."

Something brushed across the phone, probably my roommate's hand. I could hear her dry heave in the background and paper rustling. Did she just puke into one of our wastebaskets? Maybe I shouldn't have left her home alone.

"Sounds like you're the one with a problem," I said lightly, when she came back on. "How's the hangover?"

"Har, har," she said. "I'll never drink with a clurichaun again, that's for sure. But that's not why I'm calling. The office phone's been ringing off the hook. We have emergency cases, plural. I'm calling these clients back as fast as I can, and I have more calls to make, but the freaky thing is…I think the cases are all connected."

"I'm on my way," I said. I hung up and turned to Ceff. "Change of plan. I have to go in to the office."

"When was the last time you slept or ate?" he asked.

I stuck my tongue in my cheek, thinking back over the past two days.

"I caught a nap the day before yesterday, and I think I ate some toast yesterday morning," I said. I shrugged. "Duty calls."

Ceff understood all about duty. He didn't argue, though he did look at me appraisingly, scrutinizing me from head to foot.

"I will find a place to purchase human nourishment," he said. Ceff must not have liked what he saw, because he was slipping into more formal speech—a habit I'd noticed when he was stressed. "I shall return to your place of business when I am done."

"And coffee?" I asked, crossing my fingers.

He nodded and strode up the street toward an all-night pizza joint. Tomatoes and grease were good for a hangover, so it was a good choice. Jinx might be able to keep some down.

I spun on my heel and dragged myself to the offices of Private Eye, our up-and-coming detective agency. Business had been good lately, but that didn't prepare me for the crowd gathered around our door.

People were huddled in front of our office. Some were wringing their hands, others were crying or comforting the more distraught, but they all had one thing in common. Every one of the distraught clients was fae. That was unusual. We had a booming supernatural clientele since our role in finding Ceff and stopping the *each uisge* invasion of Harborsmouth, but fae, with the exception of pixies and pookas, tend not to gather in large groups. A mob made up entirely of fae was odd.

What the hell was going on?

"Excuse me," I said, approaching the crowd. "Please form an orderly line. I promise that we will meet with every one of you as soon as we can."

As soon as the gathered faeries realized who I was, they pushed forward, all talking at once. I lunged to the side, dodging grasping hands and pleading voices. I held up my hands, letting the sleeves of my jacket slide down to reveal the silver and iron of my blades.

"Stop!" I yelled. "I can't help you like this." Which wasn't a lie. If they all touched me at once, I was likely to end up a gibbering mess for days. "Please form a line at the door and wait your turn. I promise to do my best to help all of you."

I swallowed hard and held my breath, waiting to see if they'd listen. I wanted to run away and wait for the crowd to disperse, less chance of unwanted visions that way, but I didn't want to leave Jinx alone with this mess. I had no idea what had worked these fae into such frenzy, but whatever was going on it had to be bad. I crossed my arms and waited.

A few fae bared their teeth, but they all stepped back and formed a line that stretched around the block. It was then, as I examined the long line, that I noticed the items clutched in hands, tentacles, mouths, and paws. Every fae held a child's toy, blanket, or piece of clothing.

Mab's bones, I had a bad feeling about this.

With the weight of each red-rimmed eye on me, I cleared my throat and strode to the office door. I fumbled for my keys with shaking fingers, but Jinx came to my rescue. She opened the door and hurried me inside.

"Sorry, I told them to wait outside and not to touch you," she said.

Jinx looked pale, but she had showered and dressed in a clean, black and red, floral halter dress before coming to the office. The place smelled faintly of air freshener, but I avoided taking a deep breath. I pressed a hand to my mouth and stifled a sigh. Running the gauntlet of clients had left my stomach unsettled. If I smelled the underlying scent of vomit hiding below the air freshener, I'd probably foul my own wastebasket.

I dropped into the client chair facing Jinx's desk, keeping the faces of anxious fae at my back.

"Do you know why they're here?" I asked, hooking a thumb over my shoulder.

The phone rang, but Jinx let it go to voicemail. She pulled her eyes away from the blinking phone lines and chewed a ruby red lip.

"Yeah," she said, voice a whisper. Jinx cleared her throat and met my gaze. My partner didn't just look hung over, she looked haunted. "They are here because their children have gone missing."

"Wait," I said, gripping the arms of my chair with gloved hands. "You're saying that they are all parents of kidnapped kids?"

Jinx nodded.

"Dude, someone took them all," she said, voice shaking. "All in one night. These faerie kids were safe in their beds and then, poof, they were gone. How is that even freaking possible?"

I'd heard of faeries stealing human children from their beds, but not the other way around. A mass kidnapping of faerie children didn't make any sense.

"And the clients on the phone?" I asked.

"More children missing from their homes," she said. "I asked the parents to bring something from their kid's room, something for you to touch. The ones outside are the first to show up. They came faster than I expected."

I closed my eyes, dizziness making the room spin. Stress and fatigue were catching up with me. Jinx sucked in a breath and my eyes sprung open to see what was wrong now. I hoped whatever it was could wait. I couldn't face much more without a strong cup of coffee. I looked down at my wrist and sighed. The reason for her gasp was evident by the glow rising from my skin.

"Crap, I don't have time for this," I said.

"You didn't eat anything today," she said. Jinx tapped a long, red fingernail on her desk blotter and gave me the stink-eye. *Tap, tap, tap.* "You didn't sleep last night, either."

It wasn't a question, but I answered anyway.

"Nope," I said. I released my grip on the chair, pushed hair from my face, and pulled it into a messy bun. "Ceff's bringing food, sleep will have to wait."

There would be no chance for sleep until I'd interviewed every last parent standing outside my office. I glanced out the window and sighed. The crowd of fae wasn't getting any smaller.

This wasn't a case of one runaway juvenile bugbear. We were dealing with the kidnapping of dozens of fae children. To say we were unprepared and understaffed was an egregious understatement. I was glad that Ceff had decided to stay. We could use all the help we could get.

I pulled myself up and went to sit behind my desk. I wasn't running away from Jinx's reproachful stare, really.

I thumped down in my chair and prepared myself for the case. For though we had numerous clients, it was one case—it just had to be. I closed my eyes and thought about frantic parents finding the beds of their children empty this morning. I imagined frightened kids huddled somewhere cold and dark. Rage burned in my chest and I watched the sparks of gold behind my eyelids begin to disappear. I bit the inside of my cheek and remembered the families outside, desperate to save their children. I grasped my anger with both hands and held on tight.

Pain and anger had saved me before. Hopefully, they could burn away the stress, worry, and fatigue until this was all over. If embracing my anger toward the kidnapper—the true monster here, no matter what my clients looked like—helped to control my wisp powers, all the better. Walking around the city with glowing skin would make my job more difficult, especially if the fae courts stepped in.

It was hard to locate missing children while buried in a pine box.

Damn, why did it have to be children? I pounded my fist on the desk, knocking over a coffee mug filled with pens, pencils, and scissors. I flicked a glance at my reflection in a large pair of scissors that landed on my desk blotter. My skin was no longer glowing, thank Mab. It was time to get to work and bring these kids home.

I opened a drawer and pushed in the messy contents of my desk. I could sort through the detritus later. For now, I had a job to do. I lifted my chin and turned to Jinx.

"Let them in," I said.

CHAPTER 9

I met with crying gnomes, limping henkies, growling goblins, wailing banshees, and fluttering sprites—to name a few. Every faerie who approached my desk had lost a loved one—a child, sibling, or grandchild—in the night.

Though some of the fae races who visited had unsavory reputations, they all seemed genuinely distressed. Ceff was quick to remind me that all fae have difficulty conceiving. Faerie children therefore are a rare gift, treasured by their families. The raw pain on his face drove the point home. The loss of Ceff's sons had nearly destroyed him.

I didn't turn a single client away—no matter who, or what, came to us for help.

The last client walked out our door with a loud shriek, and I sighed. I rubbed my face with shaking hands. I needed a shower and a toothbrush. Too bad I didn't have the time, or the energy, for a trip upstairs.

Jinx hurried to the door, turned the lock, and flipped the sign from open to closed. She'd cancelled our regular clients for the day, rescheduling our appointments until later in the week. That meant we were double-booked, but I had bigger things to worry about than scheduling issues.

If I didn't get some sleep soon, I'd be no good to any of my clients. I'd have to ask Jinx to pencil me in for a nap. I leaned back in my chair, blowing strands of hair from my face. I rubbed gritty eyes and ran a tongue over teeth tasting of coffee and old pizza. I must look like something the cat sidhe dragged in. I pictured Sir Torn dropping me on the stoop and snorted, a giggle trying to escape.

I smoothed a gloved hand over wrinkled clothes, avoiding the looks of Ceff and Jinx. The last few hours had been a blur. Jinx and I had interviewed dozens of worried families, but the worst was yet to come.

Ceff had brought us food and coffee while we worked, a kelpie king turned office errand boy. After we ate, he cleared pizza boxes from the conference table—a flea market purchase that Jinx had insisted on for our growing business, which thankfully had no visions imprinted into the shiny pressboard and metal—and began setting up rows of plastic bags. Each bag contained a small item and was labeled with the name of the family and the missing child the item belonged to. Every bag represented a child who was missing.

The table was buried beneath them.

I've never attempted to retrieve visions from so many items, but I was about to try. I flicked my eyes away from the table, letting my gaze land on my gloved hands now fidgeting with a paper cup. Ceff had kept the coffee flowing, as if by magic. Perhaps it had been.

I drank the last sips of coffee in one gulp and tossed the cup in my overfull wastebasket. Jinx had discarded her own wastebasket in the back alley, beside the dumpster we shared with the bar that backed onto our building. We hadn't wanted to offend our clients, many of whom had a heightened sense of smell, with her fouled bin, so now we were sharing mine. The coffee cups and broken pencils spilled out onto the floor at my feet.

After hearing about a toddler, no more than twenty-four months old, stolen from his crib, I'd started waging war on office supplies. My desk was littered with fragments of wood and graphite. And pencils weren't the only casualty of the morning.

Jinx, in a fit of pique, had smashed the receiver of her retro-styled phone back into the cradle so hard, it was now held together with duct tape and nail glue. The front of our office also showed signs of abuse. It looked as if we'd corralled a herd of angry cattle into our waiting area.

It's amazing the amount of damage a mob of desperate faeries can cause. I didn't blame them, they'd lost their children and it's not like they could go to the human police for help, but we'd have to make repairs. Jinx, always the pragmatist, was adding a fee for physical damages to our bill. Of course, we'd never collect a penny if I didn't find those kids.

I swallowed hard and dragged myself from my chair. My knees creaked and my legs trembled as I walked with heavy steps to the conference table. I'd missed my morning run. That meant more laps around the Old Port and along the harbor tomorrow, if I survived the day. I tried to distract myself with plans for my altered workout schedule, but my eyes were drawn to the bags that held so much hope for the parents of the missing children.

I lowered myself onto the floor beside the table, back against a row of filing cabinets. Sitting on the floor meant I had less distance to fall, a lesson I'd learned after cracking my head more than once. I pulled my knees to my chest and looked up into Jinx's worried face.

"Hand me the first bag," I said.

I reached out, hand shaking. Too much caffeine? Maybe it was time to lay off the coffee.

Jinx bit her lip, but nodded and grabbed a plastic bag off the table. Before she could pass it to me, Ceff stepped between us. He knelt in front of me, knees almost touching my booted feet. Lines creased his brow and pinched the corners of his eyes. I wanted to reach out and wipe the lines from his face, but instead, I hugged my legs closer to my chest.

"You don't have to do this," he said, his voice barely a whisper.

"Yes, I do," I said. I looked him in the eye to let him know I was serious. "It's the job."

But this was about more than my career, he knew it and I knew it.

"You don't have to be a hero," he said.

A cold chill ran up my spine, but I held myself still. I was good at hiding my fear, had been doing it for a long time. I'd made up my mind last summer and I wouldn't back down. This city, with all its ley lines and supernatural beasties, needed a hero.

"Galliel would disagree," I said.

I lifted my lips in a grin, though my voice lacked the humor I'd intended. Galliel, a beautiful unicorn seeking sanctuary at St. Mary's church, adored me as much as I adored him. Father Michael claimed that Galliel's affection was due to two things. Unicorns are attracted to virgins and heroes. I knew that I was the former, but Father Michael had insisted that I was also the latter.

I'd never thought of myself that way until my city had been threatened by vicious *each uisge*. Since then I'd been trying my best to fill the void against evil. I hadn't known what being a hero really entailed, but I was a quick learner.

Today I was ready to live up to the priest's expectations. If it took a hero to help rescue these kids, then that's exactly what I would become.

"Ivy, I...," he said.

"I know," I said. I reached out with gloved fingers and gripped his hand, holding it for a moment. No flesh touched, but the simple act of holding Ceff's hand was intensely intimate. I was amazed that my gloves didn't burst into flame. "Me too."

The touch was a rare stolen moment. I just hoped it wasn't our last.

"You will not be swayed?" he asked.

"No," I said.

"Then what can I do to help?"

Most guys would stomp off or pout when their girlfriend did something stupid or reckless, but not Ceff. I glanced up at Jinx, standing over Ceff's shoulder. She looked at my hand on Ceff's, waggled penciled eyebrows, and winked. I pulled my hand away from Ceff and gestured to my roommate and business partner.

"Jinx is in charge," I said. "Follow her lead and do what she says, without hesitation. She knows the drill."

Jinx nodded and held out her hand to Ceff, two pieces of rubber resting on her palm.

"If you're staying, you'll need these," she said.

The brightly colored pieces of rubber were earplugs—to block out my screams.

Jinx slung a crossbow over her shoulder and set a handful of iron and silver bolts onto the table. Ceff raised an eyebrow and she poked a finger at his chest.

"Weapon up, big guy," she said. "Ivy will be completely defenseless while caught in a vision. If the person who stole these children shows up, I have her back. So should you."

It was strange having Jinx talk about me like I wasn't sitting here, just inches away. But if this was to be Ceff's first time witnessing my psychometry in action, he deserved a few pointers. And Jinx was the closest thing to an expert.

Ceff lifted his pant leg to reveal a three pronged weapon—a trident?—strapped to his ankle.

"I will protect her, no matter what comes," he said.

Ceff stared at Jinx and it seemed like they were talking about more than weapons.

"Guys?" I asked. "Can we hurry it up?"

My eyelids were heavy and the floor was beginning to feel comfortable, even with the handles of filing cabinets jabbing into my back. Jinx and Ceff ended their staring contest and Jinx stepped forward.

"Sure thing," she said.

Jinx handed me the bag. A small, stuffed animal stared out at me through the clear plastic, its smile stitched in place.

I slid my boots forward and let the bag sit on my lap. I inhaled slowly though my nose and out through my mouth. I bit my lip and stared at the pastel blue and yellow monkey smiling out at me. I had a bad feeling about this.

I unzipped the bag and pulled the child's toy onto my lap, tossing the bag aside. My hands shook, but I focused on my anger. The child who played with this toy was missing, taken from his bed. I yanked hard on my glove, pulling the leather from my skin one finger at a time.

I didn't look at Ceff, but I could feel him kneeling before me. He hadn't left my side, not yet. But I knew that what was to happen next would not be pretty. I just hoped he'd still be here when I came to, though I wouldn't blame him if he left.

My hand began to glow and I shook my head. Now was not the time to worry about Ceff. If he couldn't handle being with me, then I'd go back to being on my own. What mattered now was finding the missing children.

I reached out and touched the toy. The fabric was soft against my bare fingers, but I didn't have long to appreciate the sensation. I gasped as my skin began to tingle, as if pricked my hundreds of electrified needles. There was definitely a memory imprinted here, but it was weak. It takes strong emotion to leave a psychic imprint on an object. Either the child had not been frightened at the time of his abduction, or children leave behind weaker imprints than adults. Since this was my first case involving such young children, I had no way of knowing.

I closed my eyes and took a deep, cleansing breath. I began tensing and releasing muscles, beginning at my toes and working my way up my legs toward my head. As I performed the relaxation exercises, I cleared my mind and focused on the object in my hand. I ran my fingers over the rough stitches of the toy's smile and the room tilted as if the earth suddenly shifted on its axis.

I slid painlessly into the vision, but the perspective was disorienting. A child's mind had formed the memory which made the vision disjointed. I was in a nursery painted in pastel shades of blue and yellow similar to the toy my hand still held in the real world.

The child had recently been sleeping, the bed still warm where blankets had hastily been thrown back. The toddler's heart was racing and something—wings?—thrummed, stirring the downy curls at the back of his head.

I held my mind separate from the child mind of the vision and braced myself for what was to come next. The child swung his legs over the side of the bed, which I could now see was fashioned from a hollow tree, and reached toward something shining above him. The child toddled forward, using his wings for balance. A twinkling light beckoned from a few yards away. The glowing orb looked suspiciously familiar.

The child was being led from his home by a wisp.

The wisp ducked out through the child's bedroom door and into a hallway. The light bobbed and weaved, dancing in the air, but no matter how fast the child ran to catch it, the wisp always remained the same distance ahead. Pudgy hands reached for the pretty glowing orb, one hand clutching the toy monkey, as the light bounced and wiggled down a long hallway. At a large wooden door, the wisp shot through the keyhole. The child ran to the door and fumbled with the latch.

As the child's toy fell from his hand, the vision faded. The last image I had was of a young faerie in his pajamas, wandering off into the night.

I tried to focus on the fading image, but black smudges filled my vision. My awareness was yanked painfully upward and, with a gasping breath, I broke the surface of the vision. The last of the vision trickled away, returning me to my own body.

I ran my tongue around my mouth, tasting blood, but there didn't seem to be any lasting damage. I was even sitting upright. Go me.

I opened my eyes to see Jinx zipping the blue and yellow monkey into a plastic bag. She set the bag aside and grabbed a notepad and pen. I stole a glance at Ceff. He cleared his throat and caught my gaze.

"We are delighted at your return," he said.

"Yeah, glad to have you back," Jinx said. "Smooth ride?"

"Minimal turbulence," I said voice scratchy.

My mouth was dry and the copper taste of blood caught in my throat. But I didn't feel too bad, actually. For a vision, this one was mild.

I pulled on my glove and sagged against the metal file cabinet at my back. Jinx handed me a paper cup of water and I gulped it down. It was holy water from our water cooler, not that it tasted any different than regular water, but at that moment it seemed to come straight from Heaven. I let out a satisfied breath and Jinx held up her notepad and pen.

"Any leads?" she asked.

Mab's bones. A dancing, glowing orb had rousted the child from his bed and led him away from his home. Kaye's books were filled with stories of wisps leading men to their doom. Could wisps, my own brethren, be responsible for the missing faerie children?

"Something woke the kid, some kind of dancing light," I said. "Kid left of his own volition, but whatever that glowing orb was, it seemed to be leading him out of the house."

"Did you see where the child went to?" Ceff asked, leaning forward.

"No, sorry," I said, shaking my head. "He dropped the toy while fumbling with the latch on his front door. I just know that he followed the light outside."

I remembered wrinkled pajamas disappearing into the darkness. I squeezed the paper cup, crushing it into a tiny ball, and tossed it across the room. It dropped short of the wastebasket, another thing to worry about later.

"At least he wasn't hurt or anything, right?" Jinx asked.

"Yeah, the kid was fine last night," I said. It had been dark outside during the vision, but now daylight was streaming in through our office windows. "But that was hours ago."

Ceff rubbed the back of his neck and looked down at the floor. This had to be hard on him after losing his sons.

"What do you think the lights were?" she asked. "Some kind of spell?"

I hoped it was a spell, because if my suspicions were correct, then wisps were involved. If my own people were behind this, where did that leave me?

I'd been flinching away from the prospect of coming out as a faerie princess. But if wisps committed this crime, then I was partly responsible. My father, king of the wisps, had left our people leaderless. I had known this for months and done nothing.

I stared at the table covered in plastic bags—so many missing children. Had the same lights lured the other children from their beds? There was only one way to find out.

"I'll know more when we're done," I said. I pointed to the table. "Keep 'em coming."

Jinx gave me an understanding nod and handed me a plastic bag. Ceff's brow wrinkled and he cleared his throat.

"Are you certain?" he asked. "Couldn't we search the homes for clues? The families may have missed something."

The chances of that many families all missing something was a long shot. In the case of the winged child, he had walked out the front door himself. There had been no forced entry and the only physical intruders were the lights which floated in the air, never touching any surfaces. No, my gut told me that the answers were here in these objects, not back in the victims' homes.

"I have to do this, now," I said. "I can't put this part of the job off until later. The first few hours are the most important in any missing person case. If I don't learn anything new, then we'll try other methods, but this is our best chance of finding out what happened last night."

"She's right," Jinx said. She placed a hand on Ceff's shoulder. "This is the best way to save these kids."

"If you are both in agreement, then I acquiesce," he said. Jinx put her hand on a curvy hip and raised an eyebrow. Ceff raised his hands, palm out, and smiled. "You are the professionals. I surrender."

Professionals? I didn't feel like a professional in my wrinkled, sweat-stained clothes, but we had worked missing person cases before. I focused on the few facts we knew so far and what information we were missing.

"We need to know if the cases are connected," I said. "Maybe, just maybe, one of the kids saw something that will lead us to where they're being kept. And if we find the children, we'll need backup to get them out."

I was assuming that the children were still alive. We all were. To think that these children may already be dead was too horrible to imagine.

"I'll call Jenna," Jinx said.

The Hunters Guild wouldn't sanction a raid to extract faerie children—they only fought to protect humans—but Jenna didn't mind working a side-job, even if it was to save non-humans. For a Hunter, she was remarkably open-minded.

"I will send word to the leaders of the local water fae," Ceff said. "For now, we should all remain vigilant."

Ceff was right, fae families should be warned, but how was he going to contact the water fae? Ceff's people, kelpies, could be reached through his sentinels at the harbor and the merrows could be called through a magic shell located along the beach, but I had hoped he'd stay here with me while I endured my visions. It was selfish, but true.

Ceff rose from his crouch and looked out the picture window. He waved a hand and began flicking his fingers in an intricate series of motions. Kelpie sign language? I guess hand signals would come in handy for a species that spent most of its time under water—though I had no idea how they communicated while in horse form.

I lifted my head to look outside and saw a kelpie bodyguard standing across the street. The man stood in the shadows, his face partially hidden behind a magazine and a baseball cap pulled down low on his head. The undercover guard was pretending to read, but he was holding the magazine upside down. The guy must be wet behind the ears (water fae humor), it was a newbie mistake.

Ceff and the kelpie guard exchanged hand signals, which the guard then relayed to someone further down the street. I suppose after Ceff's abduction last summer, his guards weren't straying far from his side. When he was done signing, Ceff returned to kneel on the floor beside me.

"I have done what I can to warn my people and our allies," he said.

"Good," I said. "Let's get this show on the road. Jinx?"

My friend stepped forward, plastic bag in hand.

"Ready?" she asked.

I lifted my chin and gave her a quick nod.

"I was born ready," I said. Which, of course, wasn't true, but the white lie eased the tension in the room.

I pulled off my glove and reached inside the bag. The second my fingers touched the small blanket, the room went dark. I sank into the vision, drowning in the memory of a child with too many limbs and too many teeth following a cloud of dancing lights.

CHAPTER 10

The kidnapped fae children had been as different from one another as night and day, but every one of them had left their homes while chasing balls of light. In every vision, the glowing orbs danced and twinkled enticingly, just out of reach.

I rubbed my face and stretched cramped muscles. After subjecting myself to over two-dozen visions, I'd agreed to a shower and a nap. The visions the children left behind may have been mild compared to some I've experienced, but the vast number of them left me exhausted. The sleepless night hadn't helped matters either.

I wasn't sure if the hour of sleep had done me any good, but the shower had felt divine. Wrinkled, sweat stained clothes had been replaced with a clean pair of jeans, black tee, my spare pair of leather gloves, and black Doc Martens. My knives were already strapped into forearm sheaths, and my leather jacket, which would keep the weapons concealed in public, was tossed over the chair to my right.

Ceff sat to my left, not daring to enter the kitchen while Jinx prepared a makeshift breakfast. My roommate was as territorial as a hearth brownie and hostile as a pixie. It was best to avoid the kitchen when Jinx was cooking, especially when she was armed with a spatula.

I slouched against the kitchen counter, the smell of eggs, toast, and fresh brewed coffee bringing a smile to my face. A smile that was gone the moment Jinx opened her mouth.

"So, you think wisps kidnapped all those kids?" she asked.

I let out a heavy sigh. It was the one thought I'd tried to block out during my one hour respite. But now all of my worries came rushing back.

"I think they're involved, yeah," I said. I took a bite of toast, giving myself time to think things over.

"I agree, your description does match what we know of wisp physiology and behavior," Ceff said.

He'd also showered—the heady mix of bath gel and his own scent of salt and sea strong on his skin. Ceff smelled more delicious than breakfast. I drew in the scent of him and sighed.

"If it's wisps, then all the more reason to stop them," I said. "I'm not going to let my people go around kidnapping little kids, not if I can help it. Once we find and rescue the children, I have some new rules to enforce."

"Dude, are you serious?" Jinx asked. "You're going to come out of the faerie closet?"

"Yes," I said.

And I knew exactly the place to do just that.

A trip to Club Nexus was definitely in my future. I needed to gain control over the wisps that were currently running amok in my city. I also wanted to warn the faeries of Harborsmouth about the threat to their children. Ceff had a network for contacting water fae, but so far all the kidnappings had occurred on dry land. The fastest way to spread the word was to speak with local fae leaders and Kaye had said that the club was their gathering place. I guess what she'd said about the convergence of power was right—all roads did lead to Club Nexus.

And something that the cat sidhe, Torn, had said still niggled at me. He mentioned the dead rising from their graves to haunt the streets of Harborsmouth. I thought it was idle gossip at the time, my mind focused on Melusine and the potential threat she posed, but what if the sightings were more than rumors? Torn made it sound like harmless ghost sightings, but what if it had been something else?

If specters of the dead had not risen, then what was wandering city graveyards and cemeteries? Unfortunately, none of the possibilities were good. Graveyards attract all kinds of supernatural nasties. Vamps, ghouls, voodoo priests, black dogs, spriggans, even wisps were known to lurk in burial grounds.

What if the ghost sightings had something to do with the wisps? If the two were connected, then tracking the reported ghost sightings may lead us to the children. I had to find this guy Torn and drill him for details.

"Announcing your royal status will be dangerous," Ceff said. "The wisps may have gone without an official leader since your father's disappearance, but that does not mean someone hasn't filled the power void in his absence. Your very existence will alter the current wisp hierarchy, and that is bound to anger some."

"Noted," I said. "But if wisps are kidnapping children, then someone needs to shake that hierarchy up a bit. And, with my deadbeat dad in hiding somewhere, I'm the only one suited for the job. The wisps will have to listen to their princess."

"You said this might piss people off," Jinx said. She turned to Ceff and crossed her arms. "What exactly did you mean by that? Are we talking stacks of complaint letters, or ninja faerie assassins?"

"Assassins are a distinct possibility," he said. "Though some faeries prefer the more honorable practice of declaring a duel."

Assassins? Duels? I was in way over my head.

"We can worry about rogue wisps later," I said. "According to Kaye, Club Nexus is only open from twilight until dawn. I won't be announcing my reign until tonight. That leaves me with a few hours to check out another potential lead."

"What lead would that be?" Jinx asked.

"Something Torn said," I said. "The cat mentioned ghost sightings in graveyards and cemeteries around Harborsmouth. If humans saw unglamoured wisps floating around a graveyard, it'd make sense they'd think it was ghosts."

"You think the wisps are hiding out in a graveyard?" she asked.

"Wisps are attracted to hidden treasure and places of death," Ceff said. "Your burial grounds qualify."

"It's a long shot," I said. "But until I can question Torn, this is our best lead."

"I didn't really dress for traipsing around old graveyards," Jinx said. She looked down at her platform shoes and frowned. "Eat up. I'll go change."

"No," I said around a mouthful of eggs. "We need you here to man the phones and meet with clients. There may be parents only now realizing that their children are missing. If more families come seeking our services, there's a chance someone saw or heard something useful. Maybe we'll catch a break."

"Okay," she said. "I'll hold down the fort. If I learn anything new, I'll text you the info."

"And Jenna?" I asked. Jinx had phoned our Hunter friend while I was unconscious. She'd mentioned their conversation earlier, but I was fuzzy on the details.

"She's willing to work as backup so long as you find the kids in the next nine hours," she said. "After that, she's on official Hunter business. They're sending her to deal with some fuath infestation out in the suburbs."

I glanced at the Felix-the-Cat clock hanging on the kitchen wall. It was already past 3 o'clock. Nine hours wasn't a large window of opportunity, but my goal was to find the children before midnight. If we didn't reach them soon, chances were good that we wouldn't find them at all. Or if we did, that they wouldn't be alive—and that was unacceptable.

All the more reason to start casing local graveyards and cemeteries. I wasn't going to sit around doing nothing while I waited for Club Nexus to open its doors. I washed the last bite of toast down with coffee and slid my plate across the counter.

Break time was over.

"Can I get a printout of all the victim's street addresses?" I asked.

Jinx nodded, wiped her hands on her apron, and slapped a folder down in front of me. Not only was my roommate a great cook, she was also the most organized office assistant on the planet. Just don't make the mistake of calling her a secretary or you could end up with a split lip.

She slapped my phone down on top of the folder. The last time I remembered seeing my phone, it had been sitting on my office desk. Jinx must have picked up my phone and the case files while Ceff helped me up the stairs to our apartment. She tapped a nail on the screen, bringing up a map of Harborsmouth.

"I programmed the victims' addresses into your phone," she said. "You can see the locations in relation to other points of interest..."

"Like local graveyards?" I asked.

"Exactly," she said.

Ceff leaned in, though careful not to touch, and we studied the map. Each address was marked by a small red pin on the screen. Tapping the pin opened a window with the full name and address of the victim's family.

"You're a genius," I said.

"I know," she said. Jinx flipped her hair and grinned. "You can use Flyover to see the sites in relation to landmarks. Tap this to add field notes."

When Jinx had first insisted I upgrade my phone, I resisted. Using a touch screen was difficult while wearing gloves, but this little app had me glad I'd finally caved. This morning while talking to clients, I'd assumed the abductions were scattered randomly around the city. But the pins on the map told a different story. Fae in all city districts had been targeted, but the locations were not completely random.

The kidnappings were clustered around graveyards and cemeteries.

"Your theory appears to be correct," Ceff said. "The children who were taken all lived within walking distance of a burial ground."

The major difference between graveyards and cemeteries was that graveyards are often small and located beside a church. Cemeteries are larger, public burial places. The primary difference for supernaturals was that graveyards were always on hallowed ground. Large cemeteries, on the other hand, often had unconsecrated land where criminals were typically buried. Traditionally, this area was at the rear of the cemetery, but as cities grew so did the number of deceased. Most cemeteries now encompassed land not part of the original. If hallowed ground had been a problem for our kidnappers, then they would have stuck to the large cemeteries.

But that train of thought was a dead end. The pins indicated activity around both cemeteries and graveyards.

"Yes and our kidnappers don't have an aversion to hallowed ground," I said. I pointed to two church graveyards marked by a cross. "That rules out any demon involvement."

Some demons have a taste for human flesh. It was rumored that human children were a sought after delicacy. Knowing demons weren't involved was a relief, but it didn't bring us any closer to catching the kidnappers.

Harborsmouth was a huge, old city. There had to be hundreds of graveyards and cemeteries. Even using the app to focus on the most concentrated areas of kidnappings, we were left with too many locations to search.

I growled and slammed my fist on the counter.

"I know," Jinx said. "I spent forever dipping crossbow bolts in holy water. Why can't it ever be demons?"

My roommate was pouting because she wasn't going to get the chance to hurt some demons on this case? Some things never change. I ducked my head and stifled a laugh.

I took a deep breath and looked up into Ceff's handsome face. He tilted his head to the side and blinked at me, fork paused halfway to his mouth.

"You wish for demon involvement?" he asked.

He gave a slow, disbelieving shake of the head and this time I did laugh. Ceff wasn't aware of Jinx's love-hate relationship with demons. She loves to hate them, especially one demon in particular.

"No, I'm glad we're not dealing with demons," I said. "But if Jinx is going to fight something, she'd prefer it had pointy horns and a forked tail. You should see her at target practice."

It was true. Stick horns on the target and Jinx nailed it every time.

"You never know when a demon might walk through your door," she said, eyes gleaming. "It's best to be prepared."

Jinx patted her back where a crossbow was slung over her shoulder. The weapon looked incongruous with her frilly apron, but then again, that was Jinx all over.

"Yes, but we don't shoot clients, right?" I asked. "That was the deal."

Jinx shrugged one shoulder and cleared our plates off the counter, dumping them into a sink of soapy water. One of these days Forneus, a demon attorney and sometimes client, and Jinx were going to kill each other. I couldn't always be around to break up their fights.

I just hoped the demon didn't pick today to come through our doors. Jinx was tired, hung over, and heavily armed.

I yawned and stretched. It was time to get back to work, but where to start? I flipped through the case file one more time. Nothing helpful there. If only I could narrow down the most likely burial grounds for a wisp hideout.

"Perhaps our theory is flawed," Ceff said. He was still looking at the map displayed on my phone. "We know that the wisps acted as bait, luring the children away from their beds, but we haven't asked why. What motivation would they have to bring them to a cemetery? There are many stories of your people tricking foolish travelers, leading them deep into bogs and over cliffs, for their amusement, but why capture so many young faeries? Once at the cemetery, what do they do with the children?"

It was a good question, one I had no answer for. I sighed and ran my hands through damp hair.

"I don't know," I said. "There's too much I don't know about wisps. I've read everything I can get my hands on, and those stories involve either treasure or trickery, sometimes death, but nothing about kidnapping."

"Wisps don't eat kids, do they?" Jinx asked. "You know, like ghouls. No offense, Ivy."

I sure hoped wisps didn't feast on little kids. It was hard enough getting used to the idea of having faerie blood running through my veins without being related to cannibals. I placed a hand on my stomach, wishing I hadn't eaten an entire plate of toast and eggs.

"No, wisps are not child eaters," Ceff said. "It would seem that these wisps are either stealing children for monetary reward or amusement."

"Reward?" I asked. "As in, working for someone?"

"Yes, it's a possibility," he said. "Wisps are attracted to treasure. With your father gone, and no one to tell them differently, it's possible these wisps may have bargained their services for gold."

My chest tightened, as if a crushing weight had settled there, and I curled my hands into fists. If I had found my people and assumed my role as princess sooner, this mess may never have happened. Those children would be home safe with their families instead of huddled somewhere scared, or worse.

"So who would want a bunch of faerie children?" Jinx asked.

I shook my head. Who indeed.

Feeding on children went against vampire law, but I didn't trust bloodsuckers. For the long-lived undead, the blood of faerie children would be a potent delicacy to break the boredom of immortality. I wouldn't put it past a hungry vampire to use hired help as bait, if they had the means. And most of the dust bags I'd met were loaded. I'd have to pay a visit to the head of the local vamps. Oh. Joy.

As for fae who may wish to steal a bunch of kids, I was stumped. Faeries were known for abducting human children, not their own. The victims included both Seelie and Unseelie fae, so it wasn't a case of one court attacking the other, and the list of fae races represented by our clients was vast. I couldn't see how kidnapping such a diverse group of kids would aid in any political maneuvering, but with the fae nothing was as it seemed. I'd have to ask around, just in case. Kaye said local fae leaders gathered at Club Nexus. Maybe things would seem clearer after a trip to the club.

But I'd have to wait until dusk to interview any vamps or fae royalty. That left searching the homes where the children were abducted and nearby burial grounds. I picked up my phone and scanned the map. A large number of faeries who live in Harborsmouth reside on Joysen Hill. Many of these families were targeted by the kidnappers, and there are two large public cemeteries and three small graveyards on The Hill. With its close proximity to Club Nexus and the entrance to the head vamp's lair, it seemed like a good place to start.

I was going back to Joysen Hill. Hopefully, this time I could avoid the attentions of deadly fae and a run in with the law. With my track record, I wasn't so sure of that.

CHAPTER 11

Twenty-four hours ago, I'd juggled an armful of shopping bags while Jinx shopped on The Hill. Now I walked Market Street again, Ceff at my side. He was a lot more fun to look at than my roommate. My kelpie king boyfriend climbed the hill in a fitted dress shirt tucked into dark blue jeans that showed off some of his most attractive assets. I licked my lips, pulse racing. How did I, a grouchy half-breed, end up with such a dreamy guy?

I shook my head and turned my attention to The Hill and its inhabitants. I took a quick double-step forward to bring myself alongside Ceff. Walking behind him, and his gorgeous butt, was a distraction I couldn't afford.

We both scanned the streets for clues and any sign of Melusine, wisps, or the cat sidhe. To passersby, we probably looked like a couple out trolling for fun before hitting the bars.

I let my arms hang loose, alert to any threats. My leather jacket covered the throwing knives strapped to my wrists and the stakes tucked into my belt. I had additional anti-fae charms securely stashed in my pockets and an iron dagger in my right boot.

Ceff was also armed. Before leaving the loft, I'd asked for a closer look at the weapon he had strapped to his leg. He'd pulled up his pant leg and slid the weapon from an ankle sheath that looked suspiciously like it had been crafted from thick seaweed.

I'd been correct earlier. Ceff's weapon was a trident, a deadly three-pronged spear. With a flick of Ceff's wrist, the piercing end had shot out from a telescoping handle. The weapon, like the man, was impressive.

Now Ceff walked the street with sinuous grace, his weapon and the speed of a racehorse at the ready. I pulled my phone from my jacket pocket and double-checked the map. We were close to the first home on our list.

"This way," I said. I nodded to the street approaching on our right. "Two kids were taken from homes on Baker's Row—a bean-tighe and a nixie."

I started to turn down Baker's Row, the smell of bread and sweets making my mouth water, when I realized that Ceff was no longer at my side. I turned to see him halt mid-stride, an incredulous look on his face.

"A nixie, here?" he asked.

Nixies weren't known for city living, especially not high atop a hill away from any bodies of water. Nixies, a type of water nymph, typically lived in freshwater streams, brooks, or rivers. Joysen Hill was an unusual location for any water fae, but one of the families who called in a missing child had reported their address as the water fountain on Baker's Row.

"Yes," I said. "I think they live in the water fountain at Merrion Square."

We came to Merrion Square first. Narrow Baker's Row widened where it intersected with Grant Street, opening onto a small park. Parks were rare for this part of town and shoppers took advantage of the space. Every bench was taken, filled with people sitting with coffees and baked goods or shifty-eyed men making dubious business deals. The fountain sat directly ahead at the park's center.

"Might as well take a look around," I said.

I sighed and walked the park's perimeter. It was doubtful we'd find anything helpful. Too many people had passed through the area since the kidnapping. When the perimeter search turned up nothing, I started pacing the park, working in a classic grid pattern. Aside from discarded paper cups, condoms, and cigarette butts, I found nothing.

I joined Ceff beside the fountain where he spoke in burbling whistles and trills to a beautiful, naked woman. Long, green hair hung artfully around her body like waves, partially covering her breasts. I tilted my head, letting my own hair fall to cover my face. I could feel my cheeks and ears burn red.

In other circumstances, I might have been jealous, but the blue skinned, green haired woman was crying and wringing her hands. We had found our nixie family.

No one batted an eye at the naked woman standing in the fountain. I stole a glance from the corner of my eye and confirmed what I'd suspected. The nixie was hiding behind a glamour that only Ceff and I could see through. To passersby, the nixie was just a foamy spray of water from the fountain.

Ceff speaking to thin air in the trilling, nixie language was bound to look strange, but maybe people just thought he was making bird calls. Then again, we were on Joysen Hill. It probably didn't matter what people thought. Even during the day, people tended to mind their own business.

"She says that her child was safely beneath the water when she went to sleep last night, but this morning when she awoke, the child was gone," he said.

I nodded.

"That matches what our other clients have reported," I said. "Ask if she's noticed any suspicious activity lately around the park."

Ceff trilled the question and the nixie flapped her hands, pointing to groups of men who were obviously up to no good. When she finished, she tugged at her hair and moaned.

"She said that the humans here always act suspicious, but she thought her family was safe since they were carefully hidden behind a glamour," he said. "No human would have been able to steal her child, and the fae who live on this part of The Hill tend to keep to themselves. She wasn't aware of any danger. She thought the child was safe."

"Tell her that we'll do our best to bring her child home," I said.

My chest tightened as I walked away. I had promised to bring these kids home, but so far, I had no helpful leads, only questions. I checked the angle of the sun and sighed. The day was passing much too quickly.

Ceff drew up beside me, matching my stride as I hurried to the next address on our list. I wasn't running away from the crying nixie, really. Maybe if I kept telling myself that, I might even start to believe it.

"Did you find anything?" he asked.

"No," I said shaking my head. "This place is too public. If the kidnappers did leave any clues, they're long gone."

Searching the park and questioning the mother had been a bust.

"We must find the children," he said. He clenched his fists at his sides, eyes filled with emotion.

"Let's take a look at the bean-tighe residence," I said. I blinked rapidly and pulled out my phone to check the address.

I already knew the address by heart, but it gave me an excuse to look away. Meeting Ceff's gaze hurt too damn much. He had suffered the loss of his own children and I was feeling guilty for not claiming the wisp throne in time to stop these kidnappings. "This way."

We walked the next two blocks in silence, which was fine by me. I used the time to practice the breathing exercises Jenna had taught me. Whether battling monsters or my own emotions, the series of inhalations and exhalations helped to focus my mind and calm my racing pulse. I couldn't afford the complication of glowing skin right now. I managed to escape unnoticed yesterday, but I didn't expect my luck to hold.

I turned into the mouth of an alley that ran perpendicular to Baker's Row. Unlike most alleys on The Hill, this one was swept clean and smelled like strawberries. This was definitely the place.

The bean-tighe family lived on the third floor in a small, efficiency apartment accessed by a fire escape bolted to the brick wall. I was pretty sure that having a fire escape as the only entrance or exit was against code, which meant the building was probably owned by vampires. Vamps are prolific landlords on The Hill and their rental properties tended to be just as cold, dusty, and decayed as their owners.

The one thing vampire landlords care about is bleeding their tenants dry. The bloodsuckers didn't bother to keep their buildings up to code. If renters fall to their deaths due to a shortage of safety features, the vamps are quick to sweep the incident under the rug—and feed the body to one of their pet ghouls.

If vamps were keeping tabs on the property, it was possible that a vamp saw something the night of the kidnappings. One more question for the vampire council. Of course, if a vamp was behind the abductions, the council wasn't likely to pass along any helpful witness accounts. Vampires were experts at pulling strings and making problems disappear. Their Machiavellian machinations were legendary. I'd have to use caution when it was time to question the vamps, or they may decide to make me disappear.

I shivered and rubbed the slight bumps my knives made beneath my jacket sleeves, glad to have Ceff at my back. Ceff followed me further into the alley and I walked past the fire escape, checking the darkest corners for clues. Most of the secrets in this city could be discovered by poking around the shadowed corners of Joysen Hill.

I pulled a small penlight from my jacket and shone it along the ground and up brick walls. I reached the far corner and bent down for a closer look. The ground was worn smooth in a peculiar, circular pattern. I fanned the light over the spirals until I found what I was looking for. A shiny, green scale protruded from a crevice in the pavement.

I produced a clear, plastic baggy and tweezers from an inside pocket and wiggled the scale free. I rocked back on my heels and held it under the light. I couldn't tell if it was of fish or snake origin, but I had a bad feeling that it wasn't from any natural creature.

"Find anything?" Ceff asked.

I lowered the scale, shielding it with my body. I forced myself to grin and flashed Ceff a smile over my shoulder.

"Nothing yet," I said. "Can you go on up and get started with the bean-tighe? You're better at talking with people and I want to check the alley one more time. I'll join you in a minute."

Ceff raised an eyebrow, but nodded. I heard him pull down the fire escape and climb to the bean-tighe's window. I pretended to continue my search for clues as Ceff's voice floated down from above. After a brief conversation between Ceff and two female voices, he entered the apartment.

When I heard the window close behind him, I lowered the tweezers and the scale onto the plastic bag and took a deep breath. I had to know if the scale was related to the kidnappings, but this was something I had to do alone. If my suspicions were correct, I needed time to figure out how to break the news to Ceff. And if I was wrong, he never had to be bothered with theories that would only open old wounds.

I pulled a cheap mouthguard, the kind used for contact sports, out of my pocket and slid it between my teeth. It was a new purchase I'd only experimented with a few times, but the object made screaming nearly impossible. It made me drool like a slavering barguest, but my philosophy is that it's better to slobber all over myself than to attract unwanted attention screaming. If the mouthguard helped prevent a chipped tooth, that was a bonus.

I stole one last glance at the empty fire escape and the closed window above. Ceff would be inside for at least fifteen minutes, consoling and interviewing the bean-tighe family, before looking for me. Hopefully, I'd be done in time.

I clumsily pulled the glove from my left hand. With shaking fingers, I reached out and grasped the scale that was shining iridescent in the flashlight beam. A hissing sound roared in my ears and I used my gloved hand to steady myself against the brick wall. Reality blurred and slid, and a cascade of vertiginous images joined the hissing in my head. Bricks, mortar, pavement, fire escape, and a patch of midday sky melted and mixed together like a stirred reflection in a mud puddle, leaving only the murky depths of a vision.

I pushed past the storm of emotions raging through the vision like a tempest, and tried to open my inner eye. With an act of will, I tuned out the cacophony of hissing and rattling that assaulted my ears and focused on what I could see. The alien perspective was perplexing, but the reflection in the fog-shrouded puddle was familiar. My suspicion was correct.

The serpent scale belonged to Melusine.

A flicker of light reflected off the puddle and Melusine looked up to see a cloud of wisps exit the window above. A small bean-tighe followed, riding a broom.

That explained the difficult climb to the fourth-floor apartment. If bean-tighe can fly, then the fire escape was adequate. It also answered another question I'd had regarding these faeries. Bean-tighe are always depicted as wizened old women with rosy cheeks and wrinkled faces. Now I knew why.

Evidently, bean-tighe are born looking like miniature versions of their parents. The child astride the broom was smaller than an adult bean-tighe, but had the characteristic wrinkles on its cherubic face. A kerchief covered her head, but strands of gray hair escaped to blow in the wind. The child was smiling and chasing the wisps as they flew down the alley.

Melusine shifted through feelings of pleasure, satisfaction, pain, loss, jealousy, and rage as she slithered in the shadows. The woman was as unstable as a dwarf on a surfboard. Melusine's serpent body coiled and uncoiled rhythmically and her tail lashed the wall. The lamia seemed impatient to follow the child, but instead, she waited.

"Sssoon my sssweet," she said.

Something cold slithered over Melusine's shoulder. I held my breath as a thick bodied snake coiled around her neck. Black scales were nearly lost in the shadows, but the pale underbelly and yellow tail caught the moonlight. Melusine had herself a pet water moccasin, a venomous pit viper.

She reached out and caressed the snake affectionately on the head. Melusine was eager to chase the child, but stroking her pet seemed to calm her as she waited. The wisps exited the alley ahead of the tiny bean-tighe, and a flute began to play. I forgot all about the snake.

A beautiful, lilting melody was coming from beyond the alley. The song tugged at me, threatening to pull my soul deeper into the vision. It was a sound I could follow forever.

I couldn't see the piper, but I longed to run down the alley and dance into his or her arms. I knew, without a doubt, that they were the most wonderful person I'd ever meet. This musician was someone I'd jump off a cliff for.

I shook my ghost-like head. Running into a stranger's arms? Jumping off a cliff? That was crazy talk. I willed myself to remain rooted to where Melusine slithered in the dark, but I longed to follow the flute player to the ends of the earth.

Apparently, the alley's vermin felt the same way.

Mice and moles, even a flying squirrel, scurried to follow the music, but their numbers were nothing compared to the rats. Huge rats with long tails and big teeth poured down the walls, out of crevices, up from sewer grates, and into the alley. The ground writhed and rippled in a sea of mangy, dun brown fur.

I felt compelled to dance down the alley after them. If I hadn't been practicing my mind focusing skills recently, I may have let my soul wander, trapping me in this vision forever. It would be so easy to give in, to just let go.

Instead, I focused on Melusine. The snake at her neck scented the air with its tongue, probably wishing it could grab a tasty rodent snack for the road. But Melusine ignored her pet. She slithered from side to side, pacing the narrow width of the alley. When the flute music could no longer be heard, she rushed forward and the vision went dark.

The scale had torn from Melusine's body, becoming lodged in the small crevice in the pavement, ending the vision.

I blinked rapidly as my eyesight and hearing began to return. The world around me coalesced into blurry shapes, but sound was muffled as if my ears were stuffed with cotton wool.

I took a ragged breath and shook my head. My naked hand became visible and I flinched, dropping the serpent scale.

I pulled on my leather glove and sighed. The vision was difficult to shake, the piper's music still floating through my mind, but it could have been much worse. My suspicions had been correct. Melusine was involved in the kidnappings.

I swallowed hard, feeling the blood drain from my face. I had been lucky, this time. If the lamia hadn't shed her serpent skin recently, I could have been trapped in more than just one moment in time. Melusine had lived for millennia and she'd been crazy for at least a few hundred of those years. I had been a fool to touch anything belonging to that woman. But at least now I had a lead in the kidnapping case.

Too bad it was going to tear Ceff apart.

When no one else had seen Melusine on Market Street yesterday, I secretly hoped that she'd been a figment of my imagination. But this ghost from Ceff's past was real and she was obviously involved in the abduction of the faerie children.

I didn't have a clue as to why Melusine was stealing children, but I knew who I'd have to ask. My shoulders drooped. This wasn't a normal interrogation I was considering. If I started asking questions about Ceff's ex-wife, there was no going back.

I quickly returned the scale to the plastic bag and tucked it into my pocket. I jerked upright and headed for the nearest sewer grate. I'd have to talk to Ceff, but first I had another lead to follow up on.

Someone had been playing a flute that night and I had a nagging suspicion that the musician was fae. Faerie music has a peculiar effect on humans. Most humans, even half-breeds like me, may become overwhelmed with the urge to dance to faerie music. The compulsion can be so great that the person becomes cursed to dance until the music stops or they die from exhaustion, whichever comes first.

But I'd never heard of a faerie whose music could captivate other fae, not to mention an entire horde of rats. Were fae vulnerable to the compulsion of faerie music as children? It was something I needed to find out.

I kicked at the sewer grate, but it was securely anchored. I crouched down, shining my flashlight between the metal slats into the darkness below. No beady eyes shone back at me, no alligators in the sewer either, just filthy, stagnant water in the bottom of a large drainage pipe that branched off toward the street.

I angled the flashlight beam to the right and found something interesting. The sides of the pipe were covered in hundreds of tiny, muddy footprints like the ones a horde of rats might make. But it couldn't have been an easy climb. In fact, the broken bodies of more than one rat lay in the water below. So why had the rats abandoned their warm, wet sewer warrens for the chilly city streets?

I stood and walked back out toward Baker's Row, pacing the ground carefully. The alley had seemed clean at first glance. There were no piles of refuse, urine soaked cardboard boxes, or newspaper tumbleweeds, but I did find rodent feces. The small, dark pellets were easy to miss and easier still to explain away. If I hadn't witnessed the rats in the vision, I wouldn't have thought the scat was relevant. But the rats had been here the night of the kidnapping. I just didn't know why. Had they been lured into the alley solely by the piper's music?

I bit my lip and frowned. How did it all fit together? I knew that wisps, my kin, had enticed the fae children from their beds. In the case of the bean-tighe child's abduction, Melusine had watched from the shadows as the child was lured outside. Once away from her parents, a mysterious piper had begun to play music that seemed to compel the child, and every rodent in the vicinity, to follow.

Unfortunately, I had no way of knowing if Melusine or the piper's involvement extended to all of the kidnappings or if their presence in this one case was coincidental. I needed more information and I was running out of time.

I tilted my head up toward the third story window and sighed. I'd have to call Kaye and ask about any noteworthy fae musicians, but first I had a distraught fae family to question.

I jumped up and caught the bottom rung of the fire escape with a gloved hand and pulled the ladder down. I climbed quickly, focusing on the ache in my shoulders and calves. If I didn't think about the vision, maybe I could keep Melusine's possible involvement from Ceff just a bit longer.

At the top landing, I tapped on the window pane and waited. A wrinkled bean-tighe, wearing a tattered red shawl, which matched her rosy cheeks and red-rimmed eyes, came to the window and pushed it open. She smiled weakly and waved me inside, shuffling back toward the kitchen in her house slippers. If she were human, I'd guess that she was in her late seventies, but after seeing the wrinkled and grey-haired child, I knew this was the appearance of all bean-tighe. It was disconcerting, especially since most fae age so slowly.

I followed the faerie into the kitchen where Ceff sat at a small table eating strawberry shortcake and talking with a second bean-tighe. Strawberries are a favorite of the bean-tighe and this family was no exception. Strawberry vines grew from pots on the window sill, painted strawberries adorned white cabinets and door casings, and a fluffy, red and green, knit strawberry cozy covered the tea pot in the center of the table.

"Where are my manners?" said the bean-tighe who'd let me in. She'd started to take a seat, but jumped up and pulled another chair to the table. "Would you like a cup of tea?"

That's the thing about faeries. They're extremely polite, when they're not trying to eat your face off.

"No, thank you," I said.

I took the offered seat, but kept my hands in my lap. I would have preferred to stand, but the bean-tighe were each bent so far forward from dowager's humps that I worried they'd strain something trying to meet my eyes. As it was, they had to tilt their heads uncomfortably to avoid staring at the table.

"Myrtha and Glynda were just telling me about their daughter, Flynis," Ceff said.

He held out a sketch of a smiling bean-tighe child. All fae are careful not to be photographed in their true form, but paintings and sketches are allowed. The artist had captured the child perfectly. It was definitely the same girl from my vision.

"She's...lovely," I said. "Um, does Flynis have any fae friends or teachers who are musicians? Or perhaps a neighbor who lives in your building? I'm looking for someone who may have been a witness the night she went missing. This person is skilled at playing a woodwind instrument, perhaps a flute, panpipes, or pennywhistle."

Myrtha frowned, brow furrowed and Glynda shook her head.

"No, not that I know of," Glynda said. "Can you think of anyone, Myrtha?"

"Not a one," Myrtha said.

Oh well, it had been a long-shot.

"Was there anything unusual about last night?" I asked. "Anything at all?"

"We've been over the details so many times, but there's nothing we can remember," Glynda said. The teacup in her hand clattered against the saucer as her hand shook. Myrtha reached out and took her hand, holding it in her own. "It was such an ordinary night. We ate strawberry jam on toast with warm milk, just like we always do, and put Flynis to bed. We went to our room where Myrtha read and I worked on my knitting. I'm sorry. I wish I could remember something useful."

"That's alright," I said, standing. "You've been very helpful."

Ceff stood and thanked the bean-tighe for the shortcake and tea. As we left the kitchen, I looked back over my shoulder.

"One more thing," I said. "Do you have much trouble with rats in this part of the city?"

Ceff raised an eyebrow, but didn't ask where my strange questions were coming from. Myrtha shook her head and Glynda let out a barking laugh.

"Rats?" Glynda asked. "We keep a clean house, detective. There's nothing for those vermin here, or in the alley below. There are much better places to find food in this city. If you're looking for rats, check the docks."

It was true. The bean-tighe obviously used their brooms for more than flying. The rats had climbed up from the sewers, but why? I was afraid I was about to find out.

CHAPTER 12

I tried calling Kaye, but my witch friend was working in her spell kitchen and couldn't be disturbed. I left a message with Arachne to have Kaye get back to me and ended the call. My phone displayed the current time as forty-five minutes past six o'clock. Crap, it was later than I thought. Sunset came early during the month of March. I couldn't just wait around for Kaye to call me back. We were running out of daylight.

I had a feeling that the mysterious piper was the key to solving the case, but I'd have to look elsewhere for answers. I jumped down from the fire escape, checked that my weapons were still in place, and hurried up Baker's Row. Half a block away, Ceff caught up with me.

"Are you going to tell me what happened back there?" he asked. "You were in that alley for nearly an hour."

Oberon's eyes. My chest tightened and I swallowed hard. I'd been in the alley for an hour? That explained how it got so late. Lost time was a problem with visions, one of many.

Ceff looked cool and relaxed, thumbs in his pants pockets as he strode next to me with fluid grace, but a muscle jumped in his cheek as he clenched his jaw. I shrugged and looked away.

"I had a vision," I said. "No big deal."

I snuck a glance at Ceff as he sighed and rubbed the back of his neck. He was trying to remain calm, but a vein twitched on his forehead, matching the muscle in his cheek.

"What did you see?" he asked.

"I don't know," I said.

Unlike pureblood fae, I can tell a boldfaced lie, but neither my human nor fae blood helped to prevent the sinking feeling in my stomach. I didn't like lying to Ceff, but I wanted to protect him from the truth of Melusine's involvement as long as possible. If she was just a casual observer in the beantighe's abduction, then there'd be no reason to tell Ceff at all. Why dredge up old pain unnecessarily?

I bit my lip and kept my eyes on the street, looking for clues and potential threats. Ceff rushed me from the side and I barely had time to slide right and spin to face him. Ceff kept coming, his eyes a green so dark they looked black. I stepped away only to have my back hit a solid brick wall.

I was so busy looking for threats in the shadowed doorways and dark alleys that I missed the one walking beside me. Ceff raised muscled arms and placed his hands flat against the wall to either side of my head.

I was trapped.

"You're upset," he said. He leaned in, his breath brushing my face. "Tell me."

We were standing so close, yet not touching. It was a near thing. I could feel the chill of Ceff's kelpie skin like a balm against the burning heat emanating from my own. When had it gotten so hot?

A bead of sweat trickled down my back, but I held perfectly still. If I moved a muscle, we'd be touching. In fact, if I shifted my hips, we'd be indecent. I blushed and Ceff's eyes began to glow.

"W...wh...at?" I asked.

Ceff raised an eyebrow, a slow smile building. I licked my lips and tried to think. He had asked me something important, but I was too dizzy and light-headed to focus on the words. How could I possibly concentrate with Ceff standing so close?

Ceff dipped his head to my ear and whispered. His breath against my neck sent shivers down my spine.

"Now that I have your attention," he said. "Tell me what you saw in your vision." Ceff took one step back and lowered his arms. I gasped, trying hard not to shake. My feet didn't know if they should run away or propel me into his arms. Fear and desire waged a war within me, rooting me in place. "I can't help you if you don't let me in." I gazed into eyes that no longer glowed, but radiated concern. "You don't have to do this alone. Not anymore."

I held up my hands, palms out.

"Okay, fine," I said. "You win. But you're not going to like it."

I slid down the wall and sat cross-legged, patting the ground beside me. It was a long story, might as well get comfortable.

We sat on the sidewalk, oblivious to people walking by, as I filled Ceff in on the details of my vision. When I mentioned Melusine's suspected involvement, he placed his head in his hands. I pretended not to notice. Discovering your murderous ex was in town is bad enough. Learning that she might have a hand in the abduction of dozens of fae children was a slap in the face. If Ceff needed some time to digest the information, then that was fine by me.

I slid my phone from my pocket and checked for messages. There was nothing yet from Jinx or Kaye. I looked up to see Ceff staring at me intently. Dark rings circled his eyes, which made the skin looked bruised, but he didn't look away.

"If Melusine is involved, we must find the children," he said. "She is capable of...she..."

"I know," I said softly. "We'll find the kids. Come on. It's time to ask a friend for some answers."

I stood and offered Ceff my hand. I was wearing thick leather gloves, but for me, it was more than a hand up. I was trying to bridge the gap between us. Ceff's past and my allergy to intimacy didn't have to ruin things.

He accepted my hand, tilting his head to the side and flashing a wan smile. I lifted my chin high and smiled in return. If Melusine really was our enemy, it wouldn't be easy. But together we could face anything, even Ceff's evil ex.

CHAPTER 13

Ceff and I walked together, weaving through rush hour crowds heading home or out for a night on The Hill. I doubted any of the people around us shared our destination. We were on our way to church.

We kept the steeple of Sacred Heart in sight and walked until the stone façade of the church loomed above us. The church sat on the highest point of Harborsmouth real estate. I could see fog rolling into the harbor below to the east, the result of fast dropping temperatures. The sun hadn't fully set to the west, but lights were already twinkling on across the city.

I took the stone steps two at a time and hurried inside, Ceff a steady presence at my back. We often came here for happier reasons, but tonight we needed answers and we needed them quickly. I only hoped that Father Michael could be made to hurry. The priest was a gifted scholar, but tended toward lengthy, enthusiastic rants when asked about supernatural history.

I let my eyes adjust to the low light provided by two small lamps. One of the lamps had a flickering bulb that made our shadows dance along the narthex walls. It didn't take long for my half-fae eyes to focus. As soon as I was sure I wouldn't bang my shin on a stone bench or crack my head on a pillar, I hurried out of the lobby area and into the nave. As I suspected, the church was empty of parishioners. The only creature in sight was a sleeping unicorn.

I sprinted down the center aisle toward the altar where Galliel was resting. Even in sleep, the unicorn gave off an unearthly light. I liked to think it was the shining purity of his heart, but don't tell anyone I said that. Hanging around Galliel always turns me into a sap. Who knew my kryptonite would have doe eyes and gave wet nosed snuffles?

Galliel cracked an eye open and chuffed happily as I knelt beside him. It always amazed me to see his white, marble body come to life. Galliel was beautiful, from his long flowing tail to the tip of the spiral horn on his head. He was also the closest thing I had to a pet.

The unicorn raised his regal head, sniffed, and licked my face. I didn't even flinch. Galliel was the one creature I wasn't afraid to touch.

"Glad to see you too, big guy," I said.

I smiled and handed him a sugar cube from my pocket. All fae like sweets and Galliel was no exception. He snarfed up the treat and chewed it noisily.

"He'll get fat, you keep feeding him like that," Father Michael said.

Father Michael harrumphed as he stood, appearing from where he'd been bent over behind a podium. The priest carried a stack of books and pamphlets, his glasses balanced precariously on the end of his nose.

"Can unicorns become overweight?" Ceff asked. "I've never heard of an obese unicorn before."

"An intriguing notion," Father Michael said. "It begs the question; do other fae gain weight while in horse form? I would rather like to know. I read a treatise once on kelpie anatomy, but the scribe's penmanship left much to be desired. I'm sure you could assist with..."

Mab's bones, they had already started. It always began with an innocent question or remark from Ceff, whom Michael was entranced with, and then the mad priest would be off on a tirade of wild hypotheses and theories. Normally, I would ignore their conversation and sneak off with Galliel, but not tonight.

The lives of dozens of fae children were at stake.

"A study of fae anatomy will have to wait," I said. I sighed, standing and walking away from Galliel. "This isn't a social call. We're on a case."

"It is true, Father," Ceff said. "We are trying to locate over thirty missing children."

The priest fumbled with the books and pamphlets, setting them on a nearby pew. His hands fluttered to his head where they ran like spiders through thinning hair.

"What can I do to assist in your search?" he asked. "You wouldn't have come if you didn't think I could be of help."

It was true. The purpose of my visit was information. I placed a hand on my stomach, wishing I could push away the guilt beginning to settle there. Asking others for help didn't make me feel like much of a hero, but it was part of the job. Stomping through the case on my own would only get myself, or those kids, killed.

"Yes," I said, nodding. "I need to know everything you have on mass abductions of fae children and anything on a musician who can attract both people and rats with his music."

"Sounds like an enchanted instrument," Father Michael said. He tilted his head to the side, tapping his chin. "Do you know what kind of instrument this musician plays?"

"Woodwind," I said. "A flute or panpipe, I think."

Father Michael took off in a flurry of long arms and legs, his robes flapping out behind him like wings. Ceff and I followed close on his heels. The priest led us to his study where he searched the shelves.

He pulled down two large books, one a collection of Grimm's Fairy Tales, and set them on his desk, pushing aside a pile of yellowed scrolls. Pages fluttered and the priest bobbed his head as he found what he was looking for.

"See here, and here," he said, pointing.

The first book featured a painting of a man in traditional fool's raiment playing a flute while children danced along behind him. The second book showed an engraving of dancing skeletons alongside a medieval painting of robed, religious figures dancing hand in hand with the dead.

Cold fingers ran along my spine. Was there a connection between the dancing children and the dancing dead?

"The Danse Macabre," Ceff whispered.

"Yes," Father Michael said, head bobbing up and down. "The Danse Macabre, or Dance of Death, is a common motif found in many medieval churches and works of art. Some, like this engraving here, depict the dancing dead. While more often the works will show a circle of alternating live and dead dancers."

"What does that have to do with this musician?" I asked.

"That, my dear, is The Pied Piper of Hamelin," Father Michael said.

The name vaguely rang a bell.

"But The Piper is only legend," Ceff said. "A fiction of the Brothers Grimm."

"Ah, you know more than most that there is often truth to be found in fairy tales," Father Michael said. "Yes, many readers believe this to be only a cautionary tale, but for centuries scholars have found evidence of the true tragedy of Hamelin."

"Tragedy?" I asked. That didn't sound good.

"The story says that the town of Hamelin was overrun with rats," he said. "The Pied Piper was hired to rid the town of the vermin. He used his flute to compel the rats into the river where they drowned. But when The Pied Piper returned to collect the agreed upon payment, the townspeople refused."

"A bargain was made," Ceff said.

"Yes, part of the cautionary tale," Father Michael said. "People should always honor their side of a bargain."

My chest tightened at the mention of bargains. I'd made my share of bargains with more than one powerful fae. One day they'd come to collect.

"Before The Pied Piper left Hamelin, he vowed to get his revenge," Father Michael said. "Later that night, he returned while the townspeople were asleep in their beds. Again he played his flute, but this time he led away the city's children, who were never to be seen again. At least, that's how the fairytale goes."

"What really happened?" I asked.

"Well, that is the matter of much debate," he said. "There is evidence that the city of Hamelin truly did lose its children. A remnant of a document in the town records from the year 1384 states, 'It has been 100 years since our children left.' In addition to this document, there was a stained glass window in the Church of Hamelin that told the story, but it was destroyed in 1660."

"The fae don't like their secrets told to humans," I said.

"No, indeed, they do not," he said. "As you have guessed, I believe The Piper to be fae. The haunting, hypnotizing melodies of faerie music are known to hold power over mortals. Most humans become so overwhelmed that they are compelled to join the endless dance."

"The endless dance," I said, shaking my head. "But I thought the endless dance only took place in faerie rings and around burial mounds."

"Of course, that's why he's taking the children to the graveyards and cemeteries," Ceff said. "He doesn't need a faerie ring."

"But how is he charming full blooded faeries?" I asked.

"I believe he made a deal with a demon," Father Michael said.

Beady eyes gleamed behind his glasses. The crazy priest was obsessed with demons. I let out a heavy sigh.

"What kind of deal?" I asked.

"I don't know the terms, but I can guess what he wanted," Father Michael said.

He pointed at a figure standing outside the circle of dancers in the Dansc Macabre painting. The demon—for it was definitely a demon with red skin, cloven hooves, pointy tail, and horns—was holding a flute to his lips.

"A flute to force both the living and the dead to dance?" I asked.

"Some scholars say that the Danse Macabre is just an allegory demonstrating the fragility of life," he said.

"But?" I asked.

"But I believe the Danse Macabre is real," he said. "And that this flute can compel anyone, dead or living, mortal or fae, to join the endless dance."

"Okay, say this obsessed faerie piper makes a deal with a demon for the magic flute," I said. "Why would he want to force the faerie children into the dance? They may be immortal, but they'll tire eventually. No one can survive the endless dance."

"That I don't know," he said. "But I'd venture a guess that the master of the city may know something."

"The vampire master of the city?" I asked.

"Yes," he said. "His knowledge of raising the dead is unsurpassed. Not only do the most powerful vampires infuse the dead with their essence to create ghoul servants, but they also have the experience of their own un-death to draw upon. Ask the vampire master of the city what would happen if faerie children and the dead were to dance the Danse Macabre together, because if The Pied Piper is using the demon flute to lead the children to the endless dance, then the dead will join the dance. Perhaps he can divine The Pied Piper's purpose and have some insight as to how he can be stopped."

"Okay, I was planning on paying the vamps a visit anyway," I said. "I'll add your questions to the list."

The priest shifted from one foot to the other.

"I wish that I could tag along, but vampires detest priests, for obvious reasons," he said. He gestured to the crosses adorning his stole and the gold cross at his neck. "If you discover anything, you will tell me, won't you? For my research?"

"Sure," I said. "We should get going."

I looked up at the stained glass windows high overhead. The light filtering through the glass was faint. Was it dusk already? I started to reach for my phone to check the time, when a dark shape flit past one of the ruby, red panes of glass.

Could a bird have become trapped inside the church? The shadowy form rushed back and forth past colored glass, flying closer to a brass light fixture with each pass. The jerky pacing looked frenzied and I worried that the bird would harm itself trying to find a way to escape. Its movement appeared abnormal from my vantage point. Hopefully, it hadn't already injured a wing.

I squinted, trying to get a better look as it flew closer to the wall sconce and into the dim light. As if sensing my gaze, the creature stopped mid-flight and turned to face me. I froze, jaw dropping open.

That was no bird.

The faerie, for it was definitely fae, appeared similar to a small, three-legged lamb—if lambs could fly. Tiny wings sprouted from its sides like a chimeric My Little Pony. At least it didn't have butterflies or rainbows tattooed on its butt.

"Um, you do know you have a faerie flying around up there, don't you?" I asked.

I pointed toward the ceiling where the lamb-like creature had begun jumping through the rafters. The faerie seemed content now that it had been seen. It bleated happily as it leapt over a large, beautifully carved beam. I'd never seen anything like it, and I've seen a lot.

"What?" Father Michael asked. "Galliel is our only resident fae...Oh."

The priest's face paled and perspiration beaded on his upper lip.

"A Grim," Ceff said, in hushed tones.

"You guys can see it?" I asked.

"Unfortunately, yes," Father Michael said. He sagged, his robes suddenly seeming too heavy for his thin frame. "I can see it clearly."

Father Michael turned to me, eyes wide and watery. Hair prickled on the back of my neck. Something was definitely wrong.

"What?" I asked. "What's wrong? Is it dangerous?"

I stroked the outline of my knives, still hidden beneath the sleeves of my leather jacket, and widened my stance. I kept an eye on the faerie as it played in the shadows. It was smaller than a real lamb, about the size of a large housecat, and covered in crimped wool the color of milk. The feathers covering its wings were a pale shade of blue.

The thing was adorable, but I knew better than to trust appearances. Some of the deadliest fae were cute as a baby panda bear.

"No, it's not dangerous," he said. "At least, not to us."

"Then why the long faces?" I asked. "You guys look like you've seen a ghost."

Ceff winced, eyes haunted as they followed the faerie.

"A church grim is not predatory," Father Michael said. "They are guardians, attached to a particular church, who watch over our flock. But to see a grim means that one of my flock is in danger. They are harbingers of death...the death of a child."

I staggered backward, shaking my head.

"No, that can't be," I said. "I won't let anything happen to those kids. We're going to find them." I took a shaky breath and whispered. "We have to find them."

I had promised all of the children's parents that I would bring their kids home safe.

Galliel pressed against me, nuzzling his face under my arm until I stroked his head. Running my fingers through his mane helped me focus. The appearance of the church grim was upsetting, but I wasn't ready to give up on those kids.

The future isn't written in stone. Omens and portents have been wrong before. I had to believe that we had the power to make things right.

"I will continue to search through my library," Father Michael said. "Perhaps there is something in one of my books that can help. In the meantime, ask the vampires about The Pied Piper of Hamelin and the Danse Macabre. There is a chance that the undead may be able to deduce his whereabouts."

I glanced up to see that the stained glass windows had grown dark. The sun had finally set. It was time to interrogate some vamps.

CHAPTER 14

I sighed and pressed the doorbell. It was beginning to look less and less like vampires were involved in the kidnappings, but I hadn't ruled them out. I could get the measure of them inside their lair. But most of all, I was here to follow up on the priest's theory. If The Piper was using some demon instrument that raised the dead, then the vamps, experts on animating the dead, may have some insights.

I tapped my foot and pressed the doorbell, again. I lifted my gloved hand to knock and nearly fell as the heavy door swung inward.

I'd been expecting Stinky, the vamp boss's rotting ghoul servant, but instead, the door was held open by a tall vampire in a tailored suit. The vampire was bent slightly at the waist, arm outstretched. I didn't like having strange vamps at my back, but it would be rude to insist he walk ahead of us. I angled my body to keep one eye on the bowing vamp as I stepped inside. The vampire straightened as we walked past, but froze when he raised his eyes to mine.

It was the vamp from the waterfront, the one I pissed off the night of the *each uisge* attack. I hadn't made myself a friend in that brief meeting. The vampire had come to tell me that the council of dusty leeches was mad at me for making a bargain with The Green Lady without consulting them during the course of the battle.

He had tried to stop me, giving the message that he, "was sent to voice the displeasure of the council." Big whoop, I couldn't have cared less. The vamp had shown up while deadly water fae were attacking the harbor. I had more pressing things to worry about than a disgruntled vamp; I had a friend to find and a city to save.

It's unwise to offend a vampire, but in my defense, I didn't think I'd survive the night. I said something insulting and rushed past, leaving him to stand there like a fool. The vamp never had a chance to deliver the full message from the council. That probably hadn't endeared him to his masters.

The vamp took a step toward me and hissed. He hadn't forgotten my rudeness. The angry vampire fought to hold his pretty boy glamour, but I could have seen through his magic even if he wasn't upset. His true form—a dried, corpsified husk with fangs—frowned and flexed his claws.

Oh yeah, I'd accomplished what I did best. I'd created an enemy.

I took a deep breath and calmed my racing heartbeat. The vamp was already licking his parchment-like lips, hunger awakened by his fury. It wouldn't help matters if I rang the dinner bell. Letting my heart race was like holding up a flashing sign saying, "eat me."

The vampire was sizing me up for dinner, but I didn't run away. I slowed my pulse with another deep breath and stepped forward, into his personal space. That was the first rule of dealing with vamps; never show fear.

"I never did catch your name," I said.

"Gerald," he said.

He spat the name through lengthening fangs and I nodded, sizing him up.

"So, Gerald, you're really coming up in the world," I said. A wry smile tugged at my lips. "Who'd you piss off to get knocked down from courier to doorman?"

Okay, I shouldn't toy with someone who could snap me like kindling with his bare hands, but I liked busting this guy's chops. Watching the vamp squirm helped me forget my own problems.

Gerald stood vamp still. The problem with vampires was that the combination of their failed humanity and immortal un-death made them emotionally reactive, but on a totally different timeframe from humans. Vamps like Gerald tended to fluster easily and ruminate for days on how to respond. By the time he decided on a witty comeback, I'd be long gone.

Playing with Gerald was fun, but I was in a hurry. We needed to question the vampire master of the city and save the children before the church grim's premonition came true.

I turned and walked down the sloping tunnel cut deep into the bedrock of Joysen Hill. It felt like the narrow, rib-vault hallway was swallowing us whole. I tried not to stare at the ceiling and the tons of Harborsmouth real estate over our heads.

Ceff lengthened his stride, coming up beside me. He flashed a smile and shook his head.

"You have a strange way of asking favors," he said.

I smiled and flipped my hair.

"It's a gift," I said.

Ceff chuckled and I warmed all over.

A blur flashed past and Gerald appeared in the hall below us, ruining the mood. The vampire cleared his throat, a dry hacking sound like a zombified cat coughing up a fur ball, and waved us forward with the flick of his wrist.

"This way," he said.

Ceff started down the tunnel and I followed. He was wearing his favorite pair of jeans that hugged his butt perfectly. I let him walk ahead of me, no longer concerned about the bone crushing stone overhead or the pissed off vamp below.

Ogling a guy's butt? Trust me. It was better than speculating about the dark red stains on the walls. My skin flushed, tension melting away. I could get used to working cases with Ceff.

I nearly stumbled into Ceff when we came to an abrupt stop. We were at the doors to the vampire assembly room. Gerald stood stiffly before us, waiting for our request.

"Ivy Granger and Ceffyl Dŵr to see the master of the city," I said.

Gerald smirked and gestured to a small alcove which contained the world's most uncomfortable chair. There was no way I was sitting on that contraption again.

"I'll stand, thanks," I said. "We're in a hurry."

Gerald approached the door, but didn't go inside to announce our arrival. Instead, he stood perfectly still, his entire body going rigid, head tilted at an uncomfortable angle. A slight breeze from the wards on the council chamber doors lifted tufts of dry hair that lay in patches on his head, but the vamp didn't twitch.

Oh, right, telepathy. Apparently, the vampire servant didn't need to go inside to communicate our request for an audience. I discovered on my last visit that the master of the city and members of the vampire council had the ability to speak to one another telepathically. I hadn't been sure if young vamps had the skill, but Gerald had the entranced look the old vamps had exhibited when using their minds to converse.

I bit my lip, hoping the master of the city was in his chambers and willing to see me again. The Boss, and his vampire cronies, had ended our last meeting with veiled threats. I reached inside my jacket, gripped the lighter in my pocket, and checked the stakes at my back.

I hoped I wouldn't need my weapons, but I came prepared. Just in case.

CHAPTER 15

A tingle of magic, like static electricity, rushed over my skin and then faded as the doors to the council chamber opened. The wards had been deactivated. Gerald stepped forward and gestured for us to enter.

Apparently, the master of the city was willing to talk. If his answer had been negative, we never would have got past those doors. The wards would have blasted us into ash if we tried.

Ceff gave me a reassuring smile and we stepped over the threshold together into a large, cavernous room. I strode across the marble floor with Ceff at my side. Gerald fell into step behind us, bringing up the rear.

The room itself had not changed since my last visit, but the scene was not what I'd expected. I stopped mid-stride and blinked. The doors slammed shut behind us with a boom that sucked air from the room and made my ears pop. The wards had been reset, sealing us in with the vampire master of the city—and his friends.

The master of the city wasn't alone. Sir Gaius Aurelius, master of the city and chairman of the northeastern vampire council, sat at the head of a long table surrounded by the most powerful vamps of New England. From the looks of it, the entire vampire council was present.

Gerry, you plucky duck. I looked over my shoulder to where Gerald stood in the shadows. He was leaning against the wall and when he saw me turn, he grinned, showing more fang than usual. The vamp had known the council was in session, but brought me in anyway. I'm sure he was enjoying my discomfort.

Touché.

I sighed and returned my attention to the gathered council members. The vamps sat around a large table in the center of the lavish banquet hall. The council was made up of the most powerful vampires in the North East, and every single one of them was staring at me. I felt like a bug pinned to velvet for their amusement.

I did a quick threat assessment. *Oh yeah, we were screwed.* There were thirteen vampires seated at the table. With Gerald at my back, that made fourteen vampires total. The vamps continue to stare at me, and all but one sat eerily still.

Sir Gaius, master of the city, who I'd mentally nicknamed The Boss on my last visit, sat with fingers steepled. The tips of his fingers rustled like dead leaves as they tapped repeatedly together. Blood pounded in my ears as everyone in the room waited for the master of the city to speak.

I flexed my hands, but kept them at my sides away from my weapons. I wasn't here for a fight, but, if push came to shove, this little bug could sting. I lifted my chin and stared at Sir Gaius' forehead.

I'm not sure what Ceff saw when he looked at the assembled crowd, but I'd warned him ahead of time not to trust his eyes. Vampires change their appearance with innate magic similar to faerie glamour. Their magic portrays the image of a sexy, beautiful creature with seductive eyes, full lips, and alabaster skin—and for good reason. Vamps would never lure an easy blood meal without hiding behind their magic.

Vampires in their true form are nothing more than fanged corpses, dried out husks of flesh and bone. Their skin, the color and texture of dried parchment, is stretched tightly over bones and skulls giving each face a toothy, rictus grin. The watery parts of the body are always the first to go, and these vamps were old. They all stared out from empty eye sockets above gaping sinus cavities.

Too bad the lack of eyeballs didn't lessen the risk of mesmerism. Vampires can only permanently change memories through the introduction of their saliva—one of the few sources of moisture still produced by their bodies—but their ability to ensnare minds with a look is legendary. I wasn't about to let these creeps ensnare me with their gruesome eye sockets.

I focused on The Boss's forehead and bowed slightly.

"Corpse candle," he said.

"Sir Gaius," I said, nodding.

The master of the city had addressed me this way before, but I hadn't known who, or what, I was at the time. Corpse candle is another term for wisp. Not the most flattering address, but accurate. I wondered how the vampire knew that I was fae.

Maybe those empty eye sockets saw more than they let on.

"What could be so important that it demands our attention during a council meeting?" he asked.

There was an edge to his voice and my eyes darted to the other vamps. They continued to sit unmoving, but a flick of Gaius' wrist was all that kept the council from launching themselves at our throats. One water fae and one half-breed against thirteen vamps in a magically sealed chamber? Not good odds. Oh, make that fourteen vamps. We couldn't forget ol' Gerry in the shadows. He'd be the first on me, if I angered Sir Gaius.

I'd just have to play nice.

"I am sorry to disturb your meeting," I said. "I was unaware that the council had gathered. But now that we're here, I have a question for the master of the city that perhaps you can all assist us with."

"You put a question to the council?" Sir Gaius asked.

I flicked my eyes to Ceff, but he gave a slight head shake. The phrasing of Gaius' words sounded formal, similar to entering a bargain, but I was here to ask a question and I didn't have time for games. Ceff and I were shooting in the dark. I took a deep breath and gave a curt nod.

"Yes, I have a question," I said.

"And what do you offer us, supplicant?" Sir Gaius asked.

His lips pulled back from needle-sharp teeth. I stifled a shudder and wracked my brain for something I could offer the most powerful vampire in Harborsmouth. Not blood, that was for damn sure.

I thought back to recent bargains I had made. There had to be something I could use again.

Fetching something on a deadline? That bargain had nearly got me killed. The Cailleach was one scary old crone. Two favors to be named later? No way. I was already regretting entering into that agreement. The Green Lady was one damn savvy negotiator. My bargain with the clurichaun wasn't nearly as bad. Work a future case for free? Jinx didn't like it when I worked a case pro-bono, but it was better than bloodletting or owing surprise favors to the undead.

"I offer the vampire council the services of Private Eye detective agency," I said. "I agree to work one case of your choosing free of charge in exchange for truthful answers to our questions."

"Agreed," Sir Gaius said. The bargain settled on my soul like dead weight. I gasped for air as invisible iron bands constricted my chest. Gaius may not be fae, but I had enough faerie blood running through my veins to make the deal binding. "What is your question?"

I struggled to speak as the bargain shifted and I regained my balance.

"Over thirty faerie children have gone missing," I said.

The master of the city moved vamp fast, suddenly standing with hands splayed on the table.

"Despite our reputation as monsters, we have strict laws against feeding upon children," he said. Gaius' voice lowered to a deep whisper that sent shivers up my spine. "Do you dare accuse us of this crime in our own council room?"

I swallowed hard, but kept my eyes on the vampire's forehead.

"No, there is no evidence of vamps...um, of vampires being involved," I said. "But you are masters of the night, and these children all went missing during the darkest hours of night. You are also gifted at raising the dead, expertise that may help us answer questions about the kidnappers."

"Go on," he said.

My jugular was surprisingly still intact, but I didn't waste time beating around the bush. I'd already angered the master vamp.

"We think a lamia named Melusine and a faerie musician known as The Pied Piper may be involved," I said.

One of the council vamps hissed and I palmed one of the wooden stakes I kept tucked into my belt. I was careful to keep the stake hidden from sight. Was it something I said? I was trying to be polite, even played to the vamps vanity, but I still managed to get them riled.

"We know of The Piper," Sir Gaius said. "He is a faerie who was gifted at musical compulsion, for a half-breed. The Piper had the ability to compel both rats and humans, but apparently that power wasn't enough. There are rumors that The Piper made a deal with a demon. In exchange for an enchanted flute that gives him the ability to extend his life, The Piper gathers souls for Hell."

The Piper was a half-breed like me? That explained his desire for immortality. True blooded fae are immortal, but half-breeds with the taint of mortal blood have shorter lives than other fae. We live longer than the healthiest of humans, but we don't live forever.

I didn't like having anything in common with a sociopathic kidnapper, especially one who made deals with demons. I frowned and pushed on with my questions.

"How does this demon flute work?" I asked.

I wasn't asking for myself, not at all. But understanding the flute's magic may help us find and rescue the children.

"Legend has it that the flute was forged in the fires of Hell," Gaius said. "The instrument allows the user to compel any creature, alive or dead, to join the Danse Macabre. This dance is a perversion of the endless dance favored by faeries and uses demonic magic to animate the dead." A second vamp hissed, flashing fang. "While dancing hand in hand with the dead, the souls of living victims are pulled down to Hell. The life essence left behind is carried away on the music and absorbed into The Piper, sustaining his false immortality."

More vamps hissed and gripped the table. Apparently, the hypocrites didn't like anyone else animating the dead or cheating death. Good to know.

"How can I stop the Danse Macabre?" I asked.

"That knowledge is hidden from us," he said.

Damn. Okay, I now knew what The Piper was up to and how he would make it happen. But I still needed to know where the Danse Macabre would take place and how to stop it.

"Any idea where I can find The Piper?" I asked.

"No, but he will need a location of power near a resting place of the dead," he said.

I nodded deeply, but didn't bow.

"I thank the council for answers to my questions," I said. "Call when you have a case for me."

I stepped forward and placed a business card on the stone table.

"Oh, we will," he said.

Sinister laughter followed us as we strode out of the chamber.

CHAPTER 16

I exited the banquet hall and stopped, letting my eyes adjust to the dim light. Gerald stayed inside the council chamber, adding his chuckles to the chorus of creepy vampire laughter. I wondered briefly if we were expected to let ourselves out.

No such luck.

We were met in the hallway by the master's pet ghoul, Stinky. I'd given the ghoul the nickname on my first visit. He'd been ripe and falling apart months ago. Now Stinky more than lived up to his name.

I pinched my nose and moaned. Ceff snickered, but his skin paled as the doors closed behind us, making the stench grow tenfold.

Stinky shuffled along, leaving behind a trail of putrid slime. I dodged the foul liquid, wishing I could get ahead of the ghoul. But the narrow passageway didn't allow for much elbow room, and I wasn't sure how Stinky would react if I tried to hustle past.

If I couldn't run up ahead, then maybe I could get Stinky to speed things up.

"Um, hey, we're in a big hurry," I said. Talking? Big mistake. My mouth filled with the stench of decomposing ghoul. I covered my mouth and mumbled. "Can we pick up the pace a little?"

Stinky shrugged, the movement accompanied by the wet sound of flesh pulling off bone. I wasn't going to eat meat for a week. The ghoul didn't look back at us, but he did try to move faster. Unfortunately, that meant leaving more than a trail of liquid in his path.

"Careful of the toe," Ceff said through clenched teeth.

I dodged the chunk of rotting flesh and shook my head.

"That's toe-tally gross," I said.

I have a habit of making bad puns when I'm stressed and overtired. Ceff raised an eyebrow and I started to laugh. I choked on the intake of air and gagged, covering my mouth with a gloved hand.

I now had one hand over my mouth and the other pinching my nose. The position left me feeling exposed, the back of my neck tingling. I hoped that I wouldn't need to go for my weapons. I snuck a look over my shoulder, but the tunnel behind us was empty. The only movement was our shadows dancing on the walls. Our biggest threat was slipping in something nasty. I turned back toward Stinky, careful to watch my step.

I had to hand it to the ghoul, he was really trying. Stinky shuffled along at a near gallop, his gooey feet slapping on the stone floor. We made it to the exit in minutes.

At the top of the tunnel-like hallway, Stinky lifted a large ring of keys and unlocked the door to the outside. There was definitely something creepy about having the keyhole on the inside, so visitors couldn't escape. Thankfully, the ghoul had been given orders to let us out.

The key turned in the lock and Ceff and I rushed out the door into fresh night air. I wanted to gulp in air like a kid drinks juice, but instead, I turned to Stinky and forced a smile.

"Thanks for rushing," I said. "I appreciate it."

I tried to meet Stinky's eyes and fought to keep disgust and pity off my face. The ghoul's owner obviously didn't take care of his servants with regular feedings and yet Stinky had done his best to comply with my request for speed.

Too bad his body wasn't up to the task.

Stinky looked down at his abdomen as something started emitting a hissing sound. He was terribly bloated. The ghoul's distended belly started to move beneath the threadbare dress shirt he'd been buried in. Before I could duck for cover, the buttons of his shirt shot free of the fabric, leaving gray flesh exposed—and then Stinky exploded.

A buildup of stomach gasses had filled Stinky's abdomen like a corpse balloon. And when that balloon popped, it projected liquefied, rotten flesh all down the front of me.

I was covered in gangrenous ghoul goop. Try saying that three times fast.

"Get it off!" I choked.

Oh, Oberon's eyes, get it off. I flung my hands in the air and ran in a tight circle like a fool on fire. My eyes were watering so badly, I nearly ran into an ornamental pillar at the bottom of the stone steps.

"Hold still," Ceff said.

I froze, praying that Ceff could do something to help. For the first time ever, I needed a white knight. I wanted to be rescued.

I held my breath and stared at Ceff with wide eyes. I tried to think positive. I smelled worse than a charnel house on a hot day, but I wasn't experiencing nightmare visions. Miraculously, my skin was untouched. Too bad I couldn't say the same for my clothes.

Ceff's eyes began to glow and he cupped his hands together. A hint of a breeze brushed past my face as Ceff pulled moisture out of the air. A ball of water formed slowly between his hands.

"This may tickle," he said.

A thread of water spun out from the sphere in his hands to run across my arms and down my torso. Ceff lifted the thread higher and spread the water into a fan to cascade over me. It was the closest thing to touching we'd managed in a while and it made my skin tingle.

I stared at Ceff and a smile tugged at his lips. I bit my lip, wishing I didn't smell like the inside of a rotting corpse. After a few minutes, the water trickled to mist.

"That's all the moisture I can manage to pull from the air," he said.

"Thanks," I said. I sighed. There was no way I could go directly to Club Nexus looking and smelling like this. Making my grand entrance into fae society covered in rotting ghoul guts? Yeah, not an option. "I need a shower and a change of clothes."

I looked up and down the street. It was after dark and the night crowd was beginning to come out to play. Pretty soon someone was going to notice that I was dripping liquefied corpse intestines.

The only thing keeping me from curious eyes was the fact that I was upwind from most of the revelers and standing in shadow. But I couldn't stay that way for the entire walk home. The loft was too far away.

"If we can find a bigger water source, can you rinse more of this off?" I asked.

"Yes," he said, nodding.

I pulled a slip of paper from my jeans pocket and squinted at the address. Marvin's new digs weren't far from here. And where there's a bridge, there's usually water.

"Come on," I said.

I started walking, but turned back to see if Stinky had made it safely inside. The doors to the vampire's lair were closed and the stoop was empty. If I hadn't stopped to thank the ghoul, I might not be covered in rotting, slimy, dead guy. I shook my head ruefully and continued walking.

No good deed goes unpunished.

CHAPTER 17

Thankfully we didn't have far to go. A few people scowled and gave me a wide berth, but we stuck to the shadows and made it to the bridge without incident.

The bridge where Marvin had taken up residence was small, a single stone arch over a burbling stream. Homes and apartment buildings sat on a ridge where the land rose above on either side. The bridge itself sat low, hovering over the stream where a river had once cut its way into the earth.

As we approached, I heard snores echo from the shadows. The kid was asleep.

I made sure my booted feet hit every rock on the narrow trail that led down to the bridge. When we were only a few yards away, I called out to Marvin. The bridge troll had been attacked in his previous home and I didn't want to frighten him.

The snores ceased and the kid rolled to his feet, a baseball bat dwarfed in his huge hands. Marvin had been sleeping armed. I wasn't sure if I should be proud or cry.

"Hey, Marvin," I said.

"Poison Ivy?" he asked.

"Yeah, it's me and Ceff," I said.

"You stink," he said.

"I sure do," I said.

That was one thing about my troll friend. He got right to the point. And when a troll thinks you smell bad, you know that you seriously stink. I started to laugh and gagged, again. I'd been doing a lot of that since Stinky busted a gut all over me.

Normally, the only thing that comes between me and the contents of my stomach is a return trip to my body after a particularly nasty vision. But rotten ghoul gunk was a whole new can of maggots. I covered my mouth and tried to calm the churning in my belly. I didn't want to foul Marvin's new digs any worse than I already was.

When I caught my breath, I told Marvin about our visit to the vamp's lair and the exploding ghoul. He was still chuckling as he led us downstream.

"Clean here," he said.

"Thanks," I said. "I promise to bring a housewarming gift next time."

"Don't stink," he said.

That was a gift I could manage—so long as no more ghouls exploded on me.

Marvin flashed a gap-toothed grin and I smiled. There was something about being around the orphan bridge troll that made me feel comfortable, like coming home. We'd become each other's surrogate family since the *each uisge* attack. I was glad to see that even though Marvin's injuries were healing and he was moving on, we had managed to stay friends.

"Ready?" Ceff asked.

I nodded, stepped into the stream, and tried not to blush. My skin had tingled the first time Ceff pulled water from the air. What would happen when he tapped into an entire stream?

Ceff lifted his hands to chest level and closed his eyes. When he opened them again, his eyes shone bright green in the darkness of the streambed. Water rushed from the ground to Ceff's hands where it spooled into a large sphere.

I stood, mouth gaping, as he wove the water using his kelpie magic. With a flick of his wrist water rose from the sphere to cascade over me, my own private rain shower. I snapped my jaw shut and tried to remain still, but it was hard not to fidget. The water pouring over my body made my skin heat and left me breathless.

I met Ceff's glowing gaze and he winked. A flush ran up my neck and face and I bit my lip. I think we just discovered a way to get past our inability to touch. Too bad we were too busy to explore our options further.

Ceff lowered his hands and the water returned to the stream. I sighed and shook off, shedding water like a dog. Fun time was over. It was time to bag some bad guys.

I looked over my clothes and frowned. I'd need to wipe excess moisture off my leather jacket and give it a rubdown with mink oil, but it was salvageable. The t-shirt and jeans were soaked through. I pulled at the clothes, but the shirt stuck to me like a second skin and the jeans chafed as I stepped out of the stream. There was no way I could run or fight in these clothes.

And I still smelled like ghoul guts.

If I was going to make a trip to Club Nexus tonight, I needed to keep that appointment with my shower and a bar of soap. I sniffed my hair and winced. Make that a case of soap and bottle of shampoo. I turned to Marvin and waved.

"Thanks, Marvin," I said. "We have to run, but I promise to bring some honey next time I stop by."

"Find children?" he asked.

"Yes," I said. "I gotta stop by the loft for a change of clothes, then a trip to Club Nexus. But we'll find them."

Marvin nodded and I turned to leave. When Ceff and I made it to the top of the hill, I turned to see Marvin ducking under his bridge. It was then that I realized he was still holding the baseball bat.

A lump formed in my throat.

"I won't let bad things happen to any more fae kids," I whispered. "Not in my city."

I tightened my fists and dug the wet toes of my boots into the scree that covered the embankment. I was going to find those kids and I wouldn't let anything get in my way.

CHAPTER 18

Ceff and I hurried back to the loft as fast as we could move without attracting the wrong kind of attention. I was no longer covered in rotting blood and chunks of corpse flesh, but if a cop came too close they might notice the smell, and the fact I was soaking wet and carrying an arsenal of weapons. It's hard to keep weapons concealed when your clothes are sticking like a second skin.

The brisk walk in wet jeans had chafed the skin around both my thighs and the backs of my knees. The raw skin burned in the shower. Good thing I wasn't staying under the hot water for long. There was a hell of a lot more to do tonight and long showers weren't on the list. I dumped an entire bottle of shampoo over my head and rinsed fast.

I pulled on a clean t-shirt and stepped into a dry pair of jeans. My legs burned when I moved, but that was okay. The pain would help keep me awake and focused. I blew dry my hair and let it hang down over my shoulders to finish airing out.

Before stepping in the shower, I'd wiped down my boots, removed the insoles, and stuffed them with dry towels. I pulled out the soggy towels, tossed them into the tub, and aimed the blow dryer inside the boot shaft. The heat would be hell on the leather, but right now I was more worried about my feet. I pulled the boots on with a tug and wiggled my toes. They were damp, but if I was going to face an angry lamia, a piper with an enchanted demon flute, and a dancing ring of the animated dead, I wanted steel toes and a place to hide my dagger.

My weapons came next. I strapped a forearm sheath to each arm, and slid my throwing knives in and out, testing that they were secure, but could be pulled easily. If I needed my blades, I wouldn't have any time to spare. Every wasted second could mean my death, or the loss of someone I cared about. I thrust a dagger into my boot and shrugged on my leather jacket.

I stood and looked in the mirror. The face staring back at me didn't look at all like a princess, but it would have to do. At least I no longer smelled like rotting flesh.

I stepped out into our loft apartment and stopped dead in my tracks. While I'd been in the shower, Jinx had transformed. I may be the faerie princess, but I looked like a thug in my jeans and leathers. Jinx, my totally human best friend, was just missing a crown.

Jinx stood in a short, sequin-covered shift that reflected and caught the light in hundreds of sparkling rainbows. Her black hair was held up with wooden hair sticks that could double as stakes and she'd abandoned the matching sequined clutch for a velvet bag which she'd slung over one shoulder. The bag was large enough to carry a crossbow and a hip quiver packed with iron bolts.

Jinx had foregone matching accessories for weapons? That could only mean one thing. Jinx was going with us to Club Nexus.

My heart did a flip-flop of joy and fear. I was secretly pleased that my friend was willing to go with me, but she was only human. I didn't know what would happen to her once we stepped inside the club, or if they would even let her through the doors. I started to shake my head, but Jinx raised a hand and put the other firmly on her hip.

"I'm going with you," she said.

"But..." I said.

"No," she said, shaking a finger at me. "There is no way you're leaving me behind on this one. I am not missing my best friend's introduction to fae society."

I flicked my eyes at Ceff, who had the sense to take a step back.

"I am sorry," he said. "I thought Jinx should know where we were going, in case she needed to contact us. I didn't realize that she would wish to attend your coming out ceremony."

I narrowed my eyes. Ceff was so busted. Jinx would never miss a party. I was pretty sure that my boyfriend was well aware of that, but had told her where we were going anyway. Thing was, I had no idea why.

That made me more nervous than the thought of battling Melusine or The Piper. If Ceff thought I needed Jinx along for backup, then maybe there was more to this faerie royalty thing than I realized. But what other choice did I have?

The children were still out there somewhere. I had to find those kids tonight, but there were too many graveyards and cemeteries where The Piper could be hiding. We had to narrow down the search.

And I needed leads on Will-o'-the-Wisp. I had to track down my father if I wanted to continue taking any cases that involved leaving my apartment. I'd been lucky so far, but I didn't expect that luck to hold out. If I didn't find a way to control my wisp powers and learn to create a concealing glamour, the faerie courts would have me executed for treason—whether I was a princess or not.

I sighed.

"Okay, but I can't guarantee they'll let you inside the club," I said.

"Yes!" Jinx exclaimed.

She squeezed her eyes shut and did a little happy dance. Even her eye makeup looked fit for a princess. Jinx had applied faerie ointment so that she would have the ability to see through most faerie glamour.

Unlike Jenna who usually slathers the stuff on like petroleum jelly, Jinx uses a makeup brush. Jinx normally adds a bit of dark pigment to the ointment and uses it to line her eyes, but tonight she was going for a more dramatic look—one that would allow her to see and be seen. She'd added glitter to the dark pigment and ointment, and brushed it onto her entire eyelid in bold strokes.

The smell of clover was strong as she blinked away happy tears, showing off eyelids that looked like a starry midnight sky. I clutched the door casing, overcome by dizziness.

*****

I sank into the memory of a long forgotten night, the heady smell of clover in my nose and my eyes on the stars. I was lying on a bed of clover, staring up at the star-filled night sky. My father, Will-o'-the-Wisp, leaned over me into my line of sight.

I smiled, reaching my arms up for a hug. He lifted me into strong arms and kissed my forehead, then set me on his shoulders where I grabbed at the glowing fireflies dancing around his head. He carried me across the lawn and toward the house. It was the same house I'd grown up in with my mother and stepfather, but it looked brighter, cleaner, and larger than I remembered. Even beneath the night sky, flowers surrounded the house in full bloom.

We met my mother on the porch and I squealed as father pulled me from his shoulders. He pretended I was flying as he lowered me down to the freshly painted porch.

The house wasn't the only thing to look refreshed. My mother was fully transformed. Until now, I hadn't remembered her ever looking so happy. The perpetual lines in her forehead were gone and her eyes crinkled at the corners. For once my mother wasn't frowning. Her smile was radiant.

Her face, and my father's, began to blur. I tried to hold on, to make the memory last just a bit longer, but the happy moment was replaced by a second memory. This new memory was from a different day entirely.

"Please don't leave," my mother sobbed.

She was on the porch and I crouched inside the house, behind the half-open door. I could hear her voice shaking, but she stood just out of sight of my hiding spot. Her hands were the only part of her that I could see clearly.

My father was standing on the front lawn. He was holding a lantern that shone strangely and cast eerie shadows over his face. His shoulders were slumped and he looked like he was in pain. I wanted to run to him and ask if he was hurt, but something about the lantern in his hand frightened me.

I held my breath and listened.

"I must go," he said.

He lifted the hand that held the lantern to his head, and lowered it with a frustrated groan. He raised the other hand to run fingers through his hair and let out a lengthy sigh.

"You...you can't let it go, can you?" my mother asked.

Her hands shook where she clasped them together in front of her. I didn't think I'd be able to look at my mother's hands the same way again. The woman I knew was hard and solemn. She'd never looked so weak or upset before, but those hands, shaking and clasping each other over and over, spoke volumes. My mother was terrified.

My father demonstrated trying to set the lantern down, but could not. No matter what he tried, the lantern remained in his hand.

"I can't be rid of the cursed thing," he said. "So long as I hold this damnable lantern, I cannot escape the devil's eye. I must leave you, or risk the attention of Hell. I won't bring that on you and Ivy. I'd rather die first."

He looked worn and haggard, as if he'd aged overnight.

"There must be another way," my mother said. Her hands fisted. "What about the fae? You are a king. There must be others who can help."

"I'm sorry, love," he said. "Wisps are solitary, usually preferring their own kind. We are short on powerful allies. No, I must leave. But I promise to return when I find a way to break this fool bargain. Until then, I forbid you to speak of me. Forget."

My mother's hands fluttered, going limp, and the memory blurred. I thought I heard my father whisper, "I'm so sorry, Sarah, please forgive me," but I couldn't be sure. The memories, and the answers they may have held, were gone.

*****

I blinked rapidly, leaning against the doorframe. Jinx hovered, eyes wide.

"Dude, you okay?" Jinx asked. "What did you touch?"

What did you touch? The words took a moment to make sense. Jinx thought I'd had a vision, but this wasn't the result of my psychic gift. It was a memory, leaking past the magical barrier my father had cast on my mind. The spell had been unraveling for months, leaving my wisp abilities exposed. Now it was giving me a glimpse into my past.

"Ivy?" Ceff asked.

Ceff stood rigid, the knuckles of his fists gone white with the strain of holding himself back. He still wasn't used to my lapses of reality and was obviously worried. He looked like he wanted to scoop me up into his arms, but knew enough to keep away. Instead, he studied my face intently.

"I'm okay," I said. "It wasn't a vision. I...I remembered something from my childhood. It was a memory of my father."

I gently bit my lip and smiled. Ceff blew out a long breath and flashed a smile in return.

"A good memory?" he asked.

"Yes and no," I said. I struggled to find the right words. "My father didn't abandon us. He left to protect us."

I explained what I had seen in both memories.

"Soooooooo," Jinx said. She lifted a hand and ticked off each point with sparkly tipped fingers. "Your real dad made a deal with the devil that went south. He ended up cursed to carry some kind of tainted Hell beacon, and now he's wandering the earth looking for a cure. And if he finds one, he'll come back to you and your mom and maybe lift the memory spell."

"Yes," I said.

"So if your real dad comes back, what happens to your stepfather?" she asked.

"I have no idea," I said. "I don't know if my dad will ever come back, or find a way to break the curse. But now I know that he wasn't some fae creep who used my mom for sex and tossed her away when he got bored with her. No offense."

I aimed the last at Ceff.

"None taken," Ceff said a wry smile on his lips.

I'd spent the last few months convinced that I had a deadbeat dad who'd used his fae powers to take advantage of my mother. But now I knew the truth. My parents had loved each other. We had been a happy family before my father made a bargain with Hell. I didn't know yet if there was a way to break the curse laid upon my father, but one thing was certain.

I was prepared to do anything to get my family back.

CHAPTER 19

I'm not sure if it was the awakening of my fae blood or the awareness that the place existed, but Club Nexus wasn't difficult to find. As soon as we were within a block of the club, I could feel the energies of the place pulling me closer. In my second sight, the nightclub shone like a beacon.

I took a deep, calming breath and closed my eyes. I remembered what Kaye had said about how the club sat on a magical nexus point where lines of power intersected. I opened my eyes and gasped. Threads of neon light ran out from the location of the club in every direction.

I picked a single pink ley line and followed. My skin prickled and the hair on my arms stood on end. I continued on toward the intersection of threads, feeling energized for the first time in days. Walking along the ley line was like knocking back a shot of espresso. It was no wonder fae had chosen this place to gather.

When the club was within sight, I stopped to examine the surrounding street. The only source of light was the glow of power coming from the skein of ley lines running through the building which housed the club. There were no streetlamps in this part of town and the windows of nearby buildings stood dark. The street was empty except for the fae bouncer working the door.

A huge ogre stood outside the club, eyeing me with obvious scrutiny. The bulge in his suit jacket told me he was carrying, not that he needed a weapon. The guy had muscles the size of tree trunks. He had to be club security.

I swallowed hard, wishing I could have called Jenna for backup. But she was busy working an official cleanup job out in the burbs. Then again, maybe bringing a Hunter along would have been foolhardy. I was here to talk, not wage a war.

The ogre sniffed at the air as I started across the street. At our approach, he raised an arm which effectively blocked the door.

"Name?" he asked.

"Ivy Granger," I said.

"Court?" he asked.

"Unseelie," I said.

"Title?" he asked.

It was now or never—time to come out of the fae closet. I took a breath and lifted my chin.

"Wisp princess, daughter of Will-o'-the-Wisp, king of the wisps," I said.

The ogre raised an eyebrow and checked something off on a list that magically appeared in one hand.

"You may enter," he said.

I stepped to one side and crossed my arms, fingers brushing my throwing knives.

"I'll wait for my friends, if you don't mind," I said.

The ogre rolled his eyes, gave me a suit-yourself shrug, and turned to Ceff.

"Name?" he asked.

"Ceffyl Dŵr," Ceff said.

"Court?" he asked.

"Unseelie," Ceff said.

"Title," he asked.

"King of the kelpies," Ceff said.

"You may enter," he said.

Ceff stepped up next to me and waited. The ogre leaned toward Jinx and sniffed. I held my breath, ready to launch myself between the two if needed.

"Human?" he asked.

"She's with me," I said.

"Food or vassal?" he asked.

"Partner," I said, voice hard.

"Vassal," Ceff said.

"You may enter," he said.

The ogre stepped away from Jinx and opened the door. As we passed through the entrance he sniffed Jinx's hair and drooled.

"Too bad," he muttered.

Jinx tensed. *Jinx is not food*, my mind screamed. The grips of my throwing knives hit my palms, but weapons were unnecessary. Jinx kept walking, following us into the faerie den. The ogre sighed and returned to his post beside the door.

My best friend may have looked and smelled like a harmless human, but she had balls of steel.

We descended a spiral staircase that was both beautiful to look at and practical in terms of defense. If any unauthorized guests ever made it past the door, the tight curves of the staircase would slow an assault. It also gave the entire room an ample view of Jinx's legs as we entered the club.

The stairs cut through the ceiling of the club, giving us a bird's eye view. The space below was cavernous.

Music thumped over an invisible sound system, the stairs beneath my feet vibrating with each beat. The sensation at this height was nauseating, but I was relieved that the haunting notes of faerie compulsion were absent. The music was unusual, but decidedly human—a mix of techno, industrial, and EBM with threads of sitar and djembe drums woven throughout.

My heartbeat started to match the pulse of the music and I shifted my focus. The music may not carry a compulsion, but that didn't mean it wasn't powerful, or a dangerous distraction.

I turned my attention to the supernatural club goers. Fae of every size, shape, and court affiliation crowded the room. Nymphs, sylphs, kappa, draugr, and henkies filled the dance floor. One group of tall, slender fae dressed in old fashioned clothing moved through the steps of a waltz, dancing to their own inner music.

But not every faerie was dancing. Fae lined the walls, lounged on couches, or perched at the bar. Strobe lights from the dance floor illuminated spiral horns, beautiful eyes, perfect teeth, curled tusks, pale feathers, dripping fangs, and sharp talons—capturing bizarre Kodak moments interrupted by darkness.

I pulled my attention from the multitude of fae in the lower levels to a roped off area high above their heads. A second tier rose above the crowd and here fae gathered in small, private groupings. These gathering places were set far apart from each other, allowing for maximum privacy. To ensure that they were not disturbed, each area boasted its own security. Judging from what I could see from my aerial vantage point, the club also offered these elite clients a lavish spread of food, drink, and entertainment.

This had to be the location set aside for fae royalty.

I hurried down the stairs, ready to make a beeline for the faeries on the second tier. If Sir Torn was here, he'd be on that upper level. The club may be neutral ground, but it was organized to reflect fae hierarchy—and Torn was a cat sidhe lord.

The music stopped, the room going silent, and I froze mid-step. Every eye in the place turned to the stairs where we hung from the ceiling like flies on fly paper. If this was a trap, we were as good as dead.

I slowly lowered my foot and shifted my weight onto the balls of my feet. I scanned the room for movement, waiting for a sign from the fae below. I caught a flash of flame to my right and spun, chiding myself. I was so focused on the floor below that I hadn't searched the domed ceiling that arched just inches from our heads.

A fiery ball of flame and feathers rushed toward me. I reached for my throwing knives, but someone grabbed my sleeve, halting the movement. I risked a glance over my shoulder to see Ceff holding my jacket. He gave a quick, short shake of his head. I raised an eyebrow in question, but he was already whispering to Jinx who was reaching for her crossbow.

I lowered my hands, but kept them loose at my side. If Ceff believed the fiery ball flying toward me wasn't a threat, then I'd play along—for now.

Seconds later a winged phoenix settled on the railing beside me. It cocked its head at me, making a chirping sound low its throat. After a moment's inspection, it turned, satisfied, and faced the crowd. Flickers of flame raced along the edges of its red and gold feathers, sending up tendrils of cinnamon and myrrh scented smoke that made my eyes water. The phoenix puffed itself up, a rush of heat flowing out from its body, as it ruffled its feathers and addressed the crowd below.

"Ivy Granger, Princess, daughter of Will-o'-the-Wisp, king of the wisps," it said. "And..."

Ceff leaned forward and whispered something to the bird-like fae.

"And her *consort* Ceffyl Dŵr, king of the kelpies," it said. "And vassal."

Consort? Ceff had made our courtship official. A small, pleased smile touched my lips. Before I could turn to say anything to Ceff, the phoenix burst into flame. The crowd clapped as ash sifted over their heads like macabre confetti.

So much for making a discreet entrance.

Music began to play and the buzz of conversation filled the air. Dancers returned to the dance floor, but many fae continued to watch the three of us make our way down the spiral staircase. I made a mental note of who seemed the most openly interested and where they were located within the club.

It would have been better to have had a schematic of the place to work with, but I'd taken in the basic layout as we made our entrance. The club was laid out in a circular, spiral pattern. I used the large bar, stocked with bottles of glowing liquids, to orient myself.

When we reached the bottom of the stairs, I strode through the crowd, holding my chin high. A sea of dancers parted to make way for the two royals and their human vassal. My shoulder blades itched, feeling the eyes of strangers at my back, but I continued on toward the velvet ropes I'd seen from above.

I flipped my hair over my shoulder and stole a quick glance at my companions. Ceff looked like a man in his element. We may not have been at sea, but Ceff was used to large, royal audiences. His role as kelpie king often meant lengthy negotiations with both enemy and allied faerie delegations and the mandatory attendance of fae social functions. Ceff moved through the crowd with the strength, grace, and confidence of a champion race horse.

Jinx matched Ceff's posture though her eyes were wide and the knuckles of the hand holding the strap of her weapon's bag were white. More than one fae leaned in closer for a better look or sniff, as if they were at a wine tasting and testing Jinx's vintage. I don't know how she tolerated the behavior.

If it had been me, I might have staked them all with iron. Thankfully, my princess status demanded space—either that or I still smelled of rotting ghoul guts. The crowd of fae continued to part before me, allowing me to move unhindered. A trickle of sweat ran down my back, but I took a calming breath and tried not to think of the potential threat of nightmare visions from so many immortals.

I managed to walk confidently across the room, but by the time we reached the roped off stairs my skin had begun to glow. If I'd been on the city streets, I'd have worried. But I was in a faerie club and had come out of the proverbial closet. For once, I didn't care about my glowing skin. Let them stare.

I narrowed my eyes at the two bouncers guarding access to the upper level. A griffin stood to the right of the stairs and a boggart to my left, one light fae and one dark. I suppose in a club filled with both Seelie and Unseelie fae, it made sense to have both sides equally represented by security.

I addressed both of the bouncers, but since wisps are tied to the Unseelie court, I turned slightly toward the boggart. The creature was ugly, hairy, and smelly. Its hair was so greasy, you could use it to fuel a lamp for weeks, but I gave it my best smile.

"Ivy Granger, wisp princess, Ceffyl Dŵr, kelpie king, and our human vassal to see Sir Torn," I said.

The boggart raised his spear, but the griffin nodded and swept the rope aside. The boggart looked disappointed. I hadn't made a friend there. Maybe I shouldn't have tried smiling at the creature. I strode up the wide steps before the griffin could change his mind.

"Would you prefer I do the talking from now on?" Ceff asked.

"No," I said.

Jinx giggled and Ceff shrugged. I turned left at the top of the stairs and started scanning the booths for cat sidhe, ignoring them both. I knew deep down that Ceff was more qualified to do the talking. He was handsome, charming, and skilled at negotiating with fae from both courts. But this was my gig. The parents of those children had come to me for help, not the kelpie king. It was my responsibility to bring them home.

Bodyguards watched us intently and fingered their weapons as we sauntered along the curved walkway, though so far none had impeded our circuit. I hoped to keep it that way. As much as I wanted to run from booth to booth yelling for Torn, an altercation would only delay us further. I kept my hands out where the guards could see them and didn't make any quick, threatening motions.

We moved silently as we passed a trio of centaur guards, my boots sinking deeply into thick, spongy moss. Each section of the upper tier contained a magical microenvironment suited to the fae who were there for both business and pleasure. These microcosms spilled out onto the adjacent walkway, creating a number of potential hazards. So far we'd encountered flames, ooze, ice, and deadly looking insects, but not one cat—until now.

A small cat sidhe watched us from the shadow of a huge, elephant-ear-shaped fern. The cat was taking a chance exploring outside cat sidhe territory, but you know what they say. Curiosity killed the cat.

"Cat sidhe at two o'clock," I whispered.

Ceff nodded and Jinx gave me a thumbs up. I eased my way slowly toward the fern, pretending to admire the foliage. I didn't want to scare the cat sidhe, or give his location away to the nearby guards.

"This fern is beautiful," I said. "It looks just like an ear, but I'm actually searching for one that's Torn."

I flicked my eyes at the cat and winked. The cat sidhe blinked at me and tilted its head. Apparently, I had its attention.

"Ah, look, I found some Ivy," I said.

There wasn't any ivy in sight, but the centaur guards didn't notice. With my hand shielded by my body, I pointed to myself when I said my name. Hopefully, the cat sidhe could let Sir Torn know I was here. Or better yet, take me to him.

The cat sidhe's body faded away replaced my flickering shadows. It stepped out from under the giant fern and trotted back the way we came. I narrowed my eyes at the shadow cat and sighed. I just hoped it wasn't leading us on a wild goose, or cat, chase.

I turned and followed, though the cat sidhe was difficult to see even with my second sight. If I hadn't already known it was there, it could have passed by unseen. I kept my eyes on the cat sidhe, careful not to lose its whereabouts.

Thankfully, I didn't have to worry about dangers underfoot. The cat always seemed to know the best path, and following in its footsteps took less time than our previous trip. Where a realm of ice overlapped with a slime coated cave, the cat sidhe turned left.

It padded over to a section of ice covered stone and winked out of sight. I gasped and hurried toward where I'd last seen the cat sidhe. Ceff and Jinx followed, looking at me quizzically.

"It disappeared right here," I said, pointing at a solid wall of stone.

"Dude, this isn't a Heinlein novel, cats don't walk through walls," Jinx said.

"Maybe, in this case, they do," Ceff said.

He ran his hands over ice and stone, reaching into every notch and crevice. After a moment he smiled, finding what he was searching for.

"There's an opening here," he said.

Ceff stepped to his left and...disappeared. My heart sped up and I reached for my knives, but before they hit my palms, Ceff had reappeared. He waved his arm into an invisible entrance, the limb seeming to vanish.

Ah, there was a gap in the overlapping stone leaving the illusion of a solid wall with an entrance large enough for us to walk through single file. I couldn't see more than a foot inside, but I nodded. Cat sidhe are creatures of shadow and mystery. It made sense that the entrance to the club's representation of their world would be dark and hidden.

Ceff ducked back inside, Jinx at his heels. The cat sidhe had passed through this entrance. Hopefully, Sir Torn would be on the other side. I took one last look at the club and turned to follow my friends through the nearly invisible door.

I just hoped the exit wasn't as difficult to find.

CHAPTER 20

We slipped through the hidden doorway, leaving the ice behind. The cold of the frozen area of the club was replaced by warm, humid air as I stepped into the dark. Claws tapped on pavement and I tensed as shapes began to take form.

Fae blood gave both Ceff and me excellent night vision. Jinx wasn't so lucky. I heard her voice whisper shakily.

"Ivy?" she asked. "Remember when we agreed not to have strangers over to the loft? Well, I think this is a good time to tell you about this guy I let sleep over a few nights ago. I know you're always worried about visions, so you may not want to use your toothbrush."

My leather gloves creaked as I curled my hands into tight fists. Was this some kind of evil twist on deathbed confessions? If it was, I didn't want to hear it. I didn't have time for an argument, but when this was all over, Jinx and I were going to have a serious talk.

My skin started to glow, pushing back the shadows.

"Your friend is clever," Ceff said.

Jinx turned to me and shrugged.

"Not all of us have superhuman see-in-the-dark powers," she said. "I had to improvise."

I shook my head. Jinx was something all right.

I looked around the room, though room may not have been the correct word. We stood in an alley with what looked like night sky overhead, smog blocking out the stars. The narrow space was filled with crates, barrels, and boxes that hundreds of cats of every shape and size lounged atop, leaving no surface clear of watchful eyes.

In the far corner, a familiar cat sidhe with scar-lined fur sat on a large, overturned wood spool. The spool was the industrial type used for transporting wire. Someone had flipped it on its side like a makeshift, ghetto-style table. The cat sidhe perched atop the spool and lazily licked his paw, unbothered by our sudden appearance.

I stepped toward the scarred cat sidhe, but several cats jumped down and hissed, blocking my path. The cat sidhe stopped licking his paw and sighed. It stood and arched his back, letting out a low keening cry. The fur along his back began to ripple, replaced by skin, shadow, and black leather.

Darkness enveloped the cat and when the shadows dissipated, a handsome man sat with one leg dangling over the edge of the table. One arm leaned on a leather-clad knee and a half smile quirked his lips. We had found Sir Torn, lord of the cat sidhe.

Like many fae, the cat sidhe lord was easy on the eyes, but he lacked the perfection which so many high bloods prized. In his human guise, Torn was as damaged as he was beautiful.

Torn retained the multitude of scars I'd first noticed when he was in cat form. The faerie's face was dominated by a large, ragged scar that ran through his left brow, eyelid, and across the bridge of his nose. Additional scars crisscrossed both arms, but these were nothing compared to the damage sustained by his ears. Even in human form, the cat sidhe's left ear was filled with holes and his right ear was nothing more than a lump of scar tissue.

Instead of hiding these battle scars, Torn had embraced his imperfections. He'd adorned the many holes in his ears with bone and feather piercings, perhaps trophies from his kills. Fur, bone, and feathers also decorated the leather vest, pants, and boots that he wore. The look suited him in a wild, roguish, Beyond Thunderdome kind of way.

Torn flicked his remaining ear in a move that was completely inhuman, a signal for the cats to stand down. With a swish of tails, the cats spun away and returned to the shadows. Torn gestured to the makeshift table and smiled.

"Come, sit with me," he said.

The faerie lord continued to perch atop the table. I stood my ground, not wanting to place myself below Torn by sitting on one of the low crates. When we didn't move, he shifted his attention to our weakest link.

Torn turned yellow eyes to Jinx and winked. Her lips parted and she took a step forward. Torn ran a hand down the length of his body to pat the wood beside him. He was like a cat playing with a mouse.

I cleared my throat, snapping Jinx from Torn's spell. She took a step back and pulled something from the bag she wore slung over her shoulder. Every cat in the alley hissed, hackles raised, and I risked a glance at my friend. Jinx held a crossbow trained at the faerie lord's head. I turned back to Torn, a wry grin on my lips.

"No more games," I said. "I have questions."

"Nice to see you too, Princess," he said.

"Sorry, Torn," I said. "This isn't a social call. I don't have time for social niceties."

He tilted his head to the side and raised a scarred brow. When we'd met before, the cat sidhe claimed that he was bored. I was hoping that our mission was intriguing enough to hold his interest.

"Go on," he said.

"Two things," I said. I held up two fingers. "First, how did you know I was a princess? That didn't become common knowledge until a few minutes ago."

I scowled, remembering the phoenix perched on the stair rail announcing my royal title to the entire club below. That single moment was going to complicate my life, as if it wasn't difficult enough already.

I wasn't looking forward to marching back through that crowd when it came time to leave. Every faerie in the club was probably talking about my lackluster entrance into fae society. My mouth went dry and I focused on one of the feathers in Torn's tattered ear.

"We cat sidhe are masters of concealment," he said. To demonstrate, Torn began to fade away, obscured by shadow. Within seconds he was completely invisible. "No secret is safe from our eyes and ears."

A moment later, the shadows shifted and Torn reappeared, beginning with his amber eyes and scarred ears. He was wearing a satisfied smirk that pulled at the scar on his cheek. *Nice trick.*

"Impressive," I said.

The cat sidhe waved his hand in dismissal, as if it were nothing. But being able to walk the streets unnoticed, both in cat form and concealed by shadow, was a major talent.

Sir Torn and his subjects could have been listening any time I discussed my parentage outside the protection of The Emporium or my house wards. I'd have to learn to be more careful. I tilted my head at Torn, studying him more closely. If all cat sidhe had the ability for such stealth, they would make a powerful ally or an invincible foe. For the first time, I wondered which side the cat fae belonged to. Were cat sidhe members of the Seelie or Unseelie court?

"Cat sidhe are independent," he said. "We belong to no one."

It was as if Torn plucked the question from my mind. Oh yeah, I'd have to learn to be a lot more careful in future dealings with the cat sidhe.

"If you are such masters of secrets, then maybe you know something about my real father," I said.

I held my breath and waited. Before today, my only interest in my father was finding a cure for my life threatening wisp abilities. But after memories of my childhood had seeped past the unraveling spell on my mind, I now wanted to get to know my father. I felt a duty to help him find a way to break the curse he was under and bring him home. But I'd have to find him first.

"More than you," Torn said. I wanted to wipe the smug smile off his face with one of my blades, but instead, I waited. I rolled my shoulders and tried to look bored. I was learning a thing or two about faerie negotiations. "What will you give me for this knowledge?"

I shrugged.

"That depends on what you know," I said.

"I know that Will-o'-the-Wisp, king of the wisps, left this city twenty years ago after he made a foolish bargain with a demon," he said.

"Whatever," I said. "I knew that already. Maybe you're not as good at gathering secrets as you like to think."

"I know more, but that information comes at a price," he said.

Crap. I was hoping to keep the faerie cat boasting long enough to give something useful away for free. No such luck.

I was tired of faerie bargains and the heavy price they carried, but there was one tactic I hadn't tried yet. Since the cat sidhe were unaligned, it just might work.

"How much information would you be willing to share with an official ally?" I asked.

Torn's eyes widened for just a second, but I'd seen the reaction. I had caught the faerie lord unawares. I smiled. I was pretty sure that Torn didn't surprise easily. He returned my smile, displaying pointy white teeth.

"You are willing to ally the wisps with the cat sidhe?" he asked.

"Yes, but only in exchange for useful information about my father," I said.

"Your offer is...unprecedented," he said. Torn made a strange purring sound low in his throat and licked his lips. "I accept."

I felt the pavement shift beneath my feet as the bargain settled on my soul, but for once, there was no pain or nausea. I took that as a positive sign.

"What do you know of my father's whereabouts?" I asked.

"Liam, as I knew your father, left Harborsmouth after that foul demon bargain," he said. "He is cursed to walk the world carrying a lantern filled with an ember from the fiery pits of Hell. Will-o'-the-Wisp has become Jack o' Lantern. He carries the lantern until the curse can be broken or he hands the lantern over to another."

"But if he passes the lantern on to someone else, he's effectively cursing them, right?" I asked.

"Yes and the lantern must be taken up willingly," he said. "The role of Jack o' Lantern cannot be forced, though trickery and manipulation are permitted."

"So my father is trying to find a way to break the curse without damning someone else," I said. "Is that why he left Harborsmouth?"

"He left because the lantern is dangerous," he said. "Your father realized that the lantern he carried was a conduit to Hell. Liam did not want to harm you or your mortal mother with its presence."

My father didn't abandon us—he was trying to protect me and my mother. My heart swelled.

"Do you know where he is now?" I asked.

I bit my lip. *Please, please, please.* Torn slouched and spread his hands wide.

"I am sorry, Princess," he said. "The last known location for Jack o' Lantern was Fukushima, just before the tsunami and nuclear disaster. Many went missing that day, both fae and humans, and I lost track of your father. Locating him again will be difficult, but I will have my people look into it."

The Fukushima Daiichi nuclear disaster was known the world over. Radioactive materials had been released due to a meltdown at a nuclear power plant in Fukushima Japan. The nuclear disaster followed the Tōhoku earthquake and tsunami which caused over 15,000 casualties.

Had my father been injured during the disaster? Was he even still alive? I shook off the heavy cloak of doubt before it had a chance to suffocate me.

My mouth went dry as another thought wormed its way into my head. Had my father's presence had something to do with the Fukushima disaster? If so, the lantern he carried was more dangerous than I thought.

I sighed. I needed to talk to my father, but there was nothing to do now but wait for a lead to his whereabouts. I had no doubt that if anyone could discover where my father was hiding, it was the cat sidhe. For now, my fate, and my father's, were in Torn's hands.

The cat sidhe leaned forward, tilted his head, and studied me with open curiosity.

"And the second reason you sought me out?" he asked.

Oh, right. I'd wasted enough time on my own personal agenda. It was time to learn what I could about the walking dead. If I could trace the reports of strange lights and other supernatural activity to a specific burial ground, then we'd be one step away from rescuing those kids.

"You said that you'd heard rumors of ghost sightings in Harborsmouth," I said. "I think these sightings might be linked to a case I'm working involving missing fae kids."

Torn hissed and his eyes flashed bright yellow in the dark alley, but his anger wasn't aimed at me. Faerie children are rare and precious to the fae. I gave the guy a moment to collect himself.

"Our children are missing?" he asked.

"Yes, over thirty kids that I know of so far," I said. "The calls started pouring in this morning. We have some leads, but we're short on time."

"Tell me what you know," he said.

I gave him the Cliffs Notes version of the case. When I mentioned the rats, every cat in the alley showed their teeth and claws. Apparently, cat sidhe and their feline followers aren't besties with the rats of the city. Since most of the rats I'd seen in my vision were the size of cats, I assumed they made a dangerous foe, especially in large numbers. But if I were a betting girl, I'd put my money on the cat sidhe in a fight.

"We know that Melusine is capable of murdering children," I said. Ceff blanched, but I continued on like I hadn't noticed. It was better to get this over with fast, like ripping off a bandage. "We also know that The Piper will need to begin the Danse Macabre in order to feed off the children's life energy and to fulfill his bargain by providing Hell with their souls."

"You're running out of time," Torn said.

"Yes," I said. I swallowed hard. I just hoped we weren't already too late. "I know who the key players are, and what they want, but what I haven't been able to figure out is where they are hiding. I just know that it's likely that they are near a burial ground."

"And you think the ghost sightings might lead you to them," he said. I nodded. "Do you have a map of the city?"

"Yes," I said. I pulled up the map display on my phone.

Torn stared at the map, brow furrowed.

"Here and here," he said, pointing. "Most of the ghost sightings are reported near these two cemeteries—Ocean Overlook and Far Point."

They were the two oldest and largest cemeteries in Harborsmouth, each encompassing acres of city land. It was a lot of ground to cover, but at least Torn had helped us narrow the search to two possible locations.

"Thank you," I said.

"If you wish to thank me," he said. "Bring back our children."

I nodded and turned toward the wall where we'd entered from Club Nexus, but the door was gone. I turned to Jinx who shrugged.

"Ahem," Torn said. Torn stretched catlike and slid down from the table, his boots silent as they hit pavement. "This way."

Torn sauntered with feline grace toward the end of the alley. The sea of cats parted as we followed their leader. I wondered where they had hidden the exit. Was the door somewhere in the brick wall? The alley mouth? I just hoped it wasn't inside the dumpster.

I walked up behind Torn and he stepped aside with a flourish. We were standing facing a dark street that looked entirely real. I rubbed my forehead trying to make sense of what Torn was showing me. The energy jolt I'd received when entering the club was wearing off and I was too tired for games.

Torn pointed to my left and I gasped. The entrance to Club Nexus, still guarded by the ogre bouncer, stood a few doors down from the alley. How could that be possible?

"We aren't inside the club?" I asked.

Torn looked down at our feet standing inside the alley and lifted his eyebrows.

"Now that is a matter of opinion," he said. I stepped out onto the sidewalk, testing a theory, and turned back to Torn. He nodded and smiled. "You are most definitely outside the club."

I looked up at the night sky, a grin pulling at my lips. We'd found the answers we were looking for and saved valuable time. The strange geography of the cat sidhe's pocket of Club Nexus meant we didn't have to go back through the club to find an exit—and I wouldn't have to face the stares of snoopy curiosity seekers.

I cracked my neck and lowered my head to look at my companions. Jinx slid her crossbow into her bag and Ceff nodded.

It was time to go find those kids.

CHAPTER 21

We crouched beside a stone wall, the gates of Ocean Overlook a mass of wrought iron protruding from the gray swirls of low fog. During our walk to the cemetery, the fog had rolled in off the ocean to pool at our feet. I pulled myself upright and peered over the rock wall. Iron fencing was set deep into the stone, with sharp points aimed at the sky.

We wouldn't be climbing over the wall. Ceff was already sweating profusely from the close proximity to so much iron. No, we needed to make a run for the front gates—if I could get them open without being seen.

I scanned the cemetery grounds for a caretaker or security guards. Fog flowed between headstones like specters, but I saw no sign of humans. No telltale flashlight beams cut the night. If there was a guard on duty, he wasn't nearby.

"Looks clear," I said. "I'll be right back."

"Wait," Jinx said. She rummaged in her bag and pulled out two small plastic containers, each the size of a contact lens case. "I almost forgot. Take these."

"What are they?" I asked.

"Ear plugs," she said. "I use them when I'm out clubbing. They should muffle the flute's music."

I smiled and tucked the earplugs into a jacket pocket. Jinx was brilliant. Ceff moved more slowly to take his and I was reminded that we were in a hurry. He couldn't take much more iron exposure.

"Thanks," I said. "I'll have the gate open in just a sec."

Ceff's skin was pale, but he nodded and pulled the trident from his pant leg. He kept the handle collapsed and held it in a reverse grip, the tines of the weapon pointed toward his torso and slanted against his forearm. Jinx readied a bolt, but kept her crossbow between her body and the road. At a passing glance, they looked unarmed.

The entrance to the cemetery was on a dead-end street and we hadn't seen any traffic so far, but it was best not to take chances. We couldn't risk anyone seeing our weapons. It wouldn't do the children any good if we ended up spending the night at the police station.

I crept forward, shoulders tight. Ever since we'd left Sir Torn and the club behind, I'd had the itchy feeling that someone was watching me. When I was halfway to the gate, I spun on the ball of one foot and scanned the darkness behind me, but Jinx and Ceff were the only people in sight.

I let out a shaky breath and returned my attention to the cemetery. The gates were made of wrought iron crafted in an ornate pattern. They towered overhead at approximately seven feet at the highest point.

I pulled a bottle of clary sage from my pocket, unscrewed the cap, and squeezed a dropper full of the oil onto one of the gate hinges. The air filled with the sharp, herbal scent and I proceeded to oil the remaining hinges. Clary sage was the only oil I had on me at the moment. I hoped it would help to keep the metal silent when it came time to push the gate open.

The gates were held shut with a thick, stainless steel chain and large padlock. I unrolled the cloth containing my lock picking tools and glanced to my left and right. Satisfied that no one was coming, I began picking the padlock.

It would have been faster to cut through the chain, but I was fresh out of bolt cutters. Plus, if I got caught, trespassing was bad enough without adding vandalism to my rap sheet.

I inserted an L-shaped torsion wrench into the bottom of the keyhole. I applied tension to the lock cylinder, first clockwise and then counterclockwise. The cylinder turned a fraction of an inch counterclockwise. I applied gentle torque to the wrench in the counterclockwise direction and held it there with my left hand.

Next, I inserted a hook pick into the upper part of the keyhole. Working back to front, I pressed up with the pick, feeling each of the four pins. Starting with the pin which offered the most resistance, I pressed the pick upward setting the pin. I repeated the procedure, continuing with the final three pins. I removed the pick and turned the torsion wrench counterclockwise, holding my breath. The padlock clicked opened.

I slid the chain carefully from one of the gates and left it hanging in a loop. I'd lock up behind us when we finished. I took a deep breath and pushed the oiled gate halfway open. I needed to allow enough space for Ceff to enter without coming into contact with the iron. With one final glance at the grounds, I ducked back out onto the sidewalk and waved my friends forward.

My phone rang and my heart leapt into my throat. I rushed to answer it, chiding myself for not turning off the ringer.

"I've been researching the Danse Macabre," Father Michael said in a rush. He sounded out of breath. "I think I know how the dance can be stopped. But Ivy? I spoke with Kaye and she believes the number of fae children taken is significant. The Piper may need a particular number of fae to begin the spell. Do you know how many children have already been abducted?"

"Just a sec," I said. I jogged over to Jinx who was walking slowly toward the cemetery gate. Ceff was leaning heavily against her, the nearby iron taking its toll. "Jinx, Father Michael needs to know the number of kids who've gone missing."

Jinx raised one painted eyebrow, but didn't ask questions. She shifted Ceff to one side and pulled out her phone. She accessed her case files, tongue pressed against her cheek. Within seconds Jinx had the information we needed. I was glad that one of us was organized.

"Thirty-three," she said.

"We have thirty-three kids reported missing," I said into my phone.

I heard a quick intake of air on the other end.

"If The Piper already has thirty-three children, then you don't have much time," Father Michael said. "He has what he needs to complete the spell."

"Are you sure?" I asked.

"Yes," he said. "When Kaye told me her theory, I looked more closely at medieval paintings and carvings of the Danse Macabre. The artwork often depicts thirty-three living dancers and thirty-three of the risen dead."

Numbers, like names, hold power. I knew from spending time with Kaye that the number three was often used when casting spells. The number of children who had been taken made sense. I just wished I'd noticed that detail sooner.

"Don't worry," I said. "Torn helped narrow our search to two Harborsmouth cemeteries. We're at the gates of Ocean Overlook now. If the children aren't here, we'll head over to Far Point."

"No, you don't understand," he said, voice shrill. "There's no time. Kaye thinks that once The Piper has the thirty-three children needed to complete the spell, he will begin the dance at midnight."

Midnight? I checked the time. Talk about the eleventh freakin' hour. It was eleven forty-five. The priest was right—we were running out of time.

Far Point cemetery was too far away and both cemeteries were huge. It would be impossible to cover that much ground in fifteen, make that fourteen minutes, even if we split up.

I glanced at Ceff, his skin pale in the moonlight. He was our fastest runner, especially if he shifted to horse form, but he'd never make it through Far Point's iron gates on his own.

I set my jaw and looked my companions in the eye. We had to stick together. It was our best chance of defeating Melusine and The Piper and bringing those kids home alive. I just hoped we had the right cemetery. I waved Jinx and Ceff through the gates while continuing my conversation with the priest, voice tight.

"What else can you tell me?" I asked.

"If you find the children..." Father Michael said.

"When," I said, correcting him. I pushed the gate closed behind my friends. It would fool a casual passerby, but not someone working security. I just hoped that there were no guards on duty. "*When* we find the children."

"If the Danse Macabre has already begun, you will need a way to disrupt the spell," he said. "I found a holy verse which may cancel out the powers of the demon flute and halt the dance. Say the words, Sancte Michael Archangele, defende nos in proelio, contra nequitiam et insidias diaboli esto praesidium. Imperet illi Deus, supplices deprecamur, tuque, Princeps militiae coelestis, satanam aliosque spiritus malignos, qui ad perditionem animarum pervagantur in mundo, divina virtute, in infernum detrude. Amen."

"No offense, Father," I said. "But I suck at Latin. Can you send that to me in a text message?"

"Yes, of course," he said.

"Thanks, give Galliel a hug for me," I said. "I'll see you both when this is over."

"Ivy, the church grim is still here," he said, lowering his voice to a whisper.

"Don't worry," I said. "Omens aren't set in stone. We can always change our fate. I'll bring those kids home safe."

"I will pray for you," he said.

"Thanks, padre," I said.

I ended the call and hurried to catch up with Jinx and Ceff. I wished I believed my words to the priest. I liked to think that we could change fate, if we tried hard enough, but death omens are tricky business. We'd need the priest's prayers if we hoped to make it through the next fifteen minutes unscathed.

CHAPTER 22

We quickly left the cemetery gates behind. Color returned to Ceff's face as we put distance between us and the iron gates and he now ran without Jinx's assistance. We sprinted through the cemetery looking for sign of the children.

We moved with such speed that headstones appeared, as if by magic, in the swirling fog. I was glad for my fae-boosted night vision and quick reflexes. Jinx wasn't so lucky. Her shins and knees were bloodied from stumbling into unseen obstacles, but still she ran on.

We searched every tomb and mausoleum, but there was no sign of the children. I checked the time again—it was eleven fifty-nine. The statues of angels looked down from lofty perches atop monuments and pedestals. Their sightless eyes seemed mocking as I tried to hold out hope.

I ran faster, my breath ragged and legs burning. A light danced in the distance and I stopped. My pulse pounded in my ears as I tried to hold my breath. As I watched, more lights joined the first to dance through the air. That was no flashlight.

Those were wisps.

I'd never seen a full-blooded wisp before. Nothing, not even the glimpses in my visions, had prepared me for how captivatingly beautiful they were. Kaye had shown me artist renderings of my brethren, but the paintings and sketches hadn't done them justice. The wisps glowed like the light of the sun—and pulled at me with a star's gravity.

These were my people. *Mine.* I felt something akin to a mother's love for these beautiful spheres of light. Warmth flooded my body and flames seemed to lick at my skin. With a maternal bond comes a fierce protective instinct. I gripped my knives tightly, a growl forming deep in my chest. Melusine and The Piper had involved the wisps in their dark plans. For that, I'd make them pay.

I shook my head, pushing away thoughts of revenge. I needed to focus on the problem at hand. If the wisps were in the cemetery ahead of us, the children must be nearby. Miraculously we'd found the correct cemetery, but we were still running out of time.

Keeping an eye on the wisps, I turned to the side and waved to Jinx and Ceff who were running up behind me. I held up my hand for them to wait and pointed to the wisps. I wasn't sure if they'd seen the small faeries yet. I pointed to myself and gestured for them to stay back and let me approach first.

I crept toward the nearest wisp, heart racing. I needed to save the children and my people. If I could get close enough, I might be able to reason with the wisp, maybe. I felt the growing bond between us, but these wisps had never met their princess. And I, for all my royal blood, had never before encountered one of my people. I had no idea if we could even communicate with each other. But I had to try.

The glowing ball of light hovered above a headstone, casting the epitaph into sharp relief. When I was near enough to read the engraving, I came slowly out of my crouch and cleared my throat. The wisp ducked behind the headstone, seeming to wink in and out of existence with its speed.

"Wait," I said. I kept my voice low. If Melusine or The Piper were nearby, I didn't want to give away my position. "I am the daughter of Will-o'-the-Wisp."

A piece of me finally slid into place. I was like an old puzzle in a box with torn corners—pieces falling through the cracks. You can try to put the puzzle together, but unless you stumble on the missing pieces, the picture is incomplete. I'd found a missing piece in this unlikely place, and I would cherish it. Fulfilling my destiny as the leader of the wisps gave me an unexpected sense of calm. I smiled and took an easy breath.

"I am your princess," I said.

The wisp peeked out from behind the headstone and floated tentatively toward me. It rose to head height and twinkled happily. Though the wisp didn't communicate with words, I could feel hope, joy, and acceptance roll off its body in warm waves.

This wisp welcomed me as its leader. I just hoped the other wisps felt the same way.

"The lamia Melusine and The Piper with his demon flute are my enemies," I said. "I'm here to rescue the children. If you help me, I will forgive your role in leading them to this place."

The wisp's light dimmed in shame.

"Can you lead me to the children?" I asked.

The wisp brightened again, bobbing up and down.

"Good," I said. "Lead the way."

I waved for Jinx and Ceff to follow and turned back to the wisp. It was already dancing and weaving through the fog, nearly out of sight. That little guy could move fast.

I grinned, teeth flashing in the night. Pride surged through me, and with it returned my desire for revenge. Melusine had murdered Ceff's sons, put over thirty fae children in jeopardy, and manipulated my people. It was time to teach the lamia a lesson—payback's a bitch.

I gripped my knives and ran. Adrenaline surged through my veins as I rushed forward, heart racing. I launched myself over gravestones and urns filled with rotting flowers, all the while keeping the wisp in my sights.

As I ran more wisps joined us, but I sent them away with a quick command. Their combined glow would likely give us away. We needed to approach with stealth if we were to keep the element of surprise. With an unhinged lamia and a demon flute wielding faerie as adversaries, I'd use every possible advantage.

I remained ahead of my companions. Jinx was only human, though she'd had the sense to discard her platform shoes, and Ceff was still recovering from the effects of iron poisoning. I could hear their heavy breathing fade into the distance behind me and pushed on.

My legs ached and my lungs burned, but I never slowed. I ran along the waterfront every morning, preparing myself for moments like this. That training and my newfound speed and strength allowed me to move at a breakneck pace, but still, I was too late.

Someone blew a long, tremulous note on a flute and music began to fill the air. The sound pulled at me, making my aching feet want to dance. I shook my head and slowed my pace. Even at a distance, The Piper's music was entrancing. I had to block the sound before continuing on.

I reached into my pocket for the earplugs that Jinx had given me. I inserted the bright colored foam into my ears, immediately dampening the music. For once, I was glad that my friend enjoyed clubbing. The earplugs were high quality and made to reduce sounds even at high decibels. Since The Piper's flute played a low, haunting melody, the plugs almost completely blocked it out.

Of course, I was still a couple hundred yards away.

I checked my phone and brought up the text from Father Michael. *Sancte Michael Archangele, defende nos in proelio, contra nequitiam et insidias diaboli esto praesidium. Imperet illi Deus, supplices deprecamur, tuque, Princeps militiae coelestis, satanam aliosque spiritus malignos, qui ad perditionem animarum pervagantur in mundo, divina virtute, in infernum detrude. Amen.*

Below the Latin, Father Michael had included the words in English. *Saint Michael the Archangel, defend us in battle; be our defense against the wickedness and snares of the devil. May God rebuke him, we humbly pray. And do thou, oh prince of the heavenly host, by the power of God thrust into Hell Satan and all the evil spirits who prowl about the world for the ruin of souls. Amen.*

I repeated the phrase, securing it to memory. I slid the phone back into a secure pocket and took a deep breath. I just hoped that the priest's theory was correct.

I flipped my throwing knives, rotating each one hundred and eighty degrees to hold the blade between my fingers. I bent low and scooted closer to the music and dancing lights. When I could feel the music tugging at my body like a gale wind, I ducked behind a headstone and dug my boot heels into the turf.

I took a calming breath, centering myself like I would for a potentially nasty vision. I focused my mind and imagined bricks and mortar being laid to form a strong, impenetrable wall around my psyche, bolstering my will. I would not succumb to the demon music. Would. Not.

I opened my eyes and peeked around the headstone, careful not to let my face brush the moss covered stone. Bile rose in my throat and I ground my teeth. What I saw nearly broke my heart.

Children were huddled together on the chill, damp grass. The children, still clad in the pajamas they wore when they were abducted, shivered against the cold.

As I watched, something moved across the ground like shadows shifting through the sea of fog, heading straight for them. But these shadows were covered in skin and mangy fur. Hundreds of rats rushed toward the children, teeth and eyes flashing. The children whimpered and pulled each other closer.

I spun around the headstone and leapt to my feet, but as I rushed toward the children, the notes of the song became more urgent. The children were jerked upright, compelled by the music as if pulled by invisible puppet strings. Rats nipped at their ankles as they joined hands and began dancing in a circle.

I pulled my eyes away from the children and searched for the source of the music. A tall, slender faerie stood opposite my position, the circle of children between us. He held a flute to his lips with long, slender fingers that danced along the instrument like spiders. The man was wearing colorful pantaloons over hose and a matching vest over a loose, puffy blouse.

I'd found The Piper.

Though The Piper's unusual clothing and tall, slender build were typical for a faerie, his lined face was not. Wrinkles creased his forehead and chin and his ebony hair was streaked with white. The Piper's mortality was showing.

Coiled beside him like a cobra ready to strike was Melusine. The lamia's lips were parted in a smile of total ecstasy. The bitch was getting off on the children's terror.

"No!" Ceff yelled.

I looked over my shoulder to see Ceff rushing toward the circle. He was staring in horror at his ex-wife.

"Ah, my love," Melusine said. "I knew you would come. You always did care too much for the children."

She tut-tutted, pouting her lips. With her fangs retracted Melusine was beautiful—if you could ignore the fact she was a crazy, psycho bitch.

"How could you do this?" Ceff asked. He gave a slow, disbelieving shake of his head. "What did you possibly think you could accomplish by harming these innocent children?"

"You have only yourself to blame," she said. "I was the perfect wife and yet you loved our children more than you loved me. Children should be put in their place. They should be made to suffer for stealing what is rightfully mine."

The color drained from Ceff's face.

"You cannot fault me a father's love for his children," he said.

Melusine ignored his words, caught up in her own fantasy. The woman was truly crazy. Her hatred and jealousy had grown into an evil, festering wound that could only be healed with the suffering of more children.

That was what Melusine gained from tonight's charade. She would revel in the pain inflicted on these kids. If her ex showed up to watch, that was a bonus.

"You and I can be together again my dear," she said, eyes gleaming. "As soon as I destroy this half-breed distraction."

Melusine turned to me, fangs extending. Scratch that. She was also here to win Ceff back and kill his new girlfriend. Lucky me.

I stepped forward with my left foot, adopting a throwing stance. I bent my knees and shifted my weight to the ball of my right foot. I needed to get close enough to The Piper to disrupt his spell, but first I had to make it past Melusine.

I yawned and stretched my right arm overhead. If I kept her talking, maybe I could get my knife into position without her knowledge. I hoped she'd underestimate the lowly half-breed.

"If you're going to kill me anyway, how about you tell me how you tricked the wisps into helping you," I said.

I moved my right hand just behind my head. I hoped it looked like I was scratching my neck, not readying to toss my iron-tipped blade.

"Do not blame your foolish brethren," she said. "The wisps were promised the return of their princess for their service. And I, my dears, have delivered."

Faerie bargains; they were always filled with loopholes and trickery. I spat. I would show her what happened to those who bound my people with deception and lies. I would show them all what it meant to anger an Unseelie princess.

Melusine had to be stopped. She would never change. The fact she'd used my own people in her more recent evil machinations added to my conviction. Melusine may have been Ceffyl's queen, but she never cared about his people. The bitch cared only for herself. In a jealous fit, Melusine had murdered the heirs to their kingdom and abandoned her king. It was time she paid for her treasonous crimes against the kelpies.

Melusine shot toward me, fangs fully extended. As she rushed me, she lifted a sword and aimed it at my head. I adjusted for the change in distance and threw my knife with lightning speed, faster than I'd ever thrown a blade while practicing with Jenna. I smiled. I was drawing strength from the wisps now hovering around my head.

My knife buried itself deep in Melusine's shoulder, putting her sword arm out of commission. The sword fell from her hand, arm hanging limply at her side. Without hesitation, Melusine dipped her body and retrieved the sword with her left hand. Great, the bitch was ambidextrous—just my luck. I readied my second knife to take out her left shoulder when Ceff stepped in front of me.

"I will not let you do this," Ceff said, facing Melusine. He risked a glance at me and shouted. "Go! I'll take care of Melusine. You and Jinx rescue the children."

Ceff turned to face Melusine and widened his stance. The telescoping handle of his trident shot outward as he flicked his wrist hard, the move an open threat. If it came down to a choice between Melusine and the children, he'd pick the children, just as he'd always done. The knowledge made the tension bleed from my neck and shoulders.

I nodded and lowered my blade. I'd wounded Melusine which should slow her down. If Kaye's information was correct, lamias can only regenerate the serpent portions of their bodies. Even with the rapid healing common to full blooded fae, she wouldn't be using her right arm in this fight.

I had to trust that Ceff could handle his ex. I sent up a silent prayer and turned my attention to the children who were indeed in need of rescuing. Tiny feet stomped atop graves and gravel paths as the children's bodies lurched to The Piper's music.

The Danse Macabre had begun.

CHAPTER 23

I watched in horror as Jinx struggled to rescue children from the circle. She pulled and cajoled, but their tiny hands held firm. No matter how hard Jinx tried, the spell was too strong.

As she tugged at the hands of a young wood nymph, a bony hand burst from the ground and batted her away. Jinx stumbled, the earth roiling at her feet.

The dead were rising from their graves.

We needed to free the children from the dance. I searched recent memory and began to recite the prayer that Father Michael had given me. It was worth a shot.

"Saint Michael the Archangel, defend us in battle; be our defense against the wickedness and snares of the devil. May God rebuke him, we humbly pray. And do thou, oh prince of the heavenly host, by the power of God thrust into Hell Satan and all the evil spirits who prowl about the world for the ruin of souls," I roared. Nothing happened. I choked back my frustration and pulled my phone from a zippered pocket. Maybe the prayer had to be read in Latin. "Sancte Michael Archangele, defende nos in proelio, contra nequitiam et insidias diaboli esto praesidium. Imperet illi Deus, supplices deprecamur, tuque, Princeps militiae coelestis, satanam aliosque spiritus malignos, qui ad perditionem animarum pervagantur in mundo, divina virtute, in infernum detrude. Amen."

But the dead continued to rise. I grunted in frustration. I was too far away from The Piper and his demonic flute. I shifted the phone to my left hand, gripping a throwing knife in my right.

All around the circle, the earth burst upward in clumps of soil and sod. The dead clawed up through caskets and dirt, climbing out of their graves to scuttle like cockroaches toward the children. I kicked at the hands and heads of zombies as I made my way around the circle.

The fight between Ceff and Melusine blocked my approach on the left, so I skirted to the right. The rising dead and the horde of swarming rats slowed my progress. I kept an eye on Jinx, who was positioned between us, as she fought to free the children.

Jinx tried again to pull a small child from the circle, but it was no use. The children only parted long enough to clasp the hands of the dead, their feet never missing a beat as the zombies were welcomed into the circle.

The newly risen dead were in varying states of decay. Bony skeletons wearing nothing but shreds of rotting cloth hurried alongside the bloated corpses of the newly deceased to find their place in the dance.

Blinking away sweat and tears of frustration, Jinx grabbed the crossbow slung over her shoulder. She couldn't fire at the dead that had joined the dance, since they were positioned so close to the children. So Jinx turned away from the circle and aimed at a female zombie crawling out of her grave.

The face of the corpse had decomposed so badly that exposed teeth flashed where her cheek had been and hair hung from her scalp in stringy clumps. The woman had been dead for months, but she moved with breakneck speed. The zombie pulled herself to her feet and rushed Jinx.

Jinx fired the crossbow, but the bolt sailed straight through the rotting flesh of her assailant. The zombie kept coming. The dead woman barreled into Jinx's chest and knocked her flat on her butt.

Jinx landed with a strangled cry and I took a step toward her, prepared to lose ground if it meant saving my friend. The corpse ignored Jinx, leapt past her into the circle, and joined hands with two small fae children. The female zombie was no longer an immediate threat.

Jinx slung the crossbow back over her shoulder and stayed low, making herself a smaller target. The crossbow wasn't an effective weapon in this fight, so she started using her hands and feet. Jinx kicked and punched at both the risen dead and the sea of rats.

The rats that got past her nipped at the children's feet and ankles, drawing blood. The children cried out, but continued to dance. The sound of their cries rang out even in my earplug filled ears, making my stomach twist and churn. I turned away from Jinx and the children and focused on my target.

The spell was working. The Piper was feeding off the children's life essence. Even at this distance, I could see signs of his returning youth. The white streaks that had been in the faerie's hair were gone and his face was filling in.

I had to get closer to The Piper and interrupt the spell before he sucked these children dry. I would not let a selfish, demon flute wielding faerie steal away the lives of so many children and sentence their souls to Hell.

I choked back hot, angry tears as I sprinted around the circle. My boots crunched and I tried not to think of the rats underfoot. I kept my eyes on the objective.

A figure stumbled into my path and I batted away the rotting corpse with the flat of my blade. The zombie lurched to the left and I jinked right, avoiding its grasping hands. The thing was dressed in a threadbare suit that hung from its body in tatters and smelled almost as bad as Stinky the ghoul. I breathed through my mouth and ran faster.

I was halfway around the circle when something moved in my peripheral vision. I twisted my torso toward the movement, knife at the ready. A pack of shadows, teeth, fur, and yellow eyes rushed low across the ground heading straight toward me. When they came within throwing range, the shadows parted to my left and right, heading toward the circle. The newcomers weren't interested in me. They were here to battle The Piper's pet rats.

Our backup had arrived.

I stared, eyes wide, as more cat sidhe melted out of the fog. The first wave of faerie cats, led by a cat with torn ears, placed themselves between the children and the attacking rats. The second wave of cat sidhe flanked the rodents, darting in to snatch up the weakest rats in their teeth and claws.

Sir Torn and his army had come to battle their natural enemy, the horde of city sewer rats, and help rescue the fae children. As I watched, one cat sidhe grabbed a rat by the neck and flung it away from the children while another began using its rear claws to disembowel a second rodent. I had seen enough.

I looked away and continued sprinting toward The Piper. I now had to skirt around the perimeter of the battle between the rats and cat sidhe. This added precious time to my run, but there was nothing I could do other than push my legs to move faster. I tightened my fingers around the knife in my hand and ran.

I leapt over an injured cat sidhe and landed on a patch of grass beside The Piper. The music seemed louder here and I struggled to remain focused. I scanned the area for any immediate threats, squinting through the growing fog.

Farther away, Ceff and Melusine fought their own game of cat and mouse. Their movements were too fast to follow, but the route of their battle could be discerned by toppled gravestones and demolished mausoleums. Ceff was drawing Melusine away from me and the children.

I wouldn't let his efforts go to waste. A haunting melody buffeted my mind, but I shook my head and turned my attention to The Piper. The effects of the Danse Macabre were evident. His face was once again youthful, a thing of fae perfection.

I fumbled with my phone and prepared to read the prayer that Father Michael had sent me. I wasn't wasting time on the English version. It was time to get old school.

"Hey, douchebag!" I yelled.

The Piper opened his eyes and I gasped. The faerie's eyes glowed red—the eyes of a demon. Perhaps the demon flute exacted its own price, opening a conduit to Hell and changing the user into one of Hell's minions. The force of those eyes bored into my skull and I cried out. I needed to recite the prayer from Father Michael's text message, but I felt the phone slip from my hand.

I slid down to my knees beside the phone. I panted and shook my head, trying to fight the faerie's compulsion. But the combination of demon and faerie magic was too overpowering. I looked up into the face of The Piper and for one moment, the red eyes and youthful face were a thing of beauty.

"Poison Ivy, duck!" Marvin yelled.

When did Marvin get here? My magic-addled brain couldn't process the unexpected information.

Something large and spherical flew over my head and hit The Piper squarely in the chest. Still on my knees, my jaw dropped as a cloud of pixies enveloped The Piper's head and torso. As The Piper fought off the pixies, my head began to clear.

Marvin had thrown an entire pixie nest at The Piper. The kid had told me once before that the evil little critters didn't bother his thick troll hide, but it took guts to carry an entire nest of hibernating pixies across the city.

Pixies not only cause an itchy rash when they lick their victims, they are also equipped with a hypodermic sized stinger. Each stinger is filled with a toxin strong enough to paralyze an elephant. An entire hive of pixies was swarming The Piper, using their stingers to show their anger for the person who destroyed their nest.

Marvin had just hit The Piper with a paralyzing pixie grenade. The kid was a genius.

The Piper was playing the demon flute one-handed as he fought off the pixies, but his motions were sluggish. The faerie was quickly becoming incapacitated, but the Dance Macabre continued. The conduit to Hell was too strong.

It was time to recite the prayer.

"Saint Michael the Archangel defend us in battle!" I yelled. "Sancte Michael Archangele, defende nos in proelio, contra nequitiam et insidias diaboli esto praesidium. Imperet illi Deus, supplices deprecamur, tuque, Princeps militiae coelestis, satanam aliosque spiritus malignos, qui ad perditionem animarum pervagantur in mundo, divina virtute, in infernum detrude. Amen."

A bright, ivory light poured down from the sky illuminating the flute in The Piper's hand. As the light struck The Piper's hand, the demon flute glowed red and fell from his grasp. I could immediately feel the power of the spell dissipating.

I struggled to pull myself to my feet, but kept my distance from The Piper who was still surrounded by a swarm of angry pixies. The pixies flew in a flurry of beautiful wings, jabbing at him with their stingers. The red glow went out of The Piper's eyes and he fell to the ground paralyzed.

The beam of white light panned over the circle of children and the risen dead, continuing to break The Piper's spell. Depending on their states of decay the dead either collapsed where they stood or returned to the earth, clawing their way into nearby graves.

The children stopped dancing, halting mid-step. Jinx was immediately there to offer comfort and pull each child away from the dead and back toward the cemetery gates. I smiled. I could trust my friend to get the children safely home.

I nodded and turned back to The Piper. I had to find a way to keep the faerie incapacitated and secure the demon flute, but a long-lived murderer and a Hell-forged instrument were two things I really didn't want to come into contact with. I pocketed my phone and raked a hand through my hair. The angry pixies that continued to swarm over The Piper's body added to my unease.

I was still trying to find a solution when a corpse lumbered over to the faerie's immobile form. The zombie turned to face me and let out a hissing moan. I took a step back and bent low, retrieving the dagger from my boot. When facing an angry zombie, two knives are better than one. I held the dagger in my left hand and the throwing knife in my right.

I relaxed my stance and shifted my weight to the balls of my feet, ready to spring forward. The Piper may not be my favorite guy at the moment, but I wasn't about to let him become zombie food. If the corpse looked like he was in the mood for brains, I'd have to send him back to his grave with an empty stomach. I wasn't about to let the monster feed on someone with a bloodstream full of pixie toxin. That just wasn't a fair fight.

The zombie lunged forward, grabbing at The Piper and the pixies flew up into the air. I sighed, so much for playing nice. I sprung forward, trying to reach The Piper, but lost my footing.

The ground beneath my feet shook and I went down to my knees. I winced as rocks dug into my jeans. The ground rolled and heaved like it was in the throes of an earthquake. I dug my gloved fingers into grass and soil and held on for the ride.

I kept my eyes on the zombie, ready to launch myself forward as soon as I could stand without falling on my butt. He continued to hold The Piper by his shirt like a rag doll. With a great crack, a chasm opened between us.

My stomach twisted. I had a bad feeling about where that chasm led.

The zombie slung The Piper into a fireman's carry and jumped into the fissure. A red glow lit the faerie's face. The Piper looked at me in supplication, but in a flash of light, he was gone. I crawled forward, but in a puff of brimstone, the chasm closed, the earth swallowing the two men whole.

I coughed and sat back on my heels. Well, that was one problem solved. I was pretty sure The Piper wouldn't be stealing any more children. It seemed poetic that the man who made a deal with a demon to collect and condemn the souls of children to an eternity in Hell should now join those souls.

But The Piper's trip to Hell didn't mean the end of the devilry. I had to make sure the demon flute didn't fall into the wrong hands. I crawled back and forth searching the ground for the demon flute, but to no avail. It was gone. All that was left was a patch of scorched earth where I'd last seen The Piper and his flute. Perhaps the instrument had also been carried to Hell, returned to the forge where it had been wrought.

I pulled myself to my feet, brushing clumps of grave dirt off my jeans, and gave myself a moment to catch my breath. I let my head fall back to look at the night sky, a slow smile forming on my lips. We'd done it. The Piper and his evil Danse Macabre had been stopped. The children were safe.

I turned an ecstatic smile to Marvin. His sudden appearance and ingenious use of a pixie nest had made The Piper's defeat possible. If the kid was standing closer, I'd have given him a high-five. Coming from me, that was high praise.

Marvin began to smile and wave, but his large hand halted in mid-motion. His eyes widened and the skin at my neck prickled.

"Ivy, look out!" Marvin screamed.

I spun in time to see the fight between Melusine and Ceff steamrollering toward me. I dove aside, out of their path. I continued rolling to my right, narrowly avoiding the lamia's lashing tail. The two were locked in heated battle, and Ceff was losing.

I gasped and came up into a fighting crouch. Heart racing, I looked for an opportunity to join the fight, but Melusine and Ceff's bodies were pressed close together and moving fast. If I threw my knife, I'd risk hitting Ceff.

Melusine lunged toward Ceff's head and he struggled to take a step back and duck out of reach. Melusine didn't even appear winded, but even over the earplugs, I could hear Ceff's breath coming hard and ragged. His clothes were torn and bloodied, the shirt he wore now mere tattered scraps of fabric. Ceff was obviously still suffering from the effects of iron poisoning, that put him at a disadvantage. At the last moment, it became apparent that the lunge toward Ceff's head was just a feint, but it was too late.

Ceff's reflexes were fast, but Melusine was faster. Melusine halted the forward motion of her lunge with a jerk and swung her tail out in a foot sweep. The move took Ceff off his feet, using his momentum against him. Ceff tumbled painfully onto his back, hitting his head and knocking the air from his lungs. I tensed, still looking for an opening.

Melusine slithered atop Ceff, arms astride his shoulders. She sniffed along his body, venomous fangs inches from his skin. Her lips formed a cruel smile and she lifted one of her arms to retrieve a knife from behind her head. Her hair tumbled down to brush Ceff's face and neck. The bitch had kept the knife hidden in her hair.

Ceff's trident had fallen from his hand and he didn't move a muscle to defend himself. I studied Ceff's face, but his eyelids remained shut. His chest rose and fell slightly—he was alive—but the blow to his head must have knocked him unconscious.

"If you will not love me, then you shall pay," she said. "Goodbye, husband."

Melusine held the blade above Ceff's chest and licked her lips. Carving her ex-husband's still-beating heart from his chest was evidently Melusine's twisted version of justice—a heart for a heart. No way was I going to let that happen.

I sprinted forward, dagger in one hand, throwing knife in the other, and launched myself onto Melusine's back. She reared up, arching her back, trying to reach me with her blade. I wrapped an arm around her neck and slipped my throwing knife back into its forearm sheath in an effort to keep my hold on the thrashing lamia. I dug my left hand into her hair and held on tight.

I maintained my grip on the dagger, but it wasn't easy. Something cold and scaly brushed against my skin where the sleeve of my jacket had pulled away from my glove, leaving my wrist exposed. A vision of a mouse being dangled from Melusine's fingertips as a tasty treat intruded into my mind, but I kept my arm bent in a choke hold and held onto the dagger at her throat.

Melusine's pet snake had joined my arm around her neck. The good news was that snake brains don't make for very intense visions. I'd managed to maintain my choke hold through the minor vision. The bad news? Melusine's pet was a venomous pit viper.

"You are nothing but a half-breed, a rodent to crush and bleed," Melusine shrieked. "I will kill you and my unfaithful husband both!"

Melusine swung forward, throwing me off balance. I was slung over her shoulder to come face to face with her pet. The pit viper glared at me with slit eyes and sunk its fangs into my wrist. Indescribable pain burst through my arm as venom shot into my bloodstream. I lost my grip on my dagger and my arm fell from Melusine's neck.

I swung further forward, barely managing to hold onto Melusine's hair with one hand. I tried a spinning kick to her ribs, but didn't have enough leverage. Instead, I left my flank open to attack. Melusine struck, whipping her head down as I swung in a lazy arc. Flesh and leather tore as the lamia's fangs punctured my side.

Now I could add lamia venom to the killing cocktail in my veins.

Melusine shook her head, tearing her fangs free. Bloody spittle sprayed across my jeans with the movement. Sparks of light flashed in my peripheral vision; a likely precursor to blacking out. I noticed all of this as I fell in slow motion to hit the ground.

Strangely, I didn't feel the impact as I hit. Cold crept through my limbs as life poured from my body to soak the grass where Ceff still lay unconscious. I clamped my hand onto the wound in my side and tried to staunch the bleeding with fingers gone stiff and clumsy. I dug my boot into the turf and tried to push myself up, but something wet tore inside my gut and I gagged. *This must be what it feels like to die.*

I was so weak I could barely lift my head—and Melusine damn well knew it. With a mad gleam in her eye, Melusine spit my blood at Ceff and raised her blade a foot above his chest. The bitch was going to kill us both, but first, she'd make me watch as she cut out my boyfriend's still-beating heart.

No way was I going to let that happen. I gathered my anger to me like an old friend. I wasn't going down without a fight.

My skin flashed warm, then molten hot and began to glow. The cold slush in my veins was replaced by liquid fire.

The sparks of light that I'd mistaken for the beginning signs of unconsciousness gathered around me in a burning cloud of light—and power.

Fire rushed through my body to burn away the venom's deadly chill. Energy poured into me as I drew power from the wisps that had come to heed my call. With renewed strength, I pushed myself up into a sitting position. I slid my last throwing knife from its sheath and pinched the blade between the fingers of blood-slick gloves. I held my arm straight and raised it above my head. In one lightening fast move, I flung my arm forward and released the blade.

The knife struck Melusine between the eyes.

I gasped. The blade shouldn't have flown true. I hadn't been standing in a proper throwing stance and my gloves were slippery with blood and other fluids.

Melusine dropped the blade from her hand and toppled over, a surprised look on her face. Part of her large body fell atop Ceff and I tried to rush forward. I had to make sure that Ceff was all right. A seven-foot tall lamia was no lightweight. I staggered toward Ceff, but the strength that had filled me seconds before was gone.

I fell to the ground beside Melusine's discarded blade, vision fading. As I began my descent into the oblivion of unconsciousness, or possibly death, I sent up one last prayer that Ceff had survived unharmed.

The last thing I saw as sleep pulled me under was my own reflection in Melusine's blade—my eyes glowing like the sun.

CHAPTER 24

Nightmares tore at my mind—rats drawing blood, children dancing hand-in-hand with the dead, Marvin's cry of warning, the whip-fast lash of a serpent's tail, and fangs dripping deadly venom. The images burned like the fever raging through my body. I was caught in a typhoon of fear and fire, not sure if I'd ever find my way home.

In the distance, a man held a lantern aloft to guide my footsteps. If only I could find solid ground beneath my feet. My boots made a sucking sound with each step. The bog was pulling me under, trying to swallow me whole.

I took a step forward and plunged into cold water. I held my breath and struggled to find my way out. When my boots hit something solid, I kicked and thrashed. My head broke the surface and I coughed up foul tasting water, gasping for air.

I spun in a circle, blinking water and mud from my eyes as I searched for the man and his lantern. *There.* I swam toward the man, but the lantern flame flickered with an eerie light and I hesitated. The kind face I'd expected looked frightening in the spectral glow. This man wasn't my savior, he was a monster.

I thrashed my arms and legs, struggling to escape. Water weighted down my clothes and mud sucked at my limbs. I lost sight of the lantern light as my world was consumed by darkness and the nightmares that linger there.

Chanting and incense joined the images of my dreams and I floated, helpless, like a leaf on the surface of a raging river. I was caught by the currents of my fevered mind, condemned to smash against the rocks of my fears and memories.

Was I dying? If this was death, I wished it would get on with it already. I always thought that death would bring an end to the nightmares, but this world in between the dead and the living was even more frightening than my life had been.

If there was a chance at living, I would grab it and hold on tight. But there was no life preserver here, not even a piece of driftwood. There were only monsters hissing and growling in the dark. My heart raced and I reached for my knives, but they were gone. I had no weapons here. All I had was fear and pain and the certainty that I was in this alone.

The monsters drew closer scenting my fear like sharks drawn to a single drop of blood. My body shook as I tread water. I was without both weapons and armor. My leather jacket was gone and, in the way of nightmares, I was wearing only a camisole and panties. My skin was naked, exposed.

I tried to be quiet, but failed to hold my breath and calm the shaking. The monsters would find me soon and when they did I wasn't sure what I was afraid of most—their killing teeth and claws or the simple brush of their touch.

I slipped beneath the waves and deeper into the abyss.

*****

I emerged from the depths of my nightmares to a new series of fears. I awoke in my body, but found that I couldn't move my arms or legs or open my eyes. There was nothing except darkness and pain and the staccato beat of my heart.

My body, and the pain, seemed real. I didn't think I was still trapped in that in-between realm of fever dreams, but that didn't mean I was safe from monsters. I needed to move, to hide, and grab my weapons. I focused on trying to move my right arm and red hot needles stabbed my nerve endings. I sucked in a gasping breath and stilled, catching a familiar scent.

I sniffed at the air and my racing heart slowed. I smelled salt brine, cool skin, and sea breezes—Ceff's individual scent. I didn't like being defenseless, but at least Ceff was here, wherever here was. If someone threatened, he would protect me.

I tried to recall my last memory before I blacked out. I'd been battling Melusine in the city cemetery, but the details were blurred. I had a feeling that the fight hadn't gone well.

I needed information, and that meant opening my eyes and getting back on my feet. Maybe I could succeed if I started small—baby steps. I ignored the pain and focused on my feet. I hoped that my lower extremities hadn't been injured as badly as my arms. I tried to wiggle just my toes, but the attempt brought on a wave of nausea. I couldn't move a muscle.

Melusine and her pet snake had done a number on me. I suppose under the circumstances I was lucky to be here at all. If I was conscious, then I must have survived the fight—unless this was one of the circles of Hell.

I was a survivor; I preferred to think on the bright side. I'd fought a psycho crazed lamia and lived. Not bad for someone who'd only had a couple years of self-defense classes and a few intensive months of weapons training under her belt.

I'd begun training with Jenna back in December in the hopes that I could add the knowledge to what I knew of self-defense and use the new skills in the protection of those I cared about. After the *each uisge* invasion of my city, I'd worked hard to stay fit, but when I faced a redcap ambush over the holidays, I realized that basic self-defense wasn't enough. If I truly wanted to defend myself and my colleagues, then I needed to take Jenna up on her offer to train me in the use of weapons. The Hunter didn't come cheap, but business had been good lately—and now I'd faced a jealous lamia and lived.

It was worth every penny.

If it hadn't been for our training sessions, I'd surely be dead right now. In the past, I'd given Jenna a small, ironic bow at the beginning of each class, but as soon as I was healed enough to begin lessons again I planned to bow deeply. I owed the Hunter a great deal of respect, and the gratitude of a princess.

At least, I hoped I'd be returning to training. I hurt all over. Without the ability to move or open my eyes, I had no idea how serious my injuries were. I tried again to move my arms and legs, but all I could feel was the heavy weight of pain.

My heart raced and I struggled for breath. The world fell away beneath me, sucking me back down into unconsciousness.

*****

I woke to the sound of someone talking. The sound was muffled and I wondered if someone had forgotten to remove the earplugs I'd been wearing when I passed out. I listened more closely as my head began to clear. It sounded like Kaye's voice, but what was my witch friend doing here?

Had Father Michael sent Kaye to the cemetery? For some reason, that didn't make sense. Kaye's powers had waned since her role in the *each uisge* battle last summer. The black tattoos that crawled up her neck and twined down her arms and hands were evidence of the sacrifice she had made. No, the priest would not have sent Kaye to our aid. But then, what was she doing here?

I cracked open one eye to see the witch speaking with someone on the phone. It always looked strange to see Kaye holding a cell phone. I half expected her to keep in touch using a crystal ball.

"Yes, she'll be fine," she said. "She can go home today. Just be sure she continues to rest. No running off to be the hero—not this week."

I missed what the person on the phone said, but Kaye laughed in return and hung up. If I didn't want to have to answer questions, I'd better not let her see me awake. My head pounded with a migraine and I was pretty sure that every muscle in my body was bruised. I just needed a little longer to recuperate. Maybe after a nap...

I turned my head away from Kaye and startled, fully awake. Hob perched on the pillow beside my head. He was leaning forward, hands resting on his knees, and squinting at me with beady eyes beneath bushy eyebrows. At my movement he rose into the air, eyes wide.

Mab's bones. So much for an extra minute of shut eye.

"She's awake!" he exclaimed. He clapped knobby hands and landed on the pillow again where he danced a jig. "How do ye feel, lass?"

I tentatively lifted my arms, and did an inventory of my wounds. I had plenty of scrapes and bruises and a nasty bump on the back of my head. I was also pretty sure that my wrist was broken. But the cuts, broken bones, and throbbing headache were nothing compared to the burning in my side.

I pulled down the blanket covering me and lifted my shirt to see a large poultice wrapped in gauze.

"I'm okay," I said, forcing a smile. "But this itches like crazy."

I rubbed a gloved hand against the bandage and winced.

"Don't touch that, dear," Kaye said.

Kaye set the phone down and shuffled over to my bedside. I used the time to take in my surroundings. The old stone and wooden beams of the room were familiar. The welcome smells of herbs, incense, and wood smoke wrapped around me like a blanket. I'd been in this room hundreds of times before. I wasn't lying where I'd fallen in the cemetery. I was in Kaye's spell kitchen, near the hearth.

I suppose Hob's appearance on my pillow should have been a hint. I chalked my confusion up to a sleep-addled brain. I yawned and flinched when the movement pulled at my side. Maybe if I could just get a few hours more sleep...

I started to drift, but Kaye harrumphed and kicked the bed, jerking me awake. She placed tattooed hands on her hips and shook her head. Apparently, Kaye's recent time as a patient hadn't improved her bedside manner. If I wanted sleep, I'd have to bust out of here.

I sighed and pretended that the motion didn't cause me pain. If I wanted to get out from under Kaye's care, I'd have to pretend I was well enough to return home. She narrowed her eyes at me and I blushed. Right, trying to trick a witch was probably a dumb idea. Kaye was no fool.

With another penetrating look, Kaye lowered herself onto the low stool beside me. She took her time settling her skirts and I tried not to fidget. I didn't like lying here prone, but I figured Kaye would turn me into a toad, or worse, if I tried to sit up without permission.

I ran a gloved hand over the small wooden frame beneath me. Since the kitchen didn't have a bed, I figured they'd set me on a portable cot while Kaye nursed me back to health. When Marvin had stayed here, he'd slept in a pile of blankets on the floor. The troll was too big for a bed.

"Is Marvin alright?" I asked.

My heart raced and a cold sweat beaded on my forehead. Marvin had unexpectedly shown up during the Danse Macabre, but I couldn't remember if he made it out safely. I tried to think back to the end of the cemetery battle, but my memories were hazy.

I remembered Sir Torn arriving, leading the cat sidhe to attack the rat horde. I had uttered the Latin words just as Father Michael had instructed, weakening the compulsion of the endless dance and loosening the hold of the Danse Macabre. Ceff had battled Melusine, keeping her busy while Jinx tried to rescue children from the circle. I had fought with

The Piper…and Marvin had appeared, joining the attack. But the details were fuzzy after that.

"He be fine, lass," Hob said.

The brownie patted the blanket beside me, trying to comfort yet careful not to touch. My eyes watered and I blinked the tears away. I must be allergic to something in Kaye's kitchen. I didn't cry over bridge trolls. It wasn't my style.

"Your friends and subjects are safe," Kaye said.

Subjects. I don't think I'll ever get used to that. I let out a breath and turned my attention back to the gauze bandage taped to my side. Whatever was under the wrappings itched and burned like crazy. I felt like I'd been pixed. Maybe I had. Marvin had used a pixie nest to incapacitate The Piper long enough for me to disrupt the spell.

Memories of the battle were returning in fragments, but I still couldn't remember what I'd done to my side. I lifted my good hand and pointed at the gauze taped to my side.

"So what's up with the bandage?" I asked.

I bit my lip waiting for Kaye's reply. Hob looked worried and continued to pat the blanket beside me.

"It's time to remove the poultice," Kaye said. "I'll show you how to change the dressings and you can see for yourself."

She slid on disposable, surgical gloves and removed the medical tape from my skin. I held my breath, heart racing. My eyes slid to the black tattoos climbing up Kaye's neck, down her arms, and onto her hands; hands that were dangerously close to touching me. My heart raced, leaving me lightheaded and my skin glowing pale yellow.

"I'll be careful to avoid touching you, dear," Kaye said.

Kaye didn't look up from her work, just wiggled a gloved hand at me and continued removing tape from the edges of the bandage. She peeled back the layers of gauze and herbs to expose two round puncture holes. Jagged rips in the skin streamed out from the punctures where the flesh had been torn. A half-memory returned of Melusine shaking her head, fangs caught in my side. But was that truly memory or nightmare?

I tried to lift my head for a better look and grunted as the movement pulled at the wounds. It looked like a snake bite, if the snake was the size of a grown man, or woman.

"Melusine?" I asked.

"Yes," Kaye said. She still didn't meet my eyes. "The tips of her fangs caught you in the side as you tried to protect Ceff. If you hadn't killed her with that silver and iron blade, the lamia would have murdered you both. You are lucky to be alive."

I lay back against the pillows and squeezed my eyes shut. I'd killed my boyfriend's ex-wife. I wasn't sure how he'd feel about that. Heck, I didn't know how I felt about it. The woman was evil, but I'd murdered her in cold blood, leaving her no chance for redemption. What did that make me?

Not for the first time since discovering my Unseelie blood, I wondered if I might truly be a monster.

"Marvin say ye had no choice, lass," Hob said.

I knew the brownie was trying to help, so I nodded. But deep down inside I felt broken. Even if Ceff forgave me, which was a big if, I didn't think anything would ever make me feel better about taking a life.

I tried to swallow, but my mouth was dry and I felt like my heart was stuck in my throat. I coughed and looked away. Kaye handed me a glass of water and I sipped it slowly, postponing my next question.

"Where is Ceff?" I asked.

I'd been lying here, maybe dying, and Ceff was nowhere in sight. Lamia fangs are venomous; it was a miracle I was alive. I'd never had a boyfriend before, but I was pretty sure they were supposed to sit beside your deathbed. If he wasn't here, then he was leaving me. I'd really screwed things up this time. My insides were achingly hollow and I imagined myself falling into the void Ceff had left there.

"Calm yerself, lass," Hob said.

I opened my eyes to see Hob hovering near my shoulder and wringing his hands. My skin was glowing so bright it made my eyes water. I took a deep breath and tried not to think about Ceff and Melusine. The glowing dimmed, but didn't go away. I was too upset and had no way of hiding that fact. I was caught with my heart unguarded, raw and exposed.

"Ceff is grieving, dear," Kaye said. "Do not judge him for that. He has been here watching over you for days, but this morning I told him you were safely recovering and would be going home today. I told him to go and get some rest, but I saw the haunted look on his face when he left. At a guess, I'd say he is at the cemetery. He said he'd see you later at your apartment."

I pressed a gloved hand against my eyes and let out a shaky breath. Ceff had been at my side for days. *Thank Mab.* He hadn't left me forever. He'd left me to grieve.

"Melusine was a lot of things, but she was also the mother of his children," Kaye said. "Let the man grieve. Give him time."

Melusine was a lot of things alright—like the murderer of Ceff's sons—but Kaye's words were filled with wisdom as always. If Ceff required time to grieve, then I'd back off and give him the space he needed.

Then my sluggish brain caught up with what else Kaye had said. *He has been here watching over you for days.* I blinked rapidly and turned my head back and forth from Kaye to Hob. I'd been here for days?

"How long have I been unconscious?" I asked.

"Nearly a fortnight, lass," Hob said. "But ye be goin' home now. The Madam says so."

A fortnight was two weeks. That was a long time to be out cold. Plenty of time to lose strength and muscle tone.

"I'm going home?" I asked.

I pursed my lips together and my stomach quivered. I wanted to go home, don't get me wrong, but I wasn't sure how I was supposed to manage that with two gaping holes in my side. Monsters walk the streets of Harborsmouth and I felt as weak and vulnerable as a cat sidhe kit. I clenched my good hand, longing for my weapons. Maybe I should stay a few more days after all and build up my strength.

"You doubt my skills, girl?" she asked. Kaye lifted her chin, but there was a teasing twinkle in her eye. "I was able to draw the lamia venom from the wound at your side and administered anti-venom for the viper bite at your wrist."

Kaye pointed to the wrist I'd assumed was broken. It was wrapped tightly and hurt like the devil, but when I attempted to move my fingers they wiggled stiffly. I'd been injected with both lamia and pit viper venom. Some girls have all the luck.

"The venom brought on a terrible fever as your body tried to heal, but the fever finally broke last night," Kaye said. "You're at no risk of death now, but you'll need to rest until you recover your strength. You'll be weak as a babe, at least for a few more days."

I looked around the room, feeling lost. I was going home, but I had no idea where to begin. I wasn't used to being so dependent on others for help. There was only one person who looked after me like that, and she wasn't here.

"Where's Jinx?" I asked.

I understood why Ceff had left my side, but Jinx's absence was odd. I would have expected her to hover. For once, I would have gratefully accepted a helping hand, but my friend was nowhere in sight.

"She's back at the loft getting your room ready," Kaye said. "You know how she likes to fuss over you. The silly girl."

Kaye wasn't a big fan of my roommate. If Jinx had found a way to be of help and escape Kaye's watchful eye, she'd have been out of here in a flash of dyed hair and platform shoes.

I smiled and started the painful process of pulling myself upright. It was more difficult than I cared to admit, but with Kaye's help, I was able to stand and gather my things.

I grunted and double-checked the blades strapped in their sheaths. The leather sheath on my right arm overlapped the bandages there, but I tightened the straps and embraced the pain. Hopefully, it would keep me awake long enough to get home.

I pulled a new leather jacket over the sheaths and checked the fit in one of Kaye's scrying mirrors. The coat was a gift from Jinx. It had been folded beside the bed with a clean t-shirt and pair of jeans. A note on top of the pile said she'd procured the jacket from the clurichaun tailor...and that I owed her a new pair of shoes. Looked liked I'd be making a trip to the clurichaun's cousin soon enough.

I smoothed out the jacket, satisfied that the leather hid my weapons. I hesitated before taking up the blades. There was no way I was getting close to the weapon that killed Melusine. I would relive that moment over and over in my dreams. I didn't need visions of that night threatening to intrude into daylight as well.

I was finally convinced to take them up when Kaye assured me that the throwing knives were new. Jenna had sent them over as a get-well gift. Some people send flowers, my friends send leather and weapons.

"Time for you to be off," she said. "Humphrey will make sure you get home safe."

I limped to the door, sweating with the exertion. Kaye had warned that I'd be "weak as a babe" for a few days. Weak as a babe? That was an understatement. I was as boneless as a brollachan and pale as a vampire. Whoever Humphrey was, I hoped he walked slowly.

I'd be lucky if I made it home without passing out.

CHAPTER 25

As it turned out, Humphrey was a gargoyle. I was pretty sure he was the same gargoyle from the other day, but it was hard to tell. He sported a familiar combination of features, a mutation of dog, goat, and bat, but I had trouble examining him closely. The gargoyle was flying a few yards above me and I started to fall over each time I tilted back my head.

I shook off a wave of dizziness, put my hands in my pockets, and started the long walk home. My wrist throbbed and a burning pain stabbed my side with every step. I was pretty sure that if I had to raise my arm in a knife throwing stance, I'd pass out.

Thankfully, Kaye had provided the gargoyle escort. I may be too weak to defend myself, but I had no doubt that the half ton of living stone could keep me safe. Still, it was a long-ass walk to my apartment.

I limped along slowly, avoiding looks from passerby. When I was nearly home, my phone rang. I jumped at the sound and hissed at the pain the movement caused. The gargoyle glanced down and snorted. He seemed to find my predicament amusing. *Har, har.*

I winced and pulled my phone from my pocket. The number to our office flashed on the screen.

"Hey," I said, answering the call. "Miss me already?"

"Kaye said you were on your way home," Jinx said. "But we got a problem. I need you to stop by the office."

"Seriously?" I asked.

"Dude, I need you down here," she said, and hung up.

I stared at the blank screen and sighed. Shoulders slumped, I trudged to the office. All I wanted was my bed, but there was no rest for the wicked. Some days it sucked to be me.

I turned the corner to see a crowd assembled in front of Private Eye. The gargoyle gave a rumbling growl of warning and I looked up to see his ears lay back flat against his head. I reached into my sleeves, making sure my blades were one flick away from my hands. My right wrist was stiff, but if I ignored the pain, I could grab the throwing knife. I just hoped I didn't need my weapons. I'd be able to fight, but it wouldn't be pretty.

Faces turned toward me and I stopped dead in my tracks. For a moment, I felt a sense of déjà vu. The crowd was made up of the same fae parents from a previous morning, but the assembled fae were no longer gnashing their teeth and wringing clawed hands. This time they were smiling and waving at me, though many had tears in their eyes.

This mob wasn't here to lynch me. Considering my current state of health, that was a good thing. When Jinx saw me turn the corner, she jumped into the street and yelled, "surprise!" I slid my hands away from my weapons and gave the gargoyle a quick nod.

"It's okay Humphrey," I said. "That's my friend and business partner Jinx...and a few of our clients."

The gargoyle's stone hackles disappeared and he came to rest on a nearby building. He started licking his front paw, ignoring the people milling about below. Apparently, Humphrey was satisfied that the crowd didn't pose a threat.

I turned a stiff smile to Jinx and limped forward.

"Um, hi," I said. "What's going on?"

Jinx gestured at the crowd behind her.

"These peeps heard you were recovering and wanted to say thank you," she said. "When Kaye announced you were coming home today, we put together a little welcome home party."

A surprise party, for me? I'd spent years avoiding parties, even going so far as to beg my parents not to celebrate my birthday. Crowds and presents usually filled me with dread. But looking at the smiling faces of the parents whose children I'd helped rescue, produced an entirely different emotion.

The faeries lifted a banner above their heads to flap in the breeze. I examined the banner through joyful tears. Someone had painted "thank you" in the center of the banner in big, red letters. Around the words were numerous drawings and paintings of happy families. The families were all different, some had wings or horns or fur, but they were all drawn with smiling faces.

The children from the cemetery had each drawn a picture of themselves at home with their family, safe and happy. The children's artwork was one of the nicest gifts I'd ever received. Tears filled my eyes and I bit my lip as it began to tremble.

Most days, being a hero meant blood, sweat, and potential insanity, but then there were days like today. Days like this? They make it all worthwhile.

CHAPTER 26

I leaned back in my office chair, boots resting on my desk. I closed my eyes and sighed. I could stay here for a week.

It was getting late and Jinx and I were the only ones left in the office. The place was finally quiet. The parents of the fae children were gone, but I wasn't ready to climb the stairs to our loft apartment.

I was tired and sore, but happy. Each parent had taken the time to sit with me and tell me about the moment they heard the phone ring, knock at the door, or splash in their fountain heralding the good news that their child was alive and safe. I'd laughed, drank copious amounts of coffee, and cried as these clients shared their stories.

I usually met face to face with a client at the end of a case. I had found that it helped clients to understand my findings if I explained the details of the case in person. It also gave us closure. But I'd never had a case as satisfying to bring to an end as the case of the thirty-three missing fae children. Every child had been saved, every family reunited, and I had sat with each parent to bring the case to a close.

I hadn't realized until today just how terrified I'd been with the lives of so many children hanging in the balance. I'd tamped down my own emotions and did what had to be done. With the case solved there was no need to keep that fear and self-doubt locked inside.

The worry I hadn't allowed myself to feel while searching for the children came crashing back with the meeting of every parent. I'd spent the day with clenched fists and tight shoulders as I retold the most important events of the case, but now that it was over I felt completely relaxed.

Jinx clapped her hands together and I opened my eyes.

"Case closed," Jinx said. "I just finished logging the payments from our clients. Time to get you home and in bed."

I yawned. I had no intention of getting out of my comfy chair.

"Go on up," I said. "I'm staying here tonight."

"You can't be serious," she said. "If you sleep there, you'll get a stiff neck."

Before I could answer, someone tapped on our office door.

"If that's a client, I'm not here," I said.

"Right, and that's so convincing with you sitting there in plain sight," she muttered.

Jinx sauntered over to the door and peeked out the window. She smiled and opened the door for Ceff who stood illuminated by lamplight.

Ceff was in human form, though the large, not-so-human, dark green irises that encompassed his eyes were evident in my second sight. Except for the eyes, Ceff looked like a human male in his early thirties, one who just walked off the cover of GQ magazine. He stood in the doorway wearing an unbuttoned dress shirt and low-slung jeans. Lamplight played across a strong jaw pebbled with a five o'clock shadow. My eyes flicked down to where he stood on the brick sidewalk and I smiled. As usual, Ceff was barefoot.

"Is Ivy here?" Ceff asked.

"She's inside," Jinx said. She stepped aside and pointed to where I reclined behind my desk. "I haven't been able to get her butt out of that chair. Maybe you can talk some sense into her."

Ceff quirked an eyebrow at me and a grin touched his lips. Crap. I'd been caught enjoying the view.

I fumbled with my chair, trying to push myself to my feet. I got as far as planting my boots on the floor before a head-rush made me stop. I tried to blink away the wave of dizziness, but the entire room tilted and spun. I swallowed hard as bile rose in my throat.

Standing had been a mistake.

I rested my elbows on the arms of the chair and let my head drop into my hands. I'd have stuck my head between my legs to keep the room from spinning, but bending any farther forward wasn't an option. The wound in my side was already screaming in protest.

Ceff rushed over to where I sat slumped in my chair. I sucked air through clenched teeth and tried to ignore the coffee churning in my stomach. I may not be able to stand, but I'd sure as hell try not to throw up.

"Here," Ceff said.

His voice was rough like he'd been crying recently, but when I lifted my head his eyes were full of concern, not grief. He'd pulled the sleeve of his shirt over his hand and lifted a glass from my desk. I watched the glass fill with water and the water cooler burped air from across the room, making Jinx jump. Ceff was using his kelpie magic to draw the water to him. Jinx shook her head and went back to straightening papers on her desk.

I smiled and accepted the glass of water.

"Thanks," I said.

I sipped the water, hiding behind the glass. What do you say to the man you care about, when you've just killed his ex-wife?

"Looks like I missed the party," he said. "Sorry I'm late."

"Your loss," I said flashing Ceff a wry smile. "There was music and dancing on tables."

I waggled my eyebrows and Ceff barked a laugh not unlike a seal. I'd managed to bring a smile to his face. I smiled in return, wondering what to say next. I shifted in my seat, trying to find a comfortable position.

"Don't let her fool you," Jinx said from across the room. She paused in tidying up her desk long enough to point a fountain pen my way. *Pesky eavesdropper.* "She hasn't moved since she fell into that chair this morning."

"We shall have to remedy that situation," Ceff said.

He leaned in close, eyes flashing green. My heart raced and Ceff quirked his lips.

"T-t-there's no way I'm making it up those stairs," I said, breathless. "I can barely walk."

"No need," he said.

Ceff scooped me into his arms so fast I didn't have time to draw a weapon. It was funny that stabbing him was my first reaction to being carried. I froze, holding my breath, every muscle locked in place.

"Hey, you two, get a room," Jinx said.

"That is precisely my plan," Ceff said. He leaned his lips close to my ear and whispered. "Don't worry, I won't touch your skin and risk a vision."

His breath grazed my ear and warmth spread through my body. At a loss for words, I blinked in reply. Ceff chuckled and carried me across the room.

The last thing I saw as we left the office was Jinx flashing me two thumbs up.

CHAPTER 27

Ceff helped me get settled onto my bed. It took nearly every pillow and cushion in the apartment to prop me up into a comfortable position, but I had to admit it was better than my office chair. I pushed myself up a bit further onto the pillows with my one good hand and winced. My head pounded with the effort and I sucked air through my teeth as gauze, now stiff with dried blood, peeled away from the wound at my side.

I'd need to change the bandage soon, but first I had to tackle the sensitive topic of killing my boyfriend's ex. I fidgeted with the blankets and sighed. My life was seriously messed up.

Ceff's eyes took in my beat-up jeans, thin tank top, and the bump of gauze at my side. I'd stripped off my leather jacket, boots, and knives at the bedroom door. Without a word, Ceff turned and left the room. I could hear him rummaging in the kitchen and opening and closing cabinets. He returned a few minutes later with a shot of whiskey.

"Here, drink this," he said.

I don't usually drink hard liquor, but I made an exception. I knocked back the shot glass and set it on the bureau. The whiskey burned all the way down, but I suddenly wished he'd brought in the entire bottle. I needed the liquid courage.

"I'm so sorry about Melusine," I said.

I stared at my gloved hands in my lap, unable to meet Ceff's eyes. He froze on his way to perch on the bed beside me. He changed direction and sat on the floor, resting his head against the wall. *Way to kill the mood, Ivy.*

"It was not your fault," he said.

Dark circles ringed his eyes and I noticed for the first time that Ceff's normally impeccable clothes were rumpled. My boyfriend had spent the day mourning the death of his ex-wife. No matter what he said, I felt guilty.

"I killed her in cold blood," I said. "Her death was definitely my fault."

"She left you no choice," he said, shaking his head. "If our roles had been reversed, I would have done the same."

I thought about that. If Melusine had been inches away from killing me, Ceff would have fought to protect me. He wouldn't have held back. I nodded, accepting his words for truth.

"So we're okay?" I asked.

"Yes," he said.

"Are you...okay?" I asked.

"I will be," he said. "The hardest thing to live with is the guilt. I was angry with Mel for so long, for what she did to our sons. When I woke up and Jinx told me that Melusine was dead, I was...relieved. A part of me is happy that she's dead, and I feel guilty for that."

Ceff pulled himself up off the floor and rolled onto one knee beside the bed.

"Promise me one thing," he said.

I swallowed hard.

"Anything," I said, nodding once.

"Do not ever keep your feelings hidden from me," he said. "If you tire of my attentions, send me away. Do not hold your emotions inside where they can fester. That is what Melusine did, for hundreds of years."

Yeah, and we all know how that ended. Melusine's jealousy had driven her mad. She'd manipulated Ceff into executing their oldest son for treason and she murdered their youngest son, throwing the tiny infant into a raging fire. When she discovered Ceff had a new girlfriend, Melusine had gone off the deep end again. With the help of my wisp brethren and The Piper, she'd arranged to kidnap and murder over thirty fae children and planned to kill me as well. And if ridding Ceff of his "half-breed distraction" didn't work to win him back, she intended to kill him too.

I reached down and clasped his hand in my gloved one. I may not have a lot of dating experience, make that none, but I did know that I didn't want to build a relationship on secrets and deceit. Ceff was asking for honesty, and giving me a way out if the time came that I no longer wanted him.

"I promise," I said. I raised an eyebrow and smiled. "But I don't plan on getting sick of you any time soon."

With Ceff being water fae and me being land fae, we barely saw each other. Ceff had an ocean kingdom to run and I had cases to solve and a proclivity for trouble. We both had busy lives independent from one another. The suggestion that I'd become sick of him seemed almost comical.

"Immortality is a long time," he said.

I nodded. I knew what I needed to do, what I should have done months ago. I just hoped that my body could take the strain.

I pulled my hand away from Ceff's and peeled off the leather glove. I took a deep breath and lifted my chin to meet his curious gaze. His eyes were a green so dark they were nearly black and without his glamour the green covered his entire eye, obliterating the human white. I could lose myself in those eyes.

"No secrets," I said.

I reached out with my bare hand and brushed my fingers along Ceff's face to cup his cheek. He pulled back, wrinkling his brow.

"Are you certain?" he asked.

"Yes," I said.

Ceff pressed his face into my palm and I gasped. I saw the execution of his heir, the murder of his infant son, and his torture at the hands of the *each uisge*. His pain was palpable, bringing tears to sting my eyes and roll down my cheeks, but the visions lacked the hold they once had on my mind. I was no stranger to Ceff's memories; they were the same terrifying visions I'd received from handling Ceff's bridle. I had experienced these memories before and lived.

I would survive again.

I rode the visions, each coming faster as my mind recognized the memories and pushed the events away. But the last two visions were new. It takes strong emotion to create a vision and these had both been formed in my presence.

Something fluttered in my chest, but I held on. I wasn't sure if I'd like seeing myself through Ceff's eyes, but we had agreed—no secrets.

The first vision was from the night of the winter solstice. It was the first and last time we'd touched. The simple act of holding each other on my lumpy couch had filled Ceff's immortal heart with a love greater than anything he'd ever felt before. That scared me, just a bit. It also made me smile. The fact that that night had made such an impression told me that what I was doing now was right. I owed it to Ceff and myself.

I'd lived too long behind the walls I'd built to protect my heart. Hiding behind those walls had served me well, but I'd learned a lot about my life recently—my childhood, my parents, my abilities—and I was no longer satisfied to play it safe. Letting Ceff in was one step toward becoming the person I wanted to be.

To hell with the risk.

The final vision followed on the heels of our night of romance. Pain and fear slammed into me and I gasped for air. My mind recoiled from the assault, but I held on tight.

Through Ceff's eyes, I saw Melusine threatening the children...and me. Melusine's presence brought the painful memories of his sons' deaths to the surface, but Ceff gripped his trident and sprung forward. He wouldn't remain chained by the past. If Melusine could not be stopped peaceably, he'd do what needed to be done.

Ceff drew Melusine away from me and the circle of children, but as he tired, their fight returned to where I fought The Piper. Ceff looked at me and his heart filled with love and a fierce protective devotion. He gripped his trident and lunged for a killing blow.

Melusine danced away and swung her tail at his feet. Our fight became a blur of blood and weapons, but I'd learned an important truth. Ceff had been ready and willing to kill Melusine to protect me—just as I had been forced to kill the lamia to save him.

A weight lifted from my shoulders and I blinked rapidly as my vision cleared. I was back in my bed and Ceff's arms were around me. My hand still rested on his face as he stretched out along my side, body pressed against me. Ceff watched my face intently and I blushed.

"You're back," he said. I nodded. "And we are still touching."

Blood rushed to my face, cheeks burning. If I blushed any harder, I'd probably pass out. Ceff rubbed a finger in circles just below my ear and I forgot all about embarrassment. The heat from my face had shifted lower, much lower.

Though I was still at risk of passing out.

Ceff smiled and I bit my lip. His face was mere inches away and I had no idea what to do. Being inexperienced sucked.

His fingers trailed down my neck to a bruise at my collarbone. I gasped as Ceff leaned in and pressed his lips against the purple skin.

"Does this hurt?" he asked, lifting his eyes to my own.

Ceff stared at me through tousled hair and I struggled to catch my breath. I shook my head and Ceff returned his lips to my collarbone. His kisses were cool and soothing against my heated skin.

Ceff moved lower, leaving my skin tingling as he followed a trail of cuts and bruises along one shoulder and down my arm. When he reached my injured wrist, he blew a kiss along the bandage and lifted my arm. Ceff's body slid alongside my own moving upward as he raised my arm above my head. He set my wrist gently on a pile of pillows and held it there, fingers gliding down my arm to wrap around my uninjured bicep.

He leaned in and brushed his lips along my jaw. I turned my face toward his, but he grazed my lips with the barest hint of a kiss and smiled.

"Patience," he said.

It was easy for the sexy immortal in my bed to suggest patience—not so easy for me. I pressed my chest against Ceff and gripped his neck with my free hand, pulling him closer. I felt like I would go supernova. My lips parted and I panted as Ceff pulled away. I stared at his swollen lips, so near but unreachable, and my skin began to glow.

Ceff kissed my chin and slid down my chest, leaving a trail of kisses to my waistline. I was surprised the thin tank top between us didn't burst into flame. Ceff slid a finger under the thin cotton, teasing my skin with his touch. He smiled up at me and quirked an eyebrow in question while holding the edge of my shirt in his hand.

I'd promised to be honest with Ceff and tell him what I was feeling, but at the moment I was at a loss for words. I nodded and slid my fingers through his hair to once again grip the back of his neck. I tried to pull him to me, wanting to feel skin on skin.

No more gloves. No more weapons. No more walls—just me and Ceff.

Ceff moved his face to my stomach and I gasped. His lips caressed my skin in widening circles. He was careful not to press against the wound at my side, though right this minute I didn't care about the pain.

I'd waited so long for this moment. Feared it like a bogeyman stalking the shadows. But the fear was gone and all I wanted was to be closer to Ceff. I lifted my hips and moaned.

"Are you sure?" he asked.

Ceff's voice was husky and his eyes were glowing bright green as he studied my face. We'd agreed to be honest about our feelings and right now, I was an open book.

"Yes, I've never been so sure of anything in my life," I said.

I reached for Ceff with glowing fingers, drawing his body to my own. This time he didn't pull away.

*****

Later that night, much later if the slant of light coming through my bedroom window was any indication, I rested my head on Ceff's chest. He stroked my cheek and I closed my eyes. Shockwaves still rolled through me at his touch.

"Tired?" he asked.

"No," I said, surprised.

I had been dead to the world when Ceff carried me up to my room, but now I was bursting with energy. My skin continued to glow, giving off waves of heat. I looked down and shifted the sheet half draped across my body. I wasn't tired, but the wound at my side had started to bleed through the gauze. I was supposed to be resting, not doing mattress gymnastics. When Kaye said to spend the week in bed, I'm pretty sure this wasn't what she meant.

I sighed. I needed to change the dressing if I wanted to avoid infection.

"I'm not tired, but I do need a shower," I said.

Ceff lifted his hand and a string of water from a glass on the nightstand rose in a spiral ribbon to dance between his fingers.

"Would you like company?" he asked.

"Do pixies lick salt from your skin?" I asked.

Ceff lifted me into his arms and nuzzled my neck.

"Mmm, maybe I'm part pixie," he said.

Ceff carried me to the bathroom and kicked the door shut.

CHAPTER 28

Steam rolled out into the loft as I opened the bathroom door. My superheated skin and Ceff's water magic had filled the tiny room with steam so thick I couldn't see. Not that sight was a necessary sense for what we'd been up to.

I stepped out into the apartment and blinked at my roommate leaning against the kitchen counter. It must have been later than I thought if Jinx was out of bed. Ceff and I were still holding hands, not yet ready to break the connection of our touch. I was pretty sure that if we let go, I'd have to suffer through the visions when we touched again.

Jinx looked between us and shook her head. I was wrapped in an old robe that showed too much leg and Ceff wore a towel low on his hips. Jinx had dark circles around her eyes and held a mug of coffee to her lips.

"I want my prudish roommate back," she said. "She was much quieter and didn't hog the shower."

"Sorry," I said.

We walked over to the breakfast nook and each perched on a stool facing Jinx. When she slid two mugs of coffee across the counter, I shifted my bare foot toward Ceff's, twining our legs together at the ankle. There were a lot more ways to remain touching than just holding hands.

I flashed my friend a goofy grin and breathed in the scent of fresh coffee. My grin faltered when Jinx turned her face and I realized the dark circles weren't entirely from lack of sleep. A large, purpling bruise rose along Jinx's cheekbone.

That bruise hadn't been there yesterday, which meant it wasn't from the cemetery battle. Jinx was clumsy and no stranger to bruises, but the bruise on her face looked suspiciously like the imprint of someone's fist. I cracked my knuckles and stared at Jinx.

"Are you alright?" I asked. "What happened to your face?"

"This?" she asked. "It's nothing. You should see the other guy."

"A man did this to you?" Ceff asked.

His voice was low and threatened violence. I could feel the anger vibrate through his body where we touched. I clenched my jaw and reached for knives that weren't there. Ceff and I were in agreement. If someone did this to Jinx, they were going to pay.

Jinx shrugged.

"I went to see Hans last night while you two were trying to bring the building down," she said. "Big mistake."

Oh crap. I'd forgotten to tell Jinx about Hans' temper tantrum the night the clurichaun got her drunk. So much had happened since then that the call had totally slipped my mind, but that was no excuse.

"I am so sorry," I said. "I mentioned you'd been drinking with a clurichaun. I didn't know he was anti-fae."

"It's alright," she said. "I didn't know either. I mean, I knew he was a Hunter. But I didn't realize he was such a racist douche. When I said I'd just helped to save thirty-three fae kids, he smacked me in the face."

"I'll kill him," I said.

I broke contact with Ceff, launched myself from the barstool, and ran toward my room. This was no time for cuddling. I needed my knives. I looked down at the robe and bare legs and added clothes to the list. Ceff, moving fae fast, was pulling on jeans and grabbing his trident.

Hans was going to pay.

"No, wait," Jinx said.

She stood in the doorway and shook her head.

"I took care of it," she said. "Plus, if you two, a pure-blooded fae and a half-blood, go attacking Hans, he'll have the entire Hunter's Guild on your ass. He's not worth it."

I paused while strapping a throwing knife to my forearm.

"How did you take care of it?" I asked. "Did you shoot him with your crossbow?"

After what Hans had done to my friend's face, I wouldn't settle for anything less than painful impalement.

"Nope, stabbed him with a hair stick," she said. Jinx grinned. "I didn't have the crossbow with me, didn't think I'd need it on a date with a Hunter. I'm rethinking that for the future."

With Jinx's taste in men, that was probably a good idea. Maybe we could find a crossbow dressed up with sequins. Jinx was all about the accessories.

"I hope you also broke up with the guy," I said.

"Hell yeah," she said. "I like bad boys, not batterers."

Jinx had stabbed Hans with a hair stick. It may not have been one of my knives, but Jinx had shown the guy she wasn't a pushover. I grinned showing teeth.

"If he comes near you again, call me," I said.

"And me," Ceff said.

"Like I said, Hans would only be getting his way if my two faerie friends attacked him," she said. "I'm not getting either of you in trouble with the Hunter's Guild."

"Then call Jenna," I said. "In fact, don't wait. Call her now and tell her how Hans attacked an unarmed human."

Jinx smiled and grabbed her phone.

"Technically, I wasn't unarmed," she said. "Those hair sticks did a number on his neck. Totally ruined one of his tats."

"If you weren't carrying a blade or bow, you were unarmed," I said. "Hair accessories don't count. Call Jenna. Maybe you can keep the guy from beating another girl. The Hunter's Guild has rules and I'm pretty sure Hans just broke a few of them."

Jinx pulled up Jenna's number and sauntered into her room.

"Do you think she'll be alright?" Ceff asked.

"Yes, nothing a little revenge won't cure," I said. "Jenna will set things straight. And if that guy ever comes sniffing around here, he'll come face to face with my blades."

"You're sexy when you're angry," he said.

Ceff stood beside the door to my room raking my body with his gaze from head to toe. I blushed, realizing I was wearing nothing but a robe and the knives strapped to my wrists. I hadn't gotten around to putting clothes on yet.

My breath quickened and I licked my lips. I stepped toward Ceff, wondering how bad the visions would be this time around. I looked up into Ceff's face and his eyes flashed green. For the first time in my life, I didn't care about the potential severity of a vision.

I kicked the door shut and let the robe drop to the floor.

CHAPTER 29

"Are you sure you don't need me to come along?" I asked.

Ceff rubbed a hand over his face and sighed. He was going to visit the cemetery where Melusine had died, and now was buried. He'd been standing in the doorway to our loft, eyes distant, and I wondered if I should have dressed to go with him.

"No, this is something I have to do on my own," he said. "I must honor the dead in the way of my people. But do not worry, I'll be back by nightfall."

"I'll hold you to that," I said.

"Until tonight," he said.

Eyes that had looked sad a moment before, now held the promise of an evening of pleasure.

"Until tonight," I said.

I shivered, a breeze playing across my legs as the door closed behind him. I cinched my robe and looked around the apartment. Ceff and I hadn't left the loft in days and the place was starting to look like a boggle pit. I was behind on every one of my chores, but I couldn't bring myself to care.

I dropped onto the couch, suddenly feeling the fatigue of the past week. I was supposed to be on a week of bed rest, but so far I'd seen lots of bed and not much rest. Having Ceff gone for a few hours would do me good. I needed my beauty sleep.

Unfortunately, my over-caffeinated roommate was bored. She was suddenly single and, since we'd closed the office while I recovered from a lamia bite, had free time. Jinx skipped out of the kitchen and perched on the arm of the loveseat across from me.

"So, you ready to go out and celebrate?" Jinx asked.

"Celebrate what?" I asked.

"What are we celebrating?" she asked. "Oh, I don't know. How about the successful rescue of thirty-three faerie kids? We made bank on that case by the way, which is another reason to celebrate. And, dun dun dun! There's the whole you knockin' boots with his royal hotness. You have to fill me in on all the juicy details. Like how you got past your touch phobia in such a big way. I was starting to think you'd die a virgin."

Jinx really needed to switch to decaf.

"Let's just say I had motivation," I said. I smiled and rolled my eyes. "And that is the last we speak of it. I don't kiss and tell."

"Suuure you don't," Jinx said winking. "We'll see about that after a few drinks, and dancing."

"No way," I said. I shook my head. "I'm not going out clubbing. In case you hadn't noticed, I'm injured. I'm supposed to be in bed resting."

"Right, you were getting so much rest in your bed," she said. "Seriously, we need to go out and celebrate. I want to hear all about your hot kelpie stud. Like, was he a total stallion in bed? Does he have all his man parts? Inquiring minds want to know."

Jinx waggled her eyebrows and I blushed.

"We are not having this conversation," I said, fighting a laugh.

Man parts? Jinx really did have a way with words. A grin tugged at my lips, but I forced them down.

I crossed my arms over my chest, careful of my injured wrist. My wounds were healing fast, a benefit of Kaye's magic and my fae blood, but the puncture sites on my wrist and side still ached. I really should be resting.

"Okay, fine," she said. "I'll stop asking about the details of your steamy, hot, fae sexcapades if you agree to come out and celebrate."

I groaned and tossed my hands in the air.

"Okay, I'll go celebrate, but not tonight," I said. "I have plans with Ceff later, and tomorrow I have some unfinished business I need to take care of."

"I'm sure you two have plans," she said. Jinx waggled her eyebrows. "I can wait until after the honeymoon phase, if it doesn't take too long. How about this weekend?"

"It's a date," I said. "Ceff has to return to the sea soon. Just a few more days and you'll have your roommate back."

"Good, I was starting to think I'd created a monster," she said. "When I suggested you hook up with Ceff, I had no idea that meant an all-night light show and the need to reinforce the freaking floor. I'm seriously considering calling a contractor. We don't want you two falling in on our clients."

Jinx tapped her foot and gave the floor a significant look. We lived in the loft directly above Private Eye. Maybe we should call a contractor. My fae abilities were awakening rapidly and a newly realized perk was an increase in speed and strength—speed and strength that may someday rival Ceff's. If Ceff continued spending time in our loft, we could do some serious damage. My bed crashing through into the office below could be bad for business, not to mention embarrassing.

"Go ahead and get a quote to reinforce the floor to my bedroom...and the bathroom," I said. I felt my ears going red and fidgeted with my gloves. "You said we brought in good money on our last case. Dip into my share for the repair work."

"Will do," she said. "Anything else?"

"Yes, um, sorry about the light show," I said. "I still haven't figured out how to control my wisp abilities, but I'm working on it."

"Don't worry," she said. "If you start glowing when we go out clubbing, I'll just tell everyone that you're rockin' the latest glow-in-the-dark body paint."

Apparently, even the threat of me being sentenced to death for public glowing wouldn't stop my friend from dragging me out to the clubs this weekend. I sighed and pulled myself to my feet. I waved sleepily to Jinx, loped across the floor to my bedroom, and crawled into bed.

The pillow smelled like Ceff and I smiled, warmth spreading through my body. I relaxed, sinking into the blankets. If I closed my eyes, I could pretend he was still here with me. Light shone through my eyelids and I sighed. I'd forgotten to turn off the bedside lamp.

I opened my eyes and reached for the lamp, but the light wasn't on. The illumination was coming from me. *Mab's bones*, I had to get this under control. I was glowing more and more often now.

I needed to find my father. I planned to check in with Sir Torn and my new cat sidhe allies tomorrow, but I assumed Torn would have contacted me if he'd learned anything new. I'd hoped his network of spies would turn up something, but, according to Torn, my father's trail went cold in Fukushima.

The wisps from the cemetery had spread the word that their princess was in town. Now I received daily visits from the beautiful, glowing orbs, but I hadn't found a way to question them about my father. I wished I could communicate with my wisp brethren, but so far their language eluded me.

That left one person who might be able to help me locate my father.

CHAPTER 30

I woke the next morning eager to make some inquiries into my father's whereabouts. Torn may be looking into the matter, but that didn't mean I couldn't start my own investigation.

I slid out from under the sheets, careful not to disturb Ceff who slept on the bed beside me. His arm was thrown up over his head and his face was relaxed. The poor guy was exhausted; let him sleep.

Ceff had returned at nightfall as promised. His eyes had been red-rimmed and puffy, but when I asked how he was feeling, he smiled. He had said his goodbyes to Melusine and was ready to begin anew, with me.

I covered Ceff with a blanket and turned away from the bed. I grabbed my gear and an armful of clothes and tiptoed into the bathroom. I showered and dressed quickly, eager to get today's errands out of the way.

I pulled on jeans and a long-sleeved thermal top with sewn in thumb holes that kept my sleeves safely tucked inside my gloves. After Melusine's pet snake managed to slither against my naked wrist, I'd decided to order more shirts with the added thumb hole as insurance against unwanted visions. I added a black hoodie, leather jacket, and gloves. I immediately started to sweat, but figured the added protection outweighed the discomfort.

Next, I pulled on my boots, strapped on both throwing knives, and added a dagger in my boot. I tied my hair back out of my face and stuck a polished, wooden stake into the messy bun.

I looked fierce. I wasn't exactly dressed for a mother-daughter reunion, but the weapons and armor set me at ease. At the moment, staying calm was more important than impressing my mother. If I started glowing on the way to her house, I'd risk execution.

Tugging the hood up over my head, I slipped out of the apartment. I didn't have a lot of options for getting out to the burbs. I don't drive and taxis give me the willies, so it was either take the bus or walk. With a fresh lamia bite in my side, I chose the bus.

I caught the Route 7 metro bus at a stop on Congress Street. At this time of the morning, the outgoing bus was nearly empty. Commuters were pouring into the city on their way to work. No one except me and the bus driver were headed out to the suburbs.

I hunched down in the front seat and watched the city slip away. Brick, stone, and concrete were replaced with trees and picket fences. On the outskirts of town, I got off the bus and walked the mile to the house I'd grown up in.

I stopped on the street outside the familiar gray and white house with gingerbread trim. I shoved my hands into my jacket pockets and scanned the property for hints of the loving place I'd seen in my unlocked memories.

This was the place where it all began. My parents, my real mother and father, had been happy here once upon a time. But my father had made a deal with the devil, and lost. Burdened with carrying a cursed lantern, my father had bespelled both me and my mother in an effort to keep us safe.

I just hoped she still remembered him.

The spell cast on my mind had chained my memories, keeping my father's existence a secret. But that spell had begun to fall apart, exposing my past. Kaye speculated that this was due to the fact that memory spells are more effective on child minds. As I grew into adulthood, the spell began to unravel and the memories surfaced.

Kaye suspected that any memory spell cast on my mother would only have been temporary. My witch friend claimed that a geis had likely been placed on my mother forbidding her from ever speaking of my father. If that was true, I'd have to get creative if I wanted answers to my questions.

I set my jaw and walked steadily toward the house. My boots crunched as I strode up the gravel drive. My stepfather's car was gone, but my mother's car was parked beside his tool shed. The shed, and the garbage cans lined up against it, raised gooseflesh on my arms. This was the place I'd had my first vision. Taking the lid off the Pandora's Box of my psychic gift hadn't been pretty. That moment when my psychic gift reared its ugly head was akin to an earthquake; it shook my world apart. Even now, long after the dust has settled, I'm rocked by the aftershocks of that day.

I swallowed hard and gave the shed a wide berth. I didn't need to start glowing in front of the neighbors. I climbed up the front steps of the house and onto the wooden porch. I took a calming breath and pressed the doorbell with a gloved finger. I still had a key to the front door, but letting myself in didn't feel right. This hadn't been my home in a long time.

Footsteps sounded inside and my mother opened the door, blinking in the morning sun.

"Ivy?" she asked.

"Hi, mom," I said. "Um, can I come in?"

"Of course, come inside," she said. "I was just making a second pot of coffee."

My mother drank thick, black coffee like the stuff was ambrosia. In fact, it was the one thing we'd had in common all these years. I followed her down the hallway to the kitchen at the back of the house.

My mother looked thinner than I remembered and I made a mental note to invite her over for dinner. I didn't usually have guests over, had never invited anyone up to the loft until Ceff, but I'd make an exception for my mother. Seeing the sharp jut of her collarbone and the bony points of her shoulders through her cardigan made my throat tighten.

I hadn't been fair to my mother. She'd been unable to tell me the truth about my father and so I'd formed my own opinions. I'd judged this woman based on years of seeing her sad eyes and frowning lips without ever asking why she was so miserable. I'd assumed it was because of me. I resented my mother because I thought she hated the person I'd become when I came into my gift. I figured that having a freak for a daughter had made her bitter.

I hadn't seen the woman mourning the loss of her first love. By misjudging my mother, I'd pushed her away and forced the loss of the one connection she had left to my father. I'd been my usual hot-headed, stubborn self. I hoped it wasn't too late to fix things between us. By my own ignorance, my mother had lost not only a lover, but a daughter too.

She pulled two mugs down from the cupboard and pulled the coffee pot from the burner. I swallowed hard and cleared my throat.

"Is Stan at work?" I asked.

"Yes," she said, frowning. "Why do you ask?"

"I have something important to talk to you about...something about my real father," I said.

My mother's teeth knocked together and her mouth snapped shut. She fumbled with the coffee pot, splashing coffee onto the counter. With wide eyes, she mopped up the spill. She turned to face me, breathing hard and twisting the dish towel in her hands.

"It's okay, mom," I said. "I know who he is, what he is...what I am. And I know he put a spell on both of us. Do you know what I'm talking about?"

Yes. She nodded. Her face had gone pale and she was shaking so bad I thought she might pass out. I pulled out a chair and gestured toward it with one gloved hand.

"Come and sit down," I said. "I've got the coffees."

I topped up the mugs and carried them to the old kitchen table. My mother took the mug and held it in white-knuckled fingers.

"My friend Kaye, who's a witch, thinks dad cast a geis on you preventing you from speaking of him," I said. "Is that true?"

Yes. My mother nodded. Okay, if I could keep my questions to those with yes or no answers, I might learn something about my father. I grinned.

"You're doing great, mom," I said. "I'm going to ask you some questions. Try to shake your head yes or no. Is Will-o'-the-Wisp, king of the wisps, my real father?"

Yes.

"Did he leave us to keep us safe?" I asked.

Yes. Tears rolled down my mother's cheeks.

"Do you know where he went?" I asked.

No. She shook her head and grunted in frustration.

"Okay, scratch that," I said. "Did dad go to find a way to break the curse?"

Yes.

"Does he have any friends he might turn to for help?" I asked.

My mother frowned and threw her hands up in the air. Torn had said that my dad didn't have any friends in the fae community who were powerful enough to help him, but I wondered if Torn knew the full story. He'd liked my father, but I didn't get the impression that they were all that close. If I could just find a way to track down my father's allies, I might be able to follow his trail.

I pulled a notepad and pen out of my jacket pocket and slid it across the table to my mom. Maybe the geis wouldn't prevent her from writing down the answers to my questions. It was worth a shot.

"Write down any names you remember dad mentioning," I said.

My mother grabbed the pen and started writing. *Inari.*

A horrible snapping sound echoed across the kitchen. I looked to see what had happened and swallowed hard when I saw my mother's misshapen hand cramped around the pen. She cried out and I pulled the pen and paper away from her grasp. My mother gingerly held her right hand and bit her lip against the pain. One of her fingers was grossly disfigured. The geis had broken the bone.

A chill ran up my spine. The realization hit hard that I was dealing with something I didn't fully understand. What if the next time my mother went to nod or shake her head in answer to my questions, the spell decided to break her neck? How far would the geis go to keep my mother quiet? That was something I wasn't willing to find out.

"Mom, I'm so sorry," I said. "I had no idea the spell would do that. I swear, from now on, no more questions. Let me grab some ice and then we'll get you to a doctor."

I rushed to the fridge and pulled a tray of ice cubes from the freezer compartment. I twisted the tray and upended the cubes onto a clean dishtowel. I carried the makeshift icepack back to the table and set it beside my mother's hand.

"Thank you," she said.

"Want me to call Stan for a ride to the hospital?" I asked.

I don't drive, but I'd stay with my mom until my stepfather or a neighbor could come and pick her up.

"No, I'll be fine," she said. "Just give me a minute. I can drive myself."

"I'm sorry about the questions," I said.

"Don't be," she said. "I'm the one who should be sorry. There's so much I've wanted to tell you."

"But you couldn't," I said.

She shook her head and sighed.

"No, but now that you know the truth, there is something I'd like you to have," she said.

My mother stood, keeping the ice wrapped around her hand, and went to her bedroom. She returned with a small jewelry box.

"It's not much, but it's all I have left of your fa...," she said. *Of your father.* She coughed and cleared her throat. "Keep it safe and when you find him, tell him I love him still."

She pulled a plastic bag from a kitchen drawer and slid the box inside. My mother knew about my aversion to carrying old things and was trying to make this easier on me. She handed me the box and tears blurred my vision. I smiled and nodded.

I had come here in hopes of finding a clue to my father's whereabouts and I wasn't leaving empty handed. My mother had suffered trying to give me the information, but I now had a name—Inari. I also had the box and whatever it contained.

"I'll bring dad back to us," I said. "I promise."

My mother smiled through her tears and went to fetch her coat and purse. When she returned, she offered to drive me into the city. Since the best hospital in the area, Harborsmouth General, was in the city, I agreed. We rode in silence, lost in our own thoughts.

I held the jewelry box in my lap, eager to return to the city and continue the search for my father. I had planned on paying Kaye a visit to thank her for healing me after the cemetery battle. Now I had another reason to see my friendly neighborhood witch. If anyone had information on this Inari, it would be Kaye. I looked out the window and grinned.

For the first time since learning of my father's existence, I had a solid lead.

CHAPTER 31

I stayed with my mother at the hospital while the doctor set her finger. X-rays indicated the finger was broken, as I'd guessed. After setting the bone, the emergency room doc wrote out a script for pain meds and told my mother to ice the finger for twenty-minute intervals to control the swelling. I nodded and smiled standing at my mother's side, but I was covered in cold sweat.

Hospitals are one of my least favorite places. Aside from the obvious harried staff, frightened patients, and unpleasant smell of industrial cleaners, the place is filled with objects tainted with painful visions. I kept my hands in my pockets, hoodie and jacket collar up, and shoulders hunched. When the doctor said my mother was set to go home, I nearly ran to the exit.

I passed a banshee on my way out the door. The faerie wailed and moaned and pulled out clumps of her own hair as she hovered around a family who were huddled in the waiting area. In my peripheral vision, she looked liked a particularly distraught woman in her eighties with gray hair, pearls, and a business-casual, white dress stretched over a sagging chest and a pot belly. When I looked at the banshee directly, however, she had the telltale appearance of a death omen.

The banshee was dressed in a long, flowing dress stained with the blood of the soon to be deceased. The cute elderly woman was replaced by a fierce faerie hag with long, disheveled, gray hair and red eyes. A banshee is often loyal to one bloodline, foretelling the death of the eldest son with her keening cries. Judging by the banshee's behavior, this family was about to get some whopping bad news.

Since a banshee does not bring about death, only foretells it, there was nothing I could do for the family. I skirted past the waiting area and sprinted for the exit. Glass doors swished open and I sucked in a breath of city air laced with greasy food odors and exhaust fumes. After the antiseptic smell of the hospital, it smelled like heaven.

My stomach growled, reminding me that I'd skipped breakfast in my haste to question my mother. I turned down Mercy Ave and headed toward Congress Street, the jewelry box in my pocket thumping against my side with each step. I needed to get off the street to somewhere safe and private where I could examine the contents of the box. I could also use some food and caffeine.

I knew just the place. I was on the west side of town, not far from Fountain Square. At Congress Street, I took a shortcut through a parking garage over to Temple Ave. I held my breath against the mingling scents of sweat and urine and nodded to the ogre parking attendant. Whether it was aware of it or not, the city of Harborsmouth was an equal opportunity employer.

Once on Temple, I scooted into the Old Port quarter and followed the brick and cobbled streets to The Emporium. I owed Kaye my thanks for patching me up and nursing me back to health after the cemetery battle. I couldn't help it if that thanks was going to be followed by more questions about my father. I just hoped that Hob could spare a cup of tea and some toast.

Humphrey guarded the door from his perch on an old, stone drain spout. I waved to the gargoyle and ducked inside. It was business hours and Madam Kaye's Magic Emporium was open. No special invitation, or security escort, needed.

"Hey, Ivy," Arachne said.

The cute apprentice witch stood behind the counter removing plastic wrapping from lengths of knotted rope. The blond girl's hair was streaked with red instead of the purple she'd been fond of the past few months and she wore a bright, puffed-sleeved, button-down shirt to match.

"Hi, Arachne," I said. "Slow morning?"

"You have no idea," she said. Arachne slipped a decorative noose around her neck and tilted her head to the side, tongue hanging out of her mouth. The image was grisly, and disturbing. I hoped I never saw the teen witch like that again. The image hit too close to drawings in Kaye's books of the Burning Times. "It's totally dead in here today. Get it? Dead."

I forced a smile and tried to sound lighthearted, but I'm pretty sure I failed. Death was no laughing matter, especially where my mortal friends were concerned. I sighed. Maybe I was becoming too serious. I was having a harder time shrugging off death now that I'd been at its door more than once.

"Is Kaye around?" I asked.

"In the back," Arachne said.

Arachne let the rope drop, wearing the noose like a macabre necklace. I pulled my gaze from her neck and turned my attention to the merchandise underfoot. I made my way through the constantly shifting maze of magic ephemera to the back of the shop.

At the door to Kaye's spell kitchen, I took a calming breath and raised my hand to knock, but a noise from within made me hesitate. I listened at the door, hearing what sounded like a muffled incantation. Kaye could get cranky if I interrupted one of her spells, not to mention the unknown effect my barging in would have on a powerful casting. I decided to wait for Kaye in her office. I don't like waiting around, but it's better than being turned into a toad any day.

I loped further down the hall and let myself into the office. The room was small and crowded with Kaye's occult library, but it would provide a place to wait the time and examine my mother's jewelry box in private.

I climbed over scattered papers and random spell components, careful not to touch anything. I judiciously placed my booted feet in the rare bare spots scattered throughout the room, the trip to the one chair in the office becoming a challenging game of Twister. Thank Mab this game didn't demand Jell-O shots or I'd be ass deep in centuries of visions. And not just any visions, but the visions of madmen.

I am always careful when handling any of the books in Kaye's arcane library. This comes from a healthy dose of paranoia and a desire to keep my sanity, something the original owners of these scrolls and spell tomes often failed at. Magic, especially powerful magic, has a price. Immortals aren't the only ones who become unhinged over time. Witches who use too much magic, or who dabble in the dark arts, tend to go stark raving mad.

I eyed the towering stacks of books and shuddered. The information in these documents was invaluable to my investigations, but Kaye's filing system sucked. I wished she'd consider something safer, like glass-fronted bookcases bolted to the walls. The books were piled one on top of the other, some cover to cover and others end to end, making the act of retrieving a book a game of potentially deadly Jenga. Thankfully, I wasn't here for research. I just needed a place to sit and study the box in my pocket.

I squeezed behind Kaye's desk, a stack of books towering precariously at my back. I cautiously held the front of my jacket close to my body as I passed around the tight corner. Too bad I hadn't thought to remove the stakes at my belt.

The wood scraped and caught on something and the entire stack of books wobbled. I froze, holding my breath. I turned my head to see where I was stuck. The end of one of my stakes had become wedged into the curve of a leather binding. I bent my knees and slowly shifted a half-step, dislodging the wood. I let out a shaky breath and rested my gloved hands on the desk in front of me. That had been close, too close.

I leaned forward and slid the stakes from my belt. I sucked in my stomach to make myself as small as possible and pressed my body against the desk. This time I made it past the tower of books unscathed.

I dropped down onto the desk chair and wiped the back of my glove across my forehead. I had no idea how my witch friend navigated the office with her swirl of layered skirts and shawls. Knowing Kaye, she probably used magic.

I pulled the jewelry box from my pocket and upended the bag my mother had sealed it in. The box was made of silver and the lid was engraved with flowers and vines which twined around the corners, framing a picture set into the center. From beneath the glass panel, a happy couple smiled up at me. It was a picture of my mother and father.

My parents had been so young. Or rather, they appeared youthful. My father, an immortal fae and king of the wisps, had likely been hundreds of years old at the time the picture was taken. But to all appearances he looked to be a human in his very early twenties.

Blue eyes stared out of a heavily freckled face. Will-o'-the-Wisp was striking with pale skin, long, red hair that fell past his shoulders, and full lips most women would kill for.

In the photo, my father had his arm around my mother and his head tilted back. My mother had her face resting on his chest. Flowers were braided into her hair, which was blond at the time of the photo not gray, and she looked like she was dressed for a renaissance fair or perhaps one of the Shakespeare festivals the city holds each year down in the park.

I traced their smiles with a gloved finger. I had so few memories of my real family. My father had sealed away the memories I had of that time with his spell. I knew that he was trying to protect us, but I longed for the years that I'd lost.

I slid my gloved fingers to the sides of the box, finding a flower with larger petals than the others. I pressed the center of the flower and the box unlocked with an audible click. I don't know how I knew the secret to unlocking the box. It could have been magic keyed to my proximity to the box, or the remnants of a faded memory.

I bit my lip and lifted the lid. The box was lined with purple velvet and contained only one item, a beautiful silver key.

"Looks like your father left you the keys to the kingdom," Kaye said.

I flinched and bit my tongue. I hadn't seen or heard Kaye enter the room, but now she stood behind me hovering over my shoulder. Either I'd been too engrossed in my examination of the box and its contents or Kaye had used magic to gain entry without my notice. I flicked my eyes to her multi-layered skirts trimmed in tiny bells and the metal bangles at her wrists. It was unlikely that my friend had entered the room mundanely without making a sound. My bet was on a clandestine spell.

"What?" I asked.

"The key you have there," Kaye said gesturing to the box. "It was left to you by your father, yes?"

"Um, yeah," I said. I swallowed hard and closed the lid to the box. Kaye was eyeing the box like she was a supermodel and the key was a sandwich. "What do you mean by keys to the kingdom?"

"I mean that both literally and figuratively," she said. "If I am not mistaken, that key leads to the wisp king's demesne in the Otherworld."

"You mean this key grants me entry into FAERIE?" I asked.

I boggled at my friend's suggestion. The pathways to Faerie had been sealed, hadn't they?

"Yes, dear," she said. "Apparently, your father was unsure of his eventual return and entrusted the key into safekeeping until you matured into your powers. With your father gone, you now rule the wisps and that key gives you access to his power base. You are now the proud owner of the wisp court."

My father had left the key in my mother's safekeeping in case he could not return. That told me two things; my father had not yet broken the demon curse and he now needed me to rule in his stead.

"Wait," I said, shaking my head. "I thought the roads to Faerie were sealed."

When I'd first come to Kaye with questions about my fae heritage, I'd wondered if a trip to Faerie might be necessary to get the answers that I needed. She'd frowned and declared Faerie closed to visitors, even those with fae blood like me. I'd been relieved that a trip to Faerie, a realm rumored to be filled with all manner of monsters, was impossible.

Now I had a way down the rabbit hole, whether I wanted to go or not.

"Yes, that's partially true," Kaye said. "When Mab, Oberon, and Titania abandoned their courts, they barred the pathways into Faerie. The king and queens of Faerie sealed the land against the invasion of outsiders then disappeared. Some say that they have gone on a quest for true power, while others claim they continue to rule from afar preferring a less direct role in events. But whether out searching or in hiding, Mab, Oberon, and Titania did not leave their borders undefended in their absence. They locked Faerie away from the other planes, but left gateways that could only be opened with a special key. These keys were given to select kings and queens who ruled beneath them."

"And I have one of these keys," I said.

"Indeed," she said.

I had possession of a key to Faerie. No wonder Kaye's eyes gleamed when she looked at it. I gripped the box and started to sweat beneath Kaye's piercing gaze, but I couldn't leave yet. I still needed information. Now that I knew what the key was for, a question gnawed at my brain like a starved zombie.

If the key led to Faerie, then where was the door?

"How do I use the key to enter Faerie?" I asked. "Do you know where the entrance is?"

"That, my dear, is a closely guarded secret," she said. "I suggest you try your contacts in the fae community if you wish to discover the gate's location in the mortal world."

I sighed and sagged in the chair, letting my head hang down. Of course, it wouldn't be that easy. Nothing was ever simple when it came to the fae.

"Okay thanks, I'll ask around," I said.

I wrapped the box in the plastic bag and tucked it into a zippered jacket pocket. I took a deep breath and pushed myself to my feet. It was time to probe my fae allies for information, and I knew right where to start. I strode toward the exit, books moving out of my path. Navigating the office was much easier with Kaye's magic at hand. I turned to wave goodbye and the witch raised a tattooed hand.

"A word of advice?" she asked. "Use caution when making your inquiries. Divulging the location of the gates to the wrong person, such as a human friend and business partner, could be construed as treason, and the very existence of the keys is a closely guarded secret. If you manage to locate someone willing to talk, keep in mind that the key in your possession is extremely valuable. There are some, mortals and fae, unscrupulous enough to kill for access to Faerie."

Great, just my luck. I'd have to keep the key secret from Jinx, or risk being labeled a traitor. That was just what I needed, another reason for the faerie courts to order my execution.

As if lying to my best friend wasn't bad enough, I might get myself into hot water trying to learn the location of the door to Faerie. If I mentioned that I had my own key to the wrong person, I was as good as dead. There was nothing like carrying around an artifact that could fetch big bucks on the black market to encourage a knife in the back. I might as well paint my enemies a target.

My footsteps as I stomped out of the office were matched by the chiming of a clock. A chill ran up my spine; the sound reminded me of church bells tolling the dead.

CHAPTER 32

I was halfway up Joysen Hill when I realized I'd forgotten to ask Kaye about the name Inari. I scrubbed a gloved hand over my face and sighed. It looked like I had another question for Torn. I hoped the cat sidhe was holding court in the alley beside Club Nexus. I wasn't in the mood for a scavenger hunt.

I spied a window display showing off a huge jar of honey at a local tea shop and pulled up short. I hadn't yet thanked Marvin for saving my hide back at the cemetery and I owed the kid a bridgewarming gift.

I ducked inside the shop and haggled over the honey. The shop clerk had been surprised when I pointed to the massive jar on display, but when I flashed a handful of money I'd made on the recent missing persons case, she was happy to oblige. She even gift wrapped it for me.

The honey was heavy, but I found a renewed bounce in my step as I headed down the side street to Marvin's new digs. This was one errand I didn't dread. In fact, I couldn't wait to see the kid's face when he unwrapped the one-hundred and sixty-ounce container.

I grinned and started my descent down the scree-covered embankment in pursuit of my troll friend. I didn't have far to search. Marvin stood beside his new home, washing clothes downstream from the bridge. I made plenty of noise as I scrambled down that last yard of loose stones. Marvin turned to me and smiled wide.

"Poison Ivy," he said. Marvin hung the wet clothing over a rope he'd tied to the bridge and wiped his hands down the front of his pants. "You feeling better?"

"Yes, good as new," I said. "I'm alive, thanks to you. I don't know when you started following us, but your idea to throw an entire pixie nest at The Piper really saved the day. I owe you one."

After leaving Marvin's that night, I'd felt like someone had been watching us. I'd assumed it was a cat sidhe, or maybe one of the vamps, curious about why I smelled like the inside of a ghoul. Instead, our tail had been a teenaged troll with a killer throwing arm. He'd chucked the pixie grenade that downed The Piper long enough for me to disrupt the Dance Macabre and free the children.

"Aw, was nothing," he said.

The kid blushed and crossed one leg behind the other. I wanted to reach out and give him a hug, but settled for pulling the gift out of the shopping bag.

"Here," I said. "I promised you a proper housewarming gift the next time I stopped by."

Marvin's face lit up and he forgot all about his embarrassment. I watched him tear away wrapping paper with large hands. His smile grew when he saw what was inside.

"Thank you, Ivy," he said.

I beamed back at Marvin, glad he liked the gift. As an orphaned bridge troll, I didn't think the kid got many presents. I'd have to stop by again soon with some of his favorite candy.

"Just don't eat it all in one sitting," I said.

Marvin opened the jar and started scooping honey into his mouth with bare hands. Now that he didn't have to worry about offending Hob's sense of decorum and fanatic need for cleanliness, the kid could eat his honey in unrestrained sticky glee.

I missed seeing Marvin around the Emporium, but I was happy for him. He'd garnered the courage to leave the safe confines of Kaye's shop and found a place to call his own. I swallowed against the growing lump in my throat and flashed Marvin a smile. The kid was growing up.

I said my goodbyes, telling Marvin I had an important visit with the cat sidhe Sir Torn, and promised to return soon. I would have liked to have spent the day hanging out with the kid, but I had to chat with my new allies.

As I climbed up the embankment, a scraggly cat sat watching from the street.

"Hear that?" I asked. "You can tell Sir Torn I'm on my way."

Instead of scampering off to inform Sir Torn of my arrival, the cat blinked at me. He dropped down, spreading his hind legs in an L position with one leg up in the air, and started licking his balls.

"Ew, really?" I asked. "You think this is a good time for that? This is exactly why I will never have a cat. My unicorn would never do something so vile."

The cat stopped and glared at me, then returned to its grooming. I looked directly at the creature with my second sight to see if it was a cat sidhe in disguise, but the cat was mundane. I shook my head and ambled on toward Club Nexus. I had a date with the Lord of Cats.

As I walked, I considered the upcoming meeting. I hoped I didn't stumble on Sir Torn *in flagrante*. I didn't think I could keep the smirk off my face if I caught the cat sidhe licking his furry bits.

I chuckled and sauntered up Joysen Hill.

CHAPTER 33

I strode down the empty street, hands loose at my sides. My throwing knives could easily be drawn with a flick of the wrist and I was armed with wooden stakes at my belt, a silver cross beneath my shirt, and a pocketful of iron shavings. The club looked quiet, but the place was a center of supernatural activity. Who knew what badass monsters lurked in the shadows? Better safe than dead.

I gave a curt nod to the ogre bouncer across the street working the club door. The bouncer shifted his weight and rolled his shoulders to show off bulging muscles and the guns strapped beneath his suit jacket. The ogre was ready to rumble if anyone on the street was foolish enough to pick a fight—good to know.

I stayed upwind of the ogre's stench and crossed the street at the corner. I flashed a tentative smile at the cat sidhe kits milling about the sidewalk. The narrow alleyway where I'd previously met with Torn was right where I remembered it.

That probably shouldn't have surprised me, but it did. I half expected the entrance to the cat sidhe's alley to be limited to access through the club only. I let out a slow breath and flexed my hands. It was time to see if the faerie lord was in residence.

I stepped into the alley and halted as a large, furry tank of a cat hissed and blocked my path. I wondered idly if I should have brought some Fancy Feast or cans of tuna. I was now allied with the cat sidhe, but I had no idea what the usual customs for visiting a cat sidhe lord entailed. Another question I should have asked Kaye before leaving the Emporium.

My rescue came in the form of a man dressed in leathers decorated with fur, bones, and feathers. Sir Torn leapt down from a fire escape with a flourish. Shadows swirled around the man as he bowed mockingly, a half smile on his lips.

"And to what do I owe the honor, Princess?" he asked.

"First, I'd like to thank you and your court for coming to our aid in the battle against The Piper and Melusine," I said.

"And the rats," he said.

"Yes, of course, and the rats," I said.

I had a nagging suspicion that the opportunity to slaughter a horde of rats had tipped the scales in my favor. I doubted the cat sidhe would come to my aid if I faced, say, a barguest or a rabid loup garou.

"We are now allies," he said spreading his hands. "You will find that cat sidhe make excellent bedfellows."

Torn quirked his lips and looked like the cat that ate the canary. He leaned close and purred.

"If you'd like to continue satisfying your bedfellows, I suggest you take a step back," I said. "I don't like sharing my personal space. It's a thing."

Torn's eyes widened as he looked down to see one of my blades perilously close to his, as Jinx would say, man parts. He raised his hands and took a step back.

"You can't blame a fellow for trying, Princess," he said. "Nothing ventured, nothing gained and all that. So why are you here, alone, if not for the pleasure of my singular company?"

"My reason for coming is a confidential matter," I said. "Is there somewhere we can speak in private?"

Torn gestured for me to step forward. I held my breath and moved closer to the cat sidhe. Torn reached into a dark crevice between two bricks and pulled a shadow around us like an inky, black cloak. I could see nothing inside the shadow, but I could feel Torn's presence. I bit the inside of my cheek to keep from screaming.

"Everything is hush-hush now, Princess," he said. "You know my cat sidhe can be trusted, so why the clandestine cloak-and-dagger business? I'm guessing this shall be interesting."

In fact, I didn't trust any of the cat sidhe, but that was beside the point. This conversation was between me and Torn. What I had to say could not breach these walls, or shadows, or whatever.

"Our ears only?" I asked.

I winced and hoped the cat sidhe couldn't see me in the dark. Torn only had one tattered ear, the other was no more than a cratered lump of scar tissue. I'd have to refrain from mentioning ears if I wanted to stay on the cat lord's good side.

"Yes, Princess," he said. "It's just you and me."

I felt the cat sidhe's breath on my neck and gripped my knives.

"Touch me Torn and, allies or not, I'll carve your good ear to match," I said.

Oops. So much for not drawing attention to his disfigurements. I had a real knack for pissing people off. Jinx said it was my secret superpower, like I needed any more of those.

"Symmetry may not be such a punishment," he said. "Tyger, tyger, burning bright, in the forests of the night, what immortal hand or eye, could frame thy fearful symmetry?"

I snorted. Faeries and their damned love of poetry, it was like a disease. I was pretty sure that William Blake's tiger hadn't been a cat sidhe, but you never know. Torn's been around long enough. At least he wasn't quoting Shakespeare. Most fae are obsessed with The Bard.

"I don't have time for games, Torn," I said. "I need information."

"Yummy, I like it when you play rough, Princess," he said, purring.

"Did I mention that my blades are tipped with iron?" I said.

"Fine," he said. With a rattle of bones and a heavy sigh, Torn took a step away. "What knowledge do you seek?"

I focused on the direction of his voice and took a breath.

"I need to find a door to Faerie," I said.

"Oh, shit, is that all?" he asked, voice dripping sarcasm. "Why don't you ask for Fionn mac Cumhaill's bag of lost treasure while you're at it?"

"So you can't find out?" I asked.

"I didn't say that, Princess," he said. Torn struck a match and lit a torch he'd pulled from thin air. We were still inside the privacy shadow he'd wrapped around us. The torch flickered making light dance across the cat sidhe's scarred face. "Come with me."

"Where are we going?" I asked.

"To Mag Mell, of course," he said.

Torn grinned and sprinted away. I chased after the flickering torch, swearing under my breath. *Mab's bloody freaking bones.* I was trapped in a shadow, playing cat and mouse games with a cat sidhe.

Too bad I was the mouse.

CHAPTER 34

Sir Torn ripped a hole in the fabric of reality and leapt into the light beyond. I shielded my eyes against the sun and stumbled out onto a grassy plain. My ears popped as the shadow we'd traveled through snapped shut behind me.

I blinked as my eyes adjusted to the clear, bright day. The sun blazed from a deep cerulean sky, not a cloud marring its perfection. A breeze rustled the leaves of an orchard to my left and golden light sparkled on the surface of a placid lake to my right. I sucked in a breath at the fantastical landscape.

A white stag, with antlers streaming moss and flowering vines, drank from the lake. A cardinal perched on the stag's back, the bird a brilliant red to match the fields of flowering poppies that went on for miles in every direction.

I've a feeling we're not in Harborsmouth anymore. Maybe if I clicked my heels, I'd find a way home. On second thought, I didn't think messing with magic was a good idea in this place. With my luck, a tornado would deposit a house on my head.

Torn leaned against a tree and rubbed a shiny, red apple against the shirt beneath his leather vest.

"Want an apple, Princess?" he asked. "The food here is free for the taking. No one wants for food or drink in Mag Mell."

Mag Mell. The name sent shivers up my spine. I was on one of the mythical planes of the Celtic Otherworld. Elysium, Valhalla, these planes all existed somewhere, but the Celtic Otherworlds of Emain Ablach, Hy Brasil, Roca Barraidh, Tír na nÓg, Ynys Afallon, and Mag Mell were the ones most entwined with Faerie.

Was the door to Faerie here on the verdant plains of Mag Mell?

"W-w-what are we doing here?" I asked.

"Ah, I didn't think you were one for philosophy, Princess," Torn said. "I prefer Aristotelianism, but, then again,

I used to dine with the man. His wife Pythias could prepare a mean feast."

I sighed, jaw aching from grinding my teeth.

"I wasn't asking about the meaning of life," I said. I clenched my fists and glared at the cat sidhe. "I mean, why are we here in Mag Mell? Is the door here?"

I had wanted information about the door to Faerie, not a day trip to the Otherworld. I rubbed the place where my throwing knives were sheathed beneath my jacket. I felt woefully unprepared. What horrors lurked within the rustling poppy fields or below the still surface of the lake? Mag Mell appeared to be a land of peace and tranquility, but looks can be deceiving.

"We are here to see Béchuille, a seer," he said. "Mag Mell has long been a source of wisdom to heroes who seek knowledge." Torn spun in a circle and pointed away from the stag, placing the lake at his back. "Come, we go this way."

I dug in my heels and crossed my arms.

"Not until you tell me what I want to know," I said. I fixed Torn with a deadpan look then let the darkness from my nightmares leak out around the edges. I'd seen enough of death and torment to last a lifetime and, when I let it, it showed. "Who is this seer and what do I have to give up in bargain for her aid?"

Torn hesitated.

"Tell me," I said.

I flicked my wrist, snapping the grip of a throwing knife into my palm. The faerie would spill his guts one way or another. I grinned, showing too much teeth.

"Wait, Princess," he said. Torn raised his hands, palm out. "Let's be smart about this. If you kill me, you'll be stuck in Mag Mell forever. You need me."

My fingers itched to draw all of my blades and use Torn for target practice, but the creep was right. I had no idea how to leave this place. The cat sidhe was my ticket home. I slid the knife back into its sheath and sighed.

"Just tell me what we're dealing with," I said. I ground my teeth and shook my head. "Please."

See, I can play nice.

"Ah, perhaps you'd like to frolic a bit in the field or go skinny dipping in the lake while we chat?" he asked.

My fingers twitched and I snarled.

"Don't press your luck," I said.

"Right, probably for the best," he said. "It's not wise to dally in the Otherworlds. Shall we walk and talk?"

Torn gestured to a path I hadn't noticed before and I strode forward. His comment made my pulse quicken.

"Okay, spill," I said, walking at his side. "Who is this seer, what do I have to sacrifice to get my answers, and why is it "not wise to dally" here?"

"The seer is Béchuille, a druidess and one of the Tuatha Dé Danann," he said. "She'll do the sacrificing, not you. As for the latter, it's not wise to dally in the Otherworlds, because time moves differently here than in the mortal realm. If we don't move quickly, you could return to find your human business partner long dead."

"And if we do move quickly?" I asked.

"Then no more than a few hours will have passed," he said. "Now come along."

If we stayed too long in Mag Mell, Jinx, not to mention my mother, would be dead and gone upon my return. Didn't I say faeries were trouble? I knew I'd regret my alliance with the cat sidhe.

I took a deep breath and ran down the path.

CHAPTER 35

One of the amazing things about Mag Mell is that you never tire. According to Torn, it's part of the magic here. Nothing ever grows old, becomes ill, or dies on the plains of delight.

I ran faster than I've ever run, covering miles in a matter of minutes. Torn sighed and ran beside me, the bones dangling from his ears clattering. We reached a ring of standing stones approximately ten miles from our starting point without breaking a sweat.

I slowed, examining the menhirs that towered overhead. A huge stone placed horizontally across two of the others formed the lintel of a door. Though the circle had no walls, we made our way toward the doorway.

"So how many questions do I get to ask this seer, anyway?" I asked.

I'd done some thinking while running across the plains of Mag Mell. If I was only allowed one question, I'd rather ask where my father was instead of requesting the location of the door to Faerie. Heck, if I found Will-o'-the-Wisp, he could tell me the door's location himself. No augury necessary.

"You just get the one question, Princess," he said. Torn shrugged. "Don't ask me how it works, but Béchuille will already know what you seek. Since she is gifted with the knowledge of gates and pathways, she's most likely to give you the location of the door."

"And if that's not the information I want?" I asked.

"It's not wise to argue with one of the Tuatha Dé Danann, but do what you want," he said. "It's your funeral."

Yeah, that didn't sound ominous or anything. I guess I'd have to settle for the knowledge the druid was willing to give me. I sighed and stomped toward the circle of stones.

In the center of the circle, a woman stood over a fire singing in a strange tongue. Béchuille was not what I expected. The woman looked more like a goddess than a druid.

The Tuatha Dé was tall and slender as a supermodel, with long, blond hair that fell in waves around her body. She wore a golden torque around her neck and red robes that brushed the tops of her sandaled feet.

At our approach, the woman ceased her chanting and turned to face us. A scarlet tanager settled on her shoulder and began to sing in her ear.

"Welcome, Sir Torn and Princess Ivy," she said.

"My Lady," Torn said, bowing. "We come seeking knowledge."

"I know that which you seek," Béchuille said. "Now show me the key."

Torn turned to me with a smug grin.

"Yes, Princess," he said. "You do have the key, don't you?"

Damn, it was a bit late to be asking that. I glared at Torn and struggled to keep my hands at my waist. I wanted to strangle the cat sidhe and toss him into the cauldron that bubbled on the fire.

"Princess?" Béchuille asked.

Torn had played me well. I didn't want to admit to having a key to Faerie, but now I had no choice. If I claimed I didn't own a key, I wouldn't learn the location of the door. This trip would have been for nothing.

I lifted my chin and, with stiff movements, unzipped a jacket pocket and retrieved the jewelry box. My nostrils flared, seething, as I opened the box and lifted the key for the druid's inspection. I ignored Torn's arrogant laugh.

"Good, now let me prepare the bones," she said.

Béchuille lifted her hand to the bird on her shoulder. I thought she was going to stroke its feathers or pet its head. I gasped as she grabbed the bird roughly in both hands and deftly broke its neck. I'd bought into the Hollywood image of druids as peaceful, animal loving, hippie types who commune with nature. I chided myself for being a fool.

The druid dropped the bird to the ground at her feet and poured a ladle of steaming liquid from the cauldron over its broken body. My eyes widened as the bird was quickly reduced to bone. Whatever was in that cauldron had eaten away all sign of feathers and flesh. So much for Mag Mell being an idyllic paradise; just try telling that to the bird.

"Béchuille's cauldron contains waters taken from the Fountain of Knowledge in Tír Tairngire," Torn whispered.

A bit late for him to be informing me of that now. I inched away from the fire, putting Torn between me and the cauldron.

While I changed my position, Béchuille stuffed the bird's bones into a leather pouch. She tied the pouch and shook it, making the bones rattle inside. I bit the inside of my cheek and tried not to think about the pretty bird that had perched on the Tuatha Dé's shoulder mere seconds ago.

The druid stepped to an area beside the cauldron that was void of moss and flowers and used a wooden staff to draw a circle on the bare ground. She tossed her head back, chanting, arms lifted to the sky. Her green eyes rolled back in her head and I wondered idly what would happen if the woman fell into her own cauldron. Torn had claimed there was no such thing as death in Mag Mell, but I'd already witnessed the bird's demise.

Béchuille tossed the bones onto the ground with a clatter and I snapped my eyes back to the circle. A low moan escaped the druid's lips and Torn sidled up to me, chomping on his apple.

"I love this part," he said.

A breeze stirred the woman's golden hair and her face paled to a sickly hue. She pointed a shaking finger at me and a chill ran up my spine to creep into my scalp.

"The door you seek is one that hides," she said. "You must await midsummer tides. Upon the summer solstice when the moon doth wane, the wisp princess shall sit upon her throne again."

"Riddles?" I muttered. I should have known this wouldn't be easy.

"Shhh," Torn said.

"Muster your allies and gather your power," she said. "You must reach Tech Duinn's steps by the witching hour."

"Oh shit," Torn said.

"Shhh," I said.

"Brandish the key and do not lose heart," she said. "On solstice night the ocean shall part. Go to Martin's Point at final light of day, and the stones of Donner Isle will lead the way. Not by sea, but by land. You all will take your stand. To the house of Donn you must carry, king Will-o'-the-Wisp's key to

Faerie. Inside Donn's hearth bend your knee, close your eyes and turn the key."

The druid lowered her head, shoulders shaking, and scratched her foot across the edge of the circle. Once the circle was broken, the bones pulled together and began to sprout flesh and feathers once again. I gaped at the bird as it chirped and took wing.

Maybe death truly couldn't touch this place. After witnessing the bird's apparent death and rebirth, I didn't find that very reassuring. I was pretty sure that having your neck broken and the flesh boiled from your bones was unpleasant whether death followed or not.

"So I have to bring the key to Martin's Point at dusk on the summer solstice?" I asked.

The seer didn't answer. At closer scrutiny, I realized by the rise and fall of her chest that she'd fallen asleep on her feet.

"Let's go, Princess," Torn said.

The cat sidhe started walking toward the pathway from which we'd come. The bones and feathers adorning his leather clothing rattled as he sauntered away from the ring of standing stones. He swaggered confidently, but I wasn't fooled. Torn's face had paled at the mention of Tech Duinn.

"What is this Tech Duinn?" I asked. "And who is Donn?"

"Tech Duinn is the house of Donn," he said. Torn rubbed his chin and grimaced. "Celtic god of the dead."

For once I was in agreement with Torn. *Oh shit.*

CHAPTER 36

I stumbled into the alley and braced my gloved hands on my knees. A person may not tire while in Mag Mell, but the return trip was a doozy. I sucked in air and looked around for my unlikely travel companion. Torn rested against the dingy brick wall and waved.

"I'm famished," he said. "Later, Princess."

He grabbed hold of a rusty fire escape and pulled himself gracefully off the ground.

"Wait," I said. "I have one more question."

"What now, Princess?" he asked. "You've already ruined a perfectly good trip to the Otherworld. Give a man a break."

Right, like the druid's divination was all my fault. It's not like I chose to have the door to my kingdom accessed through an Otherworld realm of the dead.

"This question is easy," I said. "No death gods, just access to your information network. I need to find someone by the name of Inari. I think she's fae."

"THE Inari?" he asked. "As in, Inari, queen of the kitsune?"

"Um, yeah, I guess so," I said.

"Count me out, Princess," he said. "Inari and me, we have a history. I learned a lesson from my time with the kitsune queen."

"What lesson is that?" I asked.

"Don't date chicks with nine tails," he said.

Torn scampered up the fire escape and onto the roof of a neighboring building. I'd gotten all I could from the cat sidhe for one day. It was time to head home.

Time.

I bit my lip and pulled out my phone with shaking hands. Torn had said that time in the Otherworlds moved at a different pace from the mortal realm. How long had I been gone? I checked the time and date and let out the breath I'd been holding. I'd only lost six hours in Mag Mell. My human friends were still alive.

The downside? I was late for my date with Ceff.

I'd hoped to pay Jenna a visit at the dojo. I needed to see about scheduling a date to begin training again. I couldn't afford to get rusty, not now that I'd be spending the summer solstice breaking into the home of a death god.

I didn't have time now for a trip to the dojo, but at least I could give the Hunter a call. I squeezed the bridge of my nose, a headache building behind my eyes, and punched in Jenna's number. The Hunter answered on the first ring. There was nothing wrong with that girl's reflexes.

"You on a new job already?" she asked. "Jinx said you were on bed rest all week."

Jenna sounded out of breath and her words were interspersed with the clanging of metal against metal. The Hunter was talking on the phone while sparring. Show off.

"No, I'm taking it easy," I said. "Just working on something personal at the moment."

"You need someone to provide backup?" she asked.

I heard a loud thwap and a grunt and the ringing of metal ceased. Jenna had struck a victory against her opponent while chatting with me on the phone. The pint-sized redhead made being a badass look easy.

"No, I'm good," I said. *For now.* I'd need Jenna's help to survive passage through Tech Duinn, but I wasn't ready to talk about that yet. Kaye said I had to keep the door to Faerie secret from humans and the last thing I wanted was to put Jenna on the fae's hit list. "I wanted to thank you for the replacement blades and see when I can return to weapons training."

"No thanks necessary," she said. "I'll add the cost of the blades to next month's training."

That was Jenna, always practical.

"So I can return next month?" I asked.

"Sure," she said. "Stop by next week and we'll try running you through some drills. Once I assess where you're at with your recovery, I can give you some flows to practice as homework. Last thing you need is to stiffen up or lose muscle tone."

"Thanks, Jenna," I said.

"Anytime," she said. "And Ivy? Try not to get bitten by any more lamias?"

"Don't worry, I won't," I said.

That was one promise that I hoped I could keep.

CHAPTER 37

I trudged up the steps to my apartment and paused on the landing outside the door. My body felt heavy and I took a deep breath, fighting the tightness in my chest. I didn't relish the prospect of keeping secrets from Jinx.

Holding information back from Jenna was easy. There are some things that fae, even half-breeds, don't share with Hunters. But not telling Jinx about my father's key and my search for the door to Faerie felt like a terrible lie of omission. I pushed open the door to the loft with a bitter taste on my tongue.

I looked around the loft, listening for movement in any of the back rooms, and smiled. Jinx was nowhere in sight. Ceff was preparing food in the kitchen and Jinx had apparently gone out. I wouldn't have to face my roommate just yet.

I tossed my jacket over the back of the couch and strode to where Ceff was holding two empty glasses.

"Champagne?" he asked.

"Hell yes," I said.

"Bad day?" he asked.

"The worst," I said.

I explained about the visit with my mother, our trip to the hospital, the key my father left me, Kaye's instruction to keep the whole thing quiet, and Torn's trick to learn of the key's existence.

"So now I have to secretly plan how to breach the gates of Tech Duinn, break into a death god's house, and find a door hidden in his hearth," I said. "If the key opens the door, then I'll have to bring my investigation of my father's whereabouts to Faerie."

"Not tonight you don't," Ceff said. "You've visited the Otherworld and had a breakthrough in the relationship with your mother. You can begin your planning tomorrow. Tonight we dine."

Ceff waved a hand at the plates and silverware he'd set out on the bar. Candles were lit and placed around the apartment. He'd even bought flowers and arranged them in a vase set between the two place settings.

The smell of roasted meat and vegetables made my mouth water. My stomach growled and I realized I'd missed lunch while in Mag Mell. Dinner sounded fabulous, but first I needed to freshen up.

"Do I have time for a shower?" I asked.

"That depends," he said. "How much time do we need?"

Ceff's eyes began to glow and warmth spread to my belly. I licked my lips and kicked off my boots. Dinner could wait. I started walking toward Ceff, the heat rippling off my skin making the room shimmer.

"An hour," I said. "Maybe more."

Ceff turned off the oven and leaned in close. Water swirled around his body and a champagne bottle burst open behind him. Ceff lifted me onto the counter, pressing his lips against my own. When our lips met the visions of Ceff's memories came streaming through me, but, this time, they were gone in a flash.

I shed a tear when I experienced Ceff's torture at the *each uisge's* hands and then I was back in the kitchen, safe and whole. Ceff brushed the lone tear from my cheek, watching me raptly from inches away.

My breath caught as cool droplets of water and champagne skimmed across my heated skin. Ceff smiled and pulled me closer. This time when we kissed his lips pressed hard with need. Ceff opened his lips and his tongue searched my mouth with the same urgency as the rivulets of moisture which now explored my body.

I moaned and Ceff smiled against my lips. The flames of my wisp blood rose and heat flared. The dozens of liquid fingers disappeared, filling the room with steam.

"Need more water," he said.

Ceff lifted me off the counter and strode out of the kitchen. He carried me into the shower and I forgot all about secret keys, deadly missions, and death gods.

CHAPTER 38

This morning Ceff returned to the sea. He'd stayed a week while mourning the loss of his ex-wife, and exploring the new aspects of our relationship. I was sorry to see him go, but all water fae must return to water and, as king, Ceff had responsibilities he couldn't put off any longer.

At least Jinx was happy. She'd finally get a good night's sleep.

With the place to ourselves, Jinx and I tackled the job of putting our office back to rights. Anxious parents can do a number on hardwood and our lobby floor was no exception. Armed with a power sander and wood putty, we repaired the scratches and deep grooves left by hooves, claws, and talons.

I rubbed sore muscles and surveyed our handy work. Jinx said she liked the new lobby better than before. It probably says something about me that it took a mob of faeries to motivate me to give the place a make-over. I wasn't one for appearances, but I had to agree with Jinx, the place looked great.

Not bad for a day's work.

I was supposed to still be on bed rest, but I felt fine. Heck, I felt amazing. I lifted the edge of my shirt and prodded the scars on my side with gloved fingers. The skin was still pink, but I was healing faster than a normal human. At this rate, I'd be back to sparring with Jenna within the week.

Jinx tossed me a bottle of water and I caught it out of the air. Accelerated healing wasn't the only perk of being half fae. My wisp powers were awakening, bringing increased strength and speed. I was no superhero, but my fae blood was finally giving me an edge—not just pushing me to the brink.

I hoped that my new abilities would be enough to help me survive my sojourn through Tech Duinn and into Faerie. I had no idea what to expect when I reached the wisp court, but, like Ceff said, my battle plans could wait a day. The summer solstice was still months away and I'd promised Jinx we'd go out and celebrate a successful case.

Even after making repairs to the office, we had money to spend. Jinx had been frugal with our expenses lately and the case we were going out to celebrate had brought us a big payday. Gone were the days of celebrating a closed case with an extra cup of ramen noodles. We could afford to take the night off and live a little.

Plus, I couldn't let Jinx down. She was on the rebound from Hans and I had been spending nearly all of my free time with Ceff. It was high time for a girls' night.

"So, we going out tonight?" Jinx asked.

I wiped sweat from my brow and gulped down the bottle of water.

"Yeah, where to?" I asked. "Your choice."

"Really?" she asked. "Pinky swear. No take backs."

"I swear," I said.

I smiled, but didn't offer my pinky. Jinx didn't seem to mind.

I might be getting better at dealing with Ceff's visions, but that didn't mean I wanted to go around touching everybody. The thought left my mouth dry. I tipped the bottle back and finished off the last sip. No, I didn't want to live through everyone's painful memories. I had enough of my own. Plus, I owed my friend some privacy.

"I was hoping you'd say that," she said. Jinx placed a hand on her hip and winked. "There's a club I've been dying to get back into, but it seems I'm not on the guest list." Jinx pushed her full, red lips into a pout. "You really should do something about that. I'm sure Nexus would allow a human vassal through the doors if you put me on the list."

Oberon's eyes on a stick, Jinx wanted carte blanche access to Club Nexus. And she wanted to go there tonight. The room filled with the hollow, rapid-fire sound of my gloved hand crushing the empty, plastic water bottle.

"You're kidding, right?" I asked.

"How much trouble can I get into anyway?" she asked. "As your human vassal, I'm protected. Plus, there were so many hotties there the other night."

"You want to go out with a faerie?" I asked. "That's insane."

"What, think I'm not good enough for your kind?" she asked. Her chin trembled and she caught her lip between her teeth.

"No," I said, shaking my head. "Mab knows you're better than all the guys in that club combined. I'm just worried what they might do to you. The fae aren't known for their good behavior toward humans."

"They can't be much worse than the human creeps I've dated lately," she said.

Jinx had a point. Hans was moody and violent and her other boyfriends had routinely cheated on her. And I'd be a hypocrite to claim that all supernaturals were bad. I was a half-breed dating a full-blooded kelpie and I was friends with a powerful witch, a hearth brownie, and a bridge troll. Maybe Jinx was right.

"Okay," I said. "We'll go to Nexus tonight." Jinx started vibrating with excitement and I held up a hand. "But I'm not promising to sign you onto the guest list yet. Consider this a reconnaissance mission, a trial run to test security and club safety. If they don't enforce the protection of human vassals, there's no way I'm leaving you there unprotected."

In her crop top, overalls, and bandana, Jinx reminded me of the girl in the WWII propaganda posters with the slogan, "We can do it!" She was like a rockabilly Rosie the Riveter. I knew that my friend had come a long way and could take care of herself in most situations, but there was no way I was leaving her unprotected in a fae club. If I didn't like what I saw tonight, I wasn't adding her to the guest list. But that didn't mean we couldn't have fun in the meantime.

"Sure, yeah, that sounds great," she said. Jinx pulled the kerchief from her head and hurried to gather up her things. "Thanks, Ivy. You won't regret it. Scout's honor."

Jinx had never been a Girl Scout in her life, but I smiled. Her excitement was contagious. She fluttered around the room, turning off lights and grabbing her purse.

I opened my desk drawer and lifted out a vial of iron shavings and a handful of wooden stakes. If we were partying at a supernatural club tonight, I'd best be prepared for anything. I opened my jacket and slid the iron into an inner pocket and shoved the extra stakes into the belt at my waist.

I had a bad feeling about this.

CHAPTER 39

Humans have a difficult time getting into Nexus, but for tonight, Jinx was my plus one. Her eyes were lined with faerie ointment and she wore a crossbow slung across her back and a dagger strapped to her thigh. In the short, sleeveless dress that clung to her body like cling-wrap, the weapons were on display for all to see. I hoped that would be enough to keep straying hands, paws, and tentacles away from my friend.

My heart raced as I scanned the room. Yes, there were tentacles and other bizarre appendages waving around the dance floor. Faeries of every size, shape, and court were gyrating to the music. In a booth along the wall, I spied a vampire and a succubus *in flagrante delicto*. Apparently, they were feeding off each other in their own unique ways. I blushed and looked away. What the hell was I thinking agreeing to bring Jinx to this place?

I rubbed my arm where a silver and iron throwing knife was sheathed beneath my jacket. My weapons may not be on display, but that didn't mean I'd come unarmed. I wore a layer of silk underwear as a base layer to prevent unwanted visions. Over these, I'd strapped my throwing knives and wore jeans, a long sleeved t-shirt, and my leather jacket. My jacket was filled with anti-fae charms. More than a dozen slender wooden stakes were tucked into my belt and I had a dagger in each boot.

I'd tied my hair into a knot at the base of my neck where it hid my backup vial of iron shavings and a set of iron-tipped, wooden hair sticks that would double as stakes. Any fae unlucky enough to be pierced by the hair sticks would get a whopping case of iron poisoning. Overkill? Perhaps, but I wasn't taking any chances. Jinx wanted a good time and I sure as hell wasn't going to let some supernatural creep stand in her way.

I continued my scan of the room, reaching out with my newly heightened senses. An itch started between my shoulder blades and I turned to see the Green Lady. She smiled and whispered in the ear of her drinking companion. I swallowed hard and turned away. I owed the glaistig two wishes of her choosing. One of these days she'd come to collect.

The Green Lady wasn't the only familiar face in the crowd. The bar was the least crowded area in the lower section of Nexus, so I made my way to the smooth curve of black stone. The stone was polished to a high shine and reflected the backlit bottles and jars that lined the shelves behind the barkeeper. I surveyed the path to the bar and recognized the scarred face and tattered ears of Torn leaning against a tall round table.

Torn was chatting up a scantily clad sylph. As Jinx and I made our way to the bar, Torn lifted his eyes from the sylph's chest and winked. I narrowed my eyes and checked my weapons. I wasn't feeling overly loquacious toward the cat sidhe at the moment. I had questions that needed answers, namely where I could find the mysterious Inari, but I was still annoyed with my new ally. I jerked my head in a curt nod and kept moving.

As we passed, other fae smiled, nodded, bowed, or raised their glass in salute. I forced a smile and nodded to each in turn. Out on the street, it was easy to forget I was royalty, but here at Nexus, my status as princess was both known and acknowledged.

"Dude, you're like a total celebrity," Jinx said.

Yeah, too bad that attention could get me killed. So far the fae we encountered were polite, but I knew better than to let my guard down. I kept my eyes open, shoulders loose, and gloved hands ready.

I wasn't naïve enough to believe my status as wisp princess didn't come without its dangers. Fae, especially those of the Unseelie court to which I owed allegiance, never tired of political power plays. There could be hundreds in this very crowd who wished to usurp my throne. I took a steadying breath against the tightness in my chest, eyes flicking from face to face. Any one of these people could be a potential assassin.

"I think I need a drink," I said.

I guided Jinx to a cluster of empty stools at the end of the bar and put my back to the wall. I caught the bartender's eye and waved him over to take our orders. I wanted to make sure that the bartender was clear that my human vassal was not to receive any faerie wine. I let the bartender see my weapons and slipped him a fifty to guarantee he got the message.

The bartender returned with our drinks and I smiled at the pints of ale. No faerie wine in sight. Maybe this could be a fun night after all. We'd closed a difficult case, earning the respect and gratitude of dozens of faerie parents. I'd also made a breakthrough with my mother and got a lead that may help me locate my father. We did have a lot to celebrate.

For the first time since we'd entered Club Nexus, I allowed myself to relax. I was good at multitasking, and in our current location by the bar, the music wasn't even that loud. It was a nice, quiet place to kick back with a drink and people watch. I could keep an eye out for Jinx and have a bit of fun. What could possibly go wrong?

I shouldn't have asked. I only looked away from the room long enough to place my order with the bartender, but that was all the time it took for the demon to slide in beside Jinx.

I smelled sulfur and reached for my blades.

"Hello, sweetheart," Forneus said. He smiled and slid his arm around Jinx. "Buy you a drink?"

So much for a nice, relaxing evening.

Coming in 2014
The first novel in the Hunters' Guild series
set in the world of Ivy Granger

E.J. STEVENS

Hunting in Bruges

Read on for a sneak preview.

I've been seeing ghosts for as long as I can remember. Most ghosts are simply annoying; just clueless dead people who don't realize that they've died. The weakest of these manifest as flimsy apparitions, without the ability for speech or higher thought. They're like a recording of someone's life projected not onto a screen, but onto the place where they died. Most people can walk through one of these ghosts without so much as a goosebump.

Poltergeists are more powerful, but just as single-minded. These pesky spirits are like angry toddlers. They stomp around, shaking their proverbial chains, moaning and wailing about how something (the accident, their murder, or the murder they committed) was someone else's fault, and how everyone must pay for their misfortune. Poltergeists are a nuisance; they're noisy and can throw around objects for short periods of time, but it's only the strong ones that are dangerous.

Thankfully, there aren't many ghosts out there strong enough to do more than knock a pen off your desk or cause a cold spot. From what I've discovered while training with the Hunters' Guild, ghosts get their power from two things—how long they've been haunting and strength of purpose. If someone as obsessed with killing as Jack the Ripper manifests beside you on a London street, I recommend you run. If someone as old and unhinged as Vlad the Impaler appears beside you in Targoviste Romania, you better hope you have a Hunter at your side, or a guardian angel.

The dead get a bad rap, and for good reason, but some ghosts can be helpful. There was a woman with a kind face who used to appear when I was in foster care. Linda wasn't just a loop of psychic recording stuck on repeat; this ghost had free will and independent thought—and thankfully, she wasn't a sociopath consumed with bloodshed. Linda manifested in faded jeans and dark turtleneck and smelled like home, which was the other thing that was unusual about her. Most ghosts are tied to one spot, the place where they lived or died. But Linda's familiar face followed me from one foster home to another. And it was a good thing that she did. Linda the ghost saved my life more than once.

Foster care was an excellent training ground for self defense, which is probably why the Hunters' Guild uses it as a place for recruitment. Being cast adrift in the child welfare system gave me plenty of opportunities to hone my survival instincts. By the time the Hunters came along, I was a force to be reckoned with, or so I thought.

The Hunters' Guild provides exceptional training and I soon learned that my attempts at both offense and defense were child's play when compared to our senior members. I didn't berate myself over that fact; I was only thirteen when the Hunters swooped in and welcomed me into their fold. But learning my limitations did make me painfully aware of one thing. If it hadn't been for Linda the ghost, I probably wouldn't have survived my childhood.

The worst case of *honing my survival skills* had been at my last foster home, just before the Hunters' Guild intervened. I don't remember the house mother. She wasn't around much. She was just a small figure in a cheap, polyester fast food uniform with a stooped posture and downcast eyes. But I remember her husband Frank.

Frank was a bully who wore white, ketchup and mustard stained, wife-beater t-shirts. He had perpetual French fry breath and a nasty grin. It took me a few weeks to realize that Frank's grin was more of a leer. I'd caught his gaze in the bathroom mirror when I was changing and his eyes said it all; Frank was a perv.

Linda slammed the door in his face, but that didn't stop Frank. Frank would brush up against me in the kitchen and Linda would set the faucet spraying across the tiles...and slide a knife into my hand. My time in that house ended when Frank ended up in the hospital.

I'd been creeping back to the bedroom I shared with three other kids, when I saw Frank waiting for me in the shadows. I pulled the steak knife I kept hidden in the pocket of my robe, but I never got a chance to use it. Now that I know a thing or two about fighting with a blade, I'm aware that Frank probably would have won that fight.

I tried to run toward the stairs, but Frank met me at the top landing. Frank reached for me while his bulk effectively blocked my escape. That was when Linda the ghost pushed him down the stairs. I remember him tumbling in slow motion, his eyes going wide and the leering grin sliding from his face.

Linda the ghost had once again saved me, but it seemed that this visit was her last. I don't know if she used up her quota of psychic power, or if she just felt like her job here was finally done. It wasn't until years later that I realized she was my mother.

I guess I should have realized sooner that I was related to the ghost who followed me around. We both have hair the same shade of shocking red. But where mine is straight and cropped into a short bob, Linda's was wavy and curled down around her shoulders. We also share a dimple in our left cheek and a propensity for protecting the weak and innocent from evil.

Linda the ghost disappeared, a wailing ambulance drove Frank to the hospital, police arrived at my foster house, and the Hunters swooped in and cleaned up the aftermath. It was from my first Guild master that I learned of my parents' fate and put two and two together about my ghostly protector.

As a kid I often wondered why Linda the ghost always wore a dark turtleneck; now I knew. Young, rogue vamps had torn out her neck and proceeded to rip my father to pieces like meat confetti. My parents were on vacation in Belize, celebrating their wedding anniversary when it happened. I'd been staying with a friend of my mother's, otherwise I'd be dead too.

I don't remember my parents, I'd only been three when I was put into the foster care system, but I do find some peace in knowing that doing my duty as a Hunter gives me the power to police and destroy rogue vamps like the ones who killed my mother and father. When I become exhausted by my work, I think of Linda's sad face and push myself to train harder. And when I find creeps who are abusive to women and children, I think of Frank.

That's how I ended up here, standing in a Brussels airport, trying to decipher the Dutch and French signs with eyes that were gritty from the twelve hour flight. It all started when my friend Ivy called to inform me that a fellow Hunter had hit our mutual friend Jinx. Ivy didn't know how that information would push all my buttons, she didn't know about Frank or my time in the foster system, but we both agreed that striking a girl was unacceptable. She was letting me, and the Hunters' Guild, deal with it, for now.

I went to master Janus, the head of the Harborsmouth Hunters' Guild, and reported Hans' transgressions. It didn't help his case that he had a reputation as a berserker in battle. The fact that he'd hit a human, the very people we were sworn to defend against the monsters, was the nail in the coffin of Hans' career.

I was assured that Hans would be shipped off to the equivalent of a desk job in Siberia. I should have left it at that, and let my superiors take care of the problem. But Jinx was my friend. Ivy's rockabilly business partner may have had bad luck and even worse taste in men, but that didn't mean she deserved to spend her life fending off the attacks of the Franks in the world.

Hans continued his Guild duties while the higher ups shuffled papers and prepared to send him away. Hans should have skipped our training sessions, but then again, he didn't know who had ratted him out—and the guy had a lot of rage to vent. I stormed onto the practice mat and saluted Hans with my sword. It wasn't long before the man started to bleed.

We were supposed to be using practice swords, but I'd *accidentally* grabbed the sharp blade I used on hunting runs. I didn't leave any lasting injuries, but the shallow cuts made a mess of his precious tattoos. I just hoped the scars were a constant reminder of what happens when you attack the innocent.

One week later, I received a plane ticket and orders to meet with one of our contacts in Belgium. I wasn't sure if this assignment was intended as a punishment or a promotion, but I was eager to prove myself to the Guild leadership. Master Janus' parting words whispered in my head, distracting me from the voice on the overhead intercom echoing throughout the cavernous airport.

"Do your duty, Jenna," he said. Master Janus placed a large, sword-calloused hand on my shoulder and looked me in the eye. I swallowed hard, but I managed to keep my hands from shaking. "Make us proud."

"I will, sir," I said.

"Good hunting."

Ivy Granger World

Don't miss these great books set in the world of Ivy Granger.

Ivy Ganger, Psychic Detective Series

Shadow Sight
Welcome to Harborsmouth, where monsters walk the streets unseen by humans...except those with second sight, like Ivy Granger.

Blood and Mistletoe: An Ivy Granger Novella
Holidays are worse than a full moon for making people crazy. In Harborsmouth, where many of the residents are undead vampires or monstrous fae, the combination may prove deadly.

Ghost Light
Holidays are worse than a full moon for making people crazy. In Harborsmouth, where many of the residents are undead vampires or monstrous fae, the combination may prove deadly.

Club Nexus: An Ivy Granger Novella
A demon, an Unseelie faerie, and a vampire walk into a bar...

Burning Bright
Burning down the house...

Birthright
Being a faerie princess isn't all it's cracked up to be.

Hound's Bite
Ivy Granger thought she left the worst of Mab's creations behind when she escaped Faerie. She thought wrong.

Hunters' Guild Series

Hunting in Bruges
The only thing worse than being a Hunter in the fae-ridden city of Harborsmouth, is hunting vampires in Bruges.

E.J. Stevens is the author of the HUNTERS' GUILD urban fantasy series, the SPIRIT GUIDE young adult series, and the award-winning IVY GRANGER urban fantasy series. She is known for filling pages with quirky characters, bloodsucking vampires, psychotic faeries, and snarky, kick-butt heroines.

BTS Red Carpet Award winner for Best Novel, SYAE Award finalist for Best Paranormal, Best Horror, and Best Novella, winner of the PRG Reviewer's Choice Award for Best Paranormal Fantasy Novel, Best Young Adult Paranormal Series, Best Urban Fantasy Novel, and finalist for Best Young Adult Paranormal Novel and Best Urban Fantasy Series.

When E.J. isn't at her writing desk, she enjoys dancing along seaside cliffs, singing in graveyards, and sleeping in faerie circles. E.J. currently resides in a magical forest on the coast of Maine where she finds daily inspiration for her writing.

CONNECT WITH E.J. STEVENS
Twitter: @EJStevensAuthor
Website: www.EJStevensAuthor.com
Blog: www.FromtheShadows.info

Printed in Poland
by Amazon Fulfillment
Poland Sp. z o.o., Wrocław